naiyer masud

Dearest Mum,

Thank you for all the gifts.

Yours affectionately,

Asif M. Shirazi
2005

Katha Urdu Library

OTHER TITLES FROM KATHA

For Literary Connoisseurs
Katha Prize Stories, vols 1-7
A Southern Harvest
Visions-Revisions, vols 1 & 2
The Wordsmiths
Masti
Basheer
Mauni
Mapping Memories
Bazdeed (in Urdu)
Separate Journeys
Sleepwalkers

For Young Adults
A Unique Odyssey: The Story of the United Nations.
YuvaKatha, vols 1–8,

For Children

Hulgul ka Pitara (a teaching/learning kit for Hindi)
Tamasha! (a fun & development quarterly in English & Hindi)
Dhammak Dhum! (a quarterly for pre-schoolers)
Swapnasundari and the Magical Birds of Mithila (in English & Hindi)
The Secrets of Kalindi: A Jigsaw Puzzle Mystery
The Princess with the Longest Hair

Easy Readers for Adult Neo-literates (in Hindi)
Abhishaap by Pudhuvai Rã Rajani
Arjun by Mahasweta Devi
Bhola by Rajendra Singh Bedi
Do Haath by Ismat Chughtai
Faisla by Maitreyi Pushpa
Panch Parmeshwar by Premchand
Paro ki Kahani by Sughra Mehdi
Puraskar by Jaishankar Prasad
Samudra Tat Par by O V Vijayan
Sparsh by Jaywant Dalvi
Stree ka Patra by Rabindranath Tagore
Thakavat by Gurbachan Singh Bhullar
Stree Katha (a teaching/learning text, also in Gujarati, Kannada, Malayalam, Telugu and Urdu)
Stree Shakti (a teaching/learning text, also in English, Kannada and Malayalam)

Forthcoming

Katha Academic Series:
Approaches to Literature in Translation (ALT)
Anuvada: Approaches and Philosophies of Translation ed Rukmini B Nair and Shiva K Srinivasan
Alankar. On Metaphor and Translatability ed Rukmini B Nair
Desire and Sexuality in Indian Literature: Translating Desire ed Brinda Bose
Partition Narratives ed Ravi Kant and Tarun Saint
Caste Consciousness and Indian Fiction ed Tapan Basu
Ecopoetics: An Approach to Teaching Language ed Nirmal Selvamony
Women and Space ed C T Indra and Meenakshi Shivaram

Others
Katha Prize Stories, vol 8
ed Geeta Dharmarajan
Raja Rao: The Word as Mantra
ed R L Hardgrave
The Best of Raja Rao
ed Makarand Paranjape
Ambai ed Gita Krishnankutty
The Wordsmiths, vol 2

the essence of camphor

naiyer masud

Selected and Edited by
Muhammad Umar Memon

Published by

KATHA

A-3 Sarvodaya Enclave
Sri Aurobindo Marg, New Delhi 110017
Phone: 6868193, 6521752
Fax: 6514373
E-mail: DELAAB05@giasdl01.vsnl.net.in
Internet address: http://www.katha.org

First published by Katha in 1998

Distributed by Katha Mela, a distributor of quality books.
A-3 Sarvodaya Enclave, Aurobindo Marg, New Delhi 110 017

KATHA is a registered nonprofit society
devoted to enhancing the pleasures of reading.
KATHA VILASAM is its story research and resource centre.

General Series Editor: Geeta Dharmarajan
In-house Editor: Nandita Aggarwal
In-house Assistant Editor: Dipli Saikia
Cover design: Poonam Bevli Sahi, Facet

Production-in-charge: S Ganeshan
Typeset in 10.5 on 14.5 pt ElegaGaramond BT by Sandeep Kumar at Katha
Printed at Saurabh Print-o-pack, NOIDA (UP)

ISBN 81-85586-82-9 (paperback)

contents

about naiyer masud

Naiyer Masud

Naiyer Masud was born on 16 November, 1936, in Lucknow. Both his parents came from families of hakeems, but in both families the practice of traditional medicine had effectively ended with Masud's grandfathers. Naiyer Masud's father, Syed Masud Hasan Rizvi Adeeb, was a professor of Persian at Lucknow University and a renowned scholar of Persian and Urdu. His library was well regarded for its sizeable collection of rare books and manuscripts. Masud Sahab says, "I owe the greater part of my literary training to him and to this collection ... I was educated in ordinary schools and was an average student."

Naiyer Masud is mainly a short story writer. His stories have been published in three volumes – *Seemiya, Itr-e Kafoor,* and *Taus Chaman ki Maina.* He has translated the short stories and parables of Kafka, which have been published under the title *Kafka ki Afsane.* He has also translated numerous contemporary Iranian short stories which have appeared in *Quarterly Aaj.* In 1997 he received the Presidential Certificate of Honour, presented by Shri K R Narayanan, for his "outstanding contribution to Persian." In the same year he also won his second Katha Award for Creative Fiction, for his story "Sheesha Ghat" which appears in this collection. Earlier, in 1993, his story "Ray Khandan ke Asar" won him his first Katha Award.

In an interview with Asif Farrukhi, Masud Sahab says, "... I was drawn to writing short stories right from childhood. I have read more fiction than scholarly works. Later, when the new kind of short story, with its penchant for ambiguity and abstraction, moved to centre stage and was discussed vigorously in debates, I read it too. However, I didn't find it to my liking ... words should signify, and signify without equivocation."

Of his first story, Masud Sahab says, "I was so hesitant about "Nusrat" that I showed it to Farruqi Sahab (Shamsur Rahman Farruqi) as a translation, not as something I'd written. He liked it and published it."

Critics have noted that his language and atmosphere and even the characters in his stories appear markedly different from the stories of others – entirely different from mainstream Urdu fiction. Masud Sahab says, "... I had to struggle the most on language, on how to write precisely, on selecting words that would communicate my intent most accurately... For me the hardest part of writing is deciding what to keep and what to leave out, what to describe and, more importantly, what not to describe... I think a reader's impression ought to be taken as more authentic than a writer's own."

Prof Masud holds two PhD degrees, one in Urdu from Allahabad University, the other in Persian from Lucknow University, which he joined in 1965 as a professor of Persian. He has since retired and lives with his wife Mohtrima Sabiha Khatun, their three daughters, and a son, in the house his father built and appropriately named "Adabistan" ("Abode of Literature").

"Adabistan": Author's Residence

introduction

Hai ghaib-e ghaib jis-ko samajhte hain • ham shuhud
Hain • khvab mein hanuz jo jage hain • khvab mein •
(The absence of the absent: what we see is merest seeming.
It is the dreaming into which we awaken from dream.)

– Ghalib

Naiyer Masud is both a scholar of Persian and Urdu, and among the foremost contemporary Urdu short story writers. Passionately involved with fiction, he started writing stories in his early boyhood, but didn't start publishing until the 1970s. The five stories which make up his first collection, *Seemiya*, initially appeared individually in Shamsur Rahman Faruqi's literary magazine *Shab-Khun* (Allahabad) and went largely without critical comment. When they later appeared as a book they were greeted warmly. They were recognized at once as something of a phenomenon in Urdu letters, both in form and subject. And although his readers found him baffling, his work nonetheless sounded irreducibly authentic at some deeper level of perception. The world of *Seemiya* and *Itr-e Kafoor*, his second collection, pulled reader and critic alike straight into the seductive centre of what seems like an inaccessible vortex. In short, reading Naiyer Masud's stories evoked the sensation of being thrown headlong into a self-referential circularity.

Entirely un-derivative and unlike anything that preceded them in the history of Urdu fiction, these stories stand in a class by themselves. They are different from the work of the early Urdu Romantics and Didactics on the one hand, and the Social Realists such as Munshi Premchand(1880 – 1936) and the Progressive writers such as Sajjad Zaheer(d 1973), Krishan Chandar(d 1977), and Ismat Chughtai(d 1991) on the other. Strangely, they also do not approximate to anything of the modernist abstraction and symbolism that had swept over the Urdu fictional landscape in the 1960s and onwards with such relentless force.

In Masud's fiction one encounters order, neatness and decorum. These qualities dispel any idea of "unreality" in the way it has come to pervade Urdu symbolist and abstractionist writing introduced by such writers as Enver Sajjad and Surendra Prakash. His fictional world demands respect, an admission of its unique ontological orientation, but gives no clue as to what its existentialist identity or purpose might be. In the sum of its parts it does not correspond to any image of the world familiar to the reader. A mirror-image of the real world in its outer form, it nonetheless seeks to subvert that image at a deeper, more emblematic level. And even though each element in it appears palpably real, oddly, the aggregate does not add up to anything known.

The shimmering but elusive quality of the stories may derive from a number of factors. Not the least of which is the terse and highly clipped prose of the writer, one that shuns even the slightest trace of hollow rhetoric, so stark in its suppression of qualifiers that it unsettles the mind. Few idioms or none, no verbal pyrotechnics of any kind. It is Urdu all right, but it does not read like ordinary Urdu. Attenuated but overlain with invisible density and evocative of absence.

The economy, the avoidance of even an occasional exaggeration or embellishment, lend his prose an element of unfamiliarity, if not of unreality. Words are selected with extreme care, not for their meanings, but for their predisposition to evoke silence and stillness in which the elusive becomes self-evident. Rarely has Urdu seen a writer more jealously protective of his verbal choices. There is absolutely nothing arbitrary or rushed about them. Those of us who have worked in consultation with him on translations of his stories know too well his insistence on keeping the same word, often even the same order in which different verbal elements appear in a sentence. And, above all, how he hates the slightest emphasis when such emphasis could be creatively exploited in the translation. Personally, I can remember many instances when my better judgement and patience were taxed to their limits. The deliberate suppression of the expected marks all Masud's writings.

Another factor may be the use of certain elements found in narratives which employ the spatial form. For instance, key words deployed at varying intervals horizontally across the fictional space. They seek to carry the meaning – or whatever its equivalent may be in Masud's stories – incrementally forward, often even modifying it in unexpected ways, and always in a state of flux, continually evolving. Often they are woven so seamlessly in the narrative structure that one may miss them altogether. The tendency of the human mind is to fathom and move on. But Masud's narratives work as a reminder against completion and closure. One experiences things in dynamic movement, not as objects with fixed perimeters, in a state of repose or quiescence. So one cannot be done with them and move on. Circularity has no terminus. Finishing one of his stories does not bring the expected comprehension and completion. What it does bring is a continual engagement with the unsaid and the ineffable, a blurred image of which may be preserved in memory.

These qualities most likely result from an inherent tension between the expansiveness of experience as embodied in Masud's stories, its refusal to be chopped up and packaged in neat little packets, and the form in which he alludes to that experience. A tension, in other words, between content and generic expectation as understood in Urdu letters.

The tendency away from closure might itself stem from the denial, at a trans-empirical level, of linear temporality, of the divisions of time into past, present, and future. The moment, or for that matter any division of time, is simultaneously present throughout. As if it were a gathering together of all time into an eternity that is necessarily present. Experience, which can only be a single indivisible entity, is continuous, indeed it is coeval with consciousness. Eventually, the two may be the same thing.

The matter may be less abstruse from the point of view of Sufi metaphysics. Here the formula Reality = Being reduces temporality to pure non-existence, except in relation to the created world; itself devoid of reality strictly in the character of itself.

But as stories, Masud's work falls squarely within the limits of the created world. And it is here that the suspension of the defining temporal conventions creates the dizzying sensation of disjuncture. At the same time, it jars the reader into the recognition that behind the apparent multiplicity of his work lies a single concern: the experience of being. Therefore no limits or ordering perimeters or boundaries are possible. Each story is merely a variation on a single theme. Just as the present is an imaginary point along a continuum where consciousness may choose to place it, a story is a discrete embodiment only insofar as consciousness chooses to see it as such. In essence, it has no beginning and, therefore, no end.

In the process of working closely with Masud's fictional universe, I'm nowhere closer to its "meaning" today than I was some years ago when I first started. But, increasingly, I feel that to insist on some palpable meaning, or even a shard of meaning, in reflexive fiction such as Masud's, is to put the wrong foot forward. "Meaning" inevitably has to do with the domain of logic, discursive reason, empiricism. It is inherently suggestive of a split, a dichotomy, a state of divorce and rupture. Whence its inability to deal with reality except piecemeal. Our generic expectations from the short story proceed from the basic premise that objects have meaning. These expectations are not likely to be met in a perusal of Masud's short stories. These stories are preoccupied instead with being. To be, and not (so much) to mean. The maze is entered for its own sake – to become a maze – and not to subdue, to get somewhere. Keeping in mind the culture where Masud has grown up, his predilection to preface his work with quotations from Persian mystical lore predisposes me to think that the subject matter of these stories (if one could be rash enough to use the phrase "subject matter") is less accessible to the domain of reason. It is not an object to be cognized, but one can begin to get some intimation of it experientially, in something like a visionary flash in the trans-empirical realm of pure reflection. If the stories do not begin at a discrete logical point, if they don't close at the end of the day, if they fail to reach resolution and appear open-ended, it is because they do not deal with reality as something divisible or linear. Their sole purpose is perhaps to evoke silence, a stillness in which the distracted self is sufficiently calmed to begin to experience its ineffable totality, its inherent identity and synchronicity with Being.

I'm not suggesting that these stories are the product of Sufi thought or carry Sufi metaphysics forward. I'm only suggesting that we borrow a methodology which is Sufistic in its character and see whether this might lead us to the centre of the Masudian universe. In other words, to make a case for experiencing and being, for zauq-ing (tasting) – if I may be permitted this linguistic outrage – rather than knowing, as the fundamental point of entry to his work. The tension between content and form is after all the obverse of the polarity between the phenomenal and the noumenal, between time and eternity.

I recall once talking to Shamṣur Rahman Faruqi about the effect Masud's stories had on me and being amazed at his remark: "They don't go anywhere; they're like dreams." I wasn't sure how to take this remark. Coming as it did from Urdu's most astute critic, the remark, I'm inclined to believe, didn't imply a negative judgement. Faruqi Sahib rather meant to underscore the need for the construction of a fictional theory in

Urdu expansive enough to embrace Masud's work. A radically different poetics of fictional art pointed away from traditional notions of meaning and inherited form, to a trajectory more hospitable to an ethos more nearly representative of the cultural strains which make up the composite personality of a South Asian Urdu writer.

The need is both urgent and relevant. After sifting through the bulk of the Urdu short story and certainly the best of it, one is left with a curious paradox. Readily intelligible to a Westerner in most of its content, it is virtually riotous in the arbitrariness of its form. Eventually it is cut off from its own pre-modern cultural experience. Some canon formation is called for, not only to validate its peculiar South Asian flavour, but also to explain the disjuncture.

My conviction that though dimly accessible, Masud's work is much more than simply vacuous, that something was irreducibly authentic about it, prompted me to introduce it to the English reader. My hope is that it will generate useful critical discussion and open insightful ways of looking at Masud's fiction. The present volume, however, could not have materialized without the generous help and dedication of a number of friends. I'm grateful to Moazzam Sheikh, Elizabeth Bell, Sagaree Sengupta, Aditya Behl, Javaid Qazi and Shantanu Phukan for agreeing to translate a number of short stories for this volume and patiently going through several revisions to produce a translation at once faithful and readable. Ms Bell, whose help has been immense, deserves a special note of thanks for the meticulous care and industry with which she went over the text of five translations and offered many fine suggestions for improvement. And all this with a dedication and promptness which only add to my sense of gratitude.

I have been in consultation with Naiyer Masud throughout the project. His cooperation, in no small measure, contributed to ensuring that the original text has remained intact in its English incarnation. He meticulously went over eight of the translations included here, and supplied the required clarifications and explanations promptly and unstintingly. Many thanks to him.

Lastly, I'd like to thank Nandita Aggarwal, my exacting editor at Katha, without whose fine sense of the English language, her delightfully unobtrusive persuasive powers and her dedication, both this volume and I would have been the poorer. Working with her was a richly rewarding experience, especially since she shares my enthusiasm for the fictional world of Naiyer Masud.

Geeta Dharmarajan, or rather her tenacity, has been mainly responsible for the publication of this volume. On a soul-scorching day in May 1996, when I visited her in the offices of Katha, she asked me about my current and future projects, but especially about what I could do for Katha. I was in those days toying with the idea of devoting a special section of *The Annual of Urdu Studies* to Naiyer Masud translations. She immediately offered to print this selection as an independent book. Since then the awesome urgency of her reminders and her gentle remonstrations have continually kept me on my toes, foreclosing any attempt on my part to give in to the lure of procrastination, the seduction of cloying lassitude. If the book is a reality today, it is so due to her unremitting encouragement. And thank you, Geeta, for being such a good friend.

The material for this volume first appeared in a special section of *The Annual of Urdu Studies* on Naiyer Masud and is reproduced here with the *Annual*'s permission. One of the short stories, "Sheesha Ghat," I am glad to report, won the Katha Award for Creative Fiction in 1997, while its translators won the Katha Award for Translation. It appears in *Katha Prize Stories, Vol 7.* The story "Sultan Muzaffar's Chronicler of Events" originally appeared as "Sultan Muzaffar's Imperial Chronicler" in the *Annual*; the change has been made at the request of Naiyer Masud. I have also changed the title of another story. "The Woman in Black" originally appeared as "The Colour of Nothingness."

In his boyhood Masud wrote some poetry, short stories, and plays, which were published in children's magazines. Later, starting in 1965, he devoted his energies to writing research papers. His friendship with Faruqi revived his desire to write fiction. He wrote his first short story, "Nusrat," in 1971. "I'm very slow at writing," he remarks. "I've written only twenty two short stories in the last twenty five years." He is also very fond of translating, but regrets that he hasn't been able to translate as widely as he'd wanted to. "Some twenty pieces of Kafka, fifteen short stories and a few poems from Persian, that's as much as I have translated."

In the same letter he mentions his interest in calligraphy, painting, and music. "There was a time when I could play a few instruments," he writes. "I can also manage minor repair jobs around the house which have to do with plumbing, masonry, electrical work and carpentry. But I did learn the art of book-binding formally. My true occupation, at any rate, is reading and, occasionally, writing."

Masud has published some two dozen books which fall in the following categories: fiction, children's books, translations and research works.

Muhammad Umar Memon
Madison, 8 September 1998

Naiyer Masud: "When I was four or five years old, I had an attack of typhoid. The fever did not come down even after forty days which, at that time, was taken as an indication that the patient was not going to survive. My parents, in their desperation, summoned Mirza Mughal Beg, the renowned photographer of Lucknow, to get their child photographed. There was weeping and lamentation in the house while this 'last' photograph was being taken, but it turned out to be my first photograph. (My favourite ball is at my side in the photograph. It was my 'will' that the ball be left with me in my grave.)"

the essence of camphor

For on its wing was dark alloy,
And as it flutter'd – fell
An Essence – powerful to destroy
A soul that knew it well.

– Edgar Allan Poe

Gar nau-bahar ayad-o-pursad ze dustan
Gu ay saba keh an hame gulha gaya shudand
(If Spring comes asking after friends, sweet Breeze,
Say that the blossoms – ah, the blossoms turned to straw.)

– Amir Khusrau

I never learned the intricate, tenuous art of perfume making practised in ancient times, now nearly lost or perhaps already extinct; neither am I acquainted with the new methods of concocting artificial fragrances. That is why no one understands the essences I prepare, nor succeeds in imitating them. People assume that I am privy to some rare formulae, locked in my breast and bound to die with me. So they insist I preserve them, somehow, for posterity.

translated by

moazzam sheikh and elizabeth bell

I respond by remaining silent. There is nothing unique in my perfumes except that I prepare common fragrances on a base of camphor extract. In fact, every perfume I make is an extract of camphor, concealed behind a familiar scent. I have experimented with fragrances aplenty. At one point, I had gathered so many aromatic items that it was dizzying simply to be near them. The fragrance of each scent would spread and evaporate by itself. Finally, a moment would come when the matter remained but its fragrance had dissipated into the air, and I had to see or touch it in order to identify it. But camphor is very different, because it evaporates along with its odour: it is not possible for its substance to remain after its scent has vanished; though it is possible for the camphor to evaporate and the smell to remain.

In my extract, however, one does not smell camphor, or any other fragrance. It is a colourless solution inside a white, square-bottomed china jar. No fragrance of any kind wafts through the jar's narrow opening when the round lid is removed. Attempting to smell it one feels a vacant forlornness and the next time round, breathing it in more deeply, one detects something in this forlornness. At least, that's what I feel. I cannot say what others feel since no one has ever smelled the extract in its purest form, apart from me. It is true that when I prepare an essence with this foundation those who inhale it think there is something else underneath the expected fragrance. Obviously, they cannot recognize it, for there is no fragrance at all in my extract of camphor.

Like camphor, the extract of camphor, too, evaporates and dies out with its scent, or even sooner. My achievement – if one can call it that – is simply that I manage to keep the camphor from expiring with its fragrance. When I transform camphor to the solution stage, its odour becomes pronounced. Then I retain the solution, but cause its scent to vanish. Sometimes the essence perishes altogether, leaving the solution indistinguishable from plain water, and I have to toss the whole thing out. This happens only when I am distracted and my hands fumble.

Normally, my concentration is hard to break. Once absorbed in preparing the extract, I do not hear loud noises, or even nearby voices. However, the call of a distant bird or some equally faint background sound can throw me off. Then my hand stops, and as I try to turn back to my work I detect the lowest point of the fragrance curling upward like the end of a string. It rises from the solution toward the ceiling, and it just cannot be brought back. I don't mourn the loss of my labour and get back to work, resolved not to be distracted again. Soon I see the essence of the new solution as it struggles to ascend.

Slowly, slowly, I swirl the solution until a whirlpool begins to form. The fragrance revolves in the whirlpool, then rises up like a nascent tornado. I let it drift upward, its upper end spiralling to the ceiling, but at the instant its lower end is about to waft out, I quickly swirl the solution in reverse, forcing the whirlpool to reverse as well, and the wispy tornado of scent begins to descend. I can never keep an eye on the time, but I believe this takes a long while. Still, I never let my hand pause, swirling the solution in one direction, then the other, over and over. At last the rising and falling fragrance begins to get foggy. Nothing must distract me at this moment. The fragrance rises lazily and falls, and then, sometimes in a trice, disappears. After pouring the colourless solution into the square-bottomed jar, I shut the lid while deliberately diverting my attention elsewhere. In that moment of distraction my hand seems to move toward the jar of its own volition.

A feeling of forlornness, then the revealing of something in this forlornness, is now induced by inhaling the camphor essence, but whatever is revealed in this forlornness already existed before the extract's conception. Indeed, the preparing of the extract relies on its existence.

My ability to identify different kinds of birds is quite poor. During my childhood, I only knew the names of a handful of domestic birds. I would try to find out the names of the birds that chirped on the fence around our house or on a tree in the garden, from my elders, only to forget them the same day. Yet, I assigned each of the birds in my home a human name. Whenever I addressed a bird by its assigned name, it would turn toward me. In due course these birds would die. I would remember each one only for a few days after its death; later forget even the name I had given it. Now I have forgotten all the names I bestowed except one, and the one I remember happens to be neither a human name nor that of a bird. It was a name I had given to the picture of a bird.

This picture had been made by a girl from our family and since she had died a few days later it had been set on the mantel above the fireplace in the living room. So, anyone entering the house would notice it at once. Every first-time visitor to our place would look at it a good while, then examine it from up close. It was worth a good look.

The artist had glued a piece of bark, resembling a long, thin branch, on to a dark-coloured wooden board, on which she had then fashioned the bird from tufts of spotless cotton. For its outstretched wings, she had added real feathers to the cotton; a piece of red glass was used as an eye; the pointed claws were made of thorns from a bush. The bird's claws were raised in the air instead of resting on the branch, making it difficult to guess whether it was landing on the branch or flying away. Perhaps that's why it was disturbing to look at for long. My family, however, saw it simply as the picture of a bird rising from its perch.

I had named it the "kafoori sparrow." I used to feel a cool, almost frosty sensation when I looked at the clean washed cotton and the whiteness of its spotless wings. I had a similar frosty feeling whenever I saw camphor, which was always present in my house because my family prepared a camphor balm. This emollient was distributed free and was referred to as "the cool balm."

Kafoor: Camphor. **Kafoori:** Of or pertaining to camphor.

One day I sat near a woman-servant of the house as she was grinding camphor for the ointment on a stone slab. When the servant went off to run an errand, I heaped the powder on the slab into a mound and, smacking it with my palm, scattered it all over. Then the servant returned.

"Look," she complained to no one in particular, "he's spoiling the whole lot!"

I stood up, dusting my hands. When my eyes lighted on the white powder strewn on the slab, I remembered the outspread wings of the bird in the living room and the frosty feeling I had experienced when looking at it. That day I named it the kafoori sparrow and, from then on, this was the name it went by in my house – mostly because no one seemed to know its real name.

Perhaps no such bird really existed and the artist had created it from her own imagination. However, it resembled several other birds, including some birds of prey. I didn't know this until one day I came upon some guests who had just returned from a bird hunt and were chatting in the big room as they stood before the picture. Pointing to various parts of the sparrow's body, they were debating the name of the bird among themselves. I didn't understand most of their conversation, but all at once the kafoori sparrow seemed too complex a thing, and long after the guests had left I stood peering at the bird, puzzled. To all appearances, it had not been too difficult to make. I studied every aspect of it. At last, I was convinced that its maker had completed it quite simply and easily, in a relatively short time, and that I too could make one without much effort. I wondered why I hadn't tried it before, and immediately started gathering the materials necessary for my attempt.

I tried for many days to make an imitation of the kafoori sparrow. I stood in front of it holding the wooden board in my hand, but nothing seemed to come out right. Each of my efforts left me only with pieces of pinched cotton, and twisted, broken feathers that were strewn all over the living room which, since guests were brought here, was always kept neat and tidy. At last, when milder reprimands failed, I was forbidden to bring my things into the living room at all. Now I had to work within the confines of my tiny room. Every now and then, however, I would go back for a look at the picture – not a long trip, since one door of my bedroom opened on to the large room where it was kept. I would examine the kafoori sparrow in detail, then rush back to my room to add more cotton to the wooden board. Sometimes I would think I had made a portion of the bird quite accurately, but when I started on the next part, the earlier one seemed wrong, making the new portion also appear unsatisfactory.

Despite these setbacks, I still believed that I would be able to copy it quite easily. Therefore, time and again, I found myself standing in front of the picture, wondering why I couldn't duplicate it.

One afternoon, I was staring at the bird when a playmate of mine entered the room looking for me. He, too, looked at the bird for a while, and then said, "There's one just like that across the way."

"Where?" I asked.

"In the tree by the well," he said, pointing outside.

"You've been over by the well?" I asked.

He nodded. "I go there every day."

"Who lives in the house there?"

"No one. It's empty."

Pointing to the kafoori sparrow, I asked, "Is she exactly like this one?"

"It was hard to see through the leaves," he said, "but it looks like this one. Come see."

"She must have flown away by now."

"No. It's been sitting there since this morning."

My curiosity was piqued.

"Let's have a look," I said.

As we walked toward the western edge of the compound, I asked again, "You're sure no one's living there?"

"I told you, it's empty."

The house, the only one besides ours in that large field, usually stood empty. Its main door opened on to the road, but the small door of its large walled back-yard was directly across from our main door. The panels of this door had come loose and were nearly sunk into the earth. A boy of my size could squeeze through the panels. If my friends and I found the house empty when playing in the field, we would often slip into the yard through this loose double door.

Now, my friend and I slipped through the panels one by one and entered the enclosure. Despite my hurry to reach the tree, I stopped at the door and scanned the yard. Heaped with rubbish and overgrown with weeds, it had the appearance of a forest. The people who had lived there had left mementos of their occupancy everywhere, in the form of piles of rubbish. Glancing around, I asked my companion, "Where is it?"

He silenced me with a finger to his lips, and we both tiptoed around to one side of the well. It was nearly overflowing with soil, trash and broken tree branches; only the top two or three circular layers of the six-cornered bricks were free of debris.

The tree stood between the left-hand wall and the well. Since the wall obstructed its growth in one direction, the tree had leaned over the well. We had never climbed this tree. Though its heavy branches appeared strong at first sight, they were the sort that often wouldn't bear the slightest weight. Its large round leaves had a light fuzz of permanent dust on them, which made one's body itch if one accidentally brushed against it. There was no wind now, and the tree looked still and lifeless. When the wind blew, the entire tree swayed, seeming, in motion, to be somehow even more devoid of life. A strong wind could easily make the tree sway, causing a branch to snap and fall to the ground.

Craning his neck, my friend stood under the tree and stared into the branches in deep concentration. I tiptoed near him, leaned against the trunk and looked up at the tree. Its leaves had withered and were about to fall. In certain areas, the whiteness of the sky showed through the web of leaves. I kept thinking I could see a bird in the patches of light. Finally, my companion nudged me with his elbow and pointed upward. I had thought the little body, half-visible, half-hidden by three or four large leaves, was just another patch of sky. Then I saw that one edge of the whiteness had the ridged contour of a wing. The bird was not very high up, its face hidden by leaves. I gestured to my friend that I was going to climb the tree. He signalled back for me not to, but my foot was already on the trunk.

I had started up that tree once before, on a bet with my playmates, but had come down right away when they ran off on seeing I was going to win. Nonetheless, I had been able to assess that the tree could be climbed if too much weight were not exerted on it. This in mind, I began moving up, keeping to the thickest branches. At last I was high enough to grab the bird with my right hand. I grasped a branch with my left hand, planted my feet firmly on a lower branch, and leaned my torso toward the bird. From my vantage point, only one wing was visible, and I wanted to seize both wings in one swoop so it would have no chance of fluttering away. To do so, I moved one foot slightly forward. The branch creaked ominously. My friend called urgently to me from below. I clamped one arm around the branch above and abruptly lifted both feet. My hand was inches from the bird. The lower branch squeaked again, and the whole tree seemed to rock. My playmate called again, plaintively, but now the bird was in my hand.

I glanced down at the groaning branch and tested all the others one by one, but their weakness was apparent at the slightest touch of my foot. I held the bird in my outstretched hand, which all of a sudden was itching furiously. Hanging on with only one hand, I slipped down with difficulty, barely keeping my balance. As my friend hastened around the well to meet me, a large branch crashed down to the well's edge with a great cracking sound, trapping my friend lightly. I grabbed his hand and helped him out from under the branch, and we stood together a few steps away from the well.

"Did you get it?" asked my friend, dusting off his clothes. I looked at my fist. There were tiny red ants crawling all over my hand. The bird had been dead for days; it was hollow inside. A web of tangled leaves was caught in its pointed claws; its head rested on its chest; and its eyes were completely eaten away. I quietly lamented my lost labour as I threw the bird in my friend's direction and started to blow the crawling ants off my hand. Then I heard a strangled scream from my friend. The bird was lying under one of his feet, which he held, frozen, over it. Then I remembered that he was frightened of dead things and that he would go rigid when he'd had a fright. I pulled him gently toward me. He remained stunned for a moment, then jerked away, staring blankly at me. He looked down at his feet and backed away a few more steps. I started toward him but he spun around and ran out through the back door.

I made to follow him, but when I reached the door it occurred to me that I hadn't taken a good look at the bird, so I turned back. I approached the bird and bent over it. It had been flattened by my friend's foot. Had there been a wooden board beneath it instead of the soft earth I would have thought I'd created a slapdash copy of the kafoori sparrow.

After that, I lost interest in the kafoori sparrow and once again set to making other things.

Even when I was very small I would put together ill-assorted pieces of things picked up here and there, and then ask people to guess what it was. My family would name something or the other, and I would really believe I had made what they said I had, even convincing myself that it was, indeed, what I had set out to make all along. I would display the new sample of my craftsmanship on the mantel and consider my work the equal of the kafoori sparrow. I never admitted that the things I made were toys, and once when I had tied two or three blocks of wood together and was told that I had made a remarkable car, I insisted for days that my family use it to go out for a drive. But soon I would forget my latest creation and someone would discreetly remove it from the mantel. Gradually, I collected quite a few tools and other implements with which I fashioned many different objects. Their resemblance to their real life counterparts was slim, but recognizable. Underneath the bed in my small room I stowed all kinds of tools, pieces of wood, snippets of gaily coloured cloth, scraps of tin, metal wire, even fruit pits. I could put out my hand and touch any of the objects I wished, even in the dark.

In my fervour to duplicate the kafoori sparrow, I had quite forgotten all these items, but now they reclaimed my attention more intensely than before. Though the noise of things being hammered and banged about began to erupt from my room at all hours of the day and night, disturbing the rest of the household, no restrictions were imposed on me, as I was the darling son of the house. When I accidentally injured my hands, however, my work would come to a halt for a day or two. After I had injured myself often enough, a big bottle of kafoor balm was kept in my room permanently, although such salves were usually used for serious injuries and old wounds. My cuts were ordinary and temporary, and any remedy from the market would have healed them, but I was, as I said, the darling of the house. The objects I made were displayed on the mantelpiece without any prompting from me and were made much of to guests. Sometimes, when I couldn't think of anything to make, I would go up to the roof, from where one could clearly see the top of the other house and the wall of its back-yard across the field. There, I would sometimes sense, in the soft pulse of the breeze, the embrace of some familiar or unfamiliar fragrance, and a picture would form in my mind, only to disappear at once. As I experienced these forming and dissolving images, I would suddenly be seized with the desire to make something and hurry down to lock myself up in my room.

One day, after the long season of scorching heat and white-hot winds, I stood on the roof of my house watching the clouds that had been gathering in the sky since the morning. Near me stood the same friend who had earlier been frightened by the dead bird. We both enjoyed getting wet in the first rain of the season, and seeing the signs of an imminent shower he had come up to the roof to look for me. We pointed out shapes made by large and small clumps of drifting clouds. Here and there the blue of the sky peered between them, but as we stood there, the patchy clouds congealed into a smooth sheet of dark grey. I forgot my playmate in my anticipation of the strong wind and falling rain. Shortly, little puffs of wind began to blow. One of them seemed to bear a fragrance as cold as ice, but this scent somehow met my eyes instead of my nostrils, appearing before me like the dangling end of a white string that pulled upward and then vanished. Just then I heard my friend:

"That looks just like the other one."

He was looking up. I did the same. A bird was hovering above our heads. Circling with it was a white string.

"What is that string?" I asked myself aloud.

"She must have picked it up," said my friend, "to make her nest."

The bird descended slightly, then rose up again.

"No," I said, "the string is tied to her claws."

"Then she must have broken free from somewhere," my friend observed. "I wonder whose bird it is."

We continued to stare at it in silence. The pattern of its flight spoke of a great weariness. Flapping its wings slowly, it hovered near the roof as though searching for a resting place. Finally, it landed on the turret that rose from the roof to the left of where we were standing. It seemed to be staring at something straight ahead, oblivious to our presence. I motioned to my companion to be silent and began edging slowly toward the turret. I stopped very near it. I could not see the bird, but the string was dangling before me, within reach of my hand.

I turned toward my friend and gestured for him to be silent once again, but just then I heard the rustling of feathers, and when I spun back to the turret, the end of the string had risen beyond my reach. I returned to my friend's side. The bird was now flying swiftly toward the other house, veering left and right like someone staggering across the ground, the white string wavering behind it like a snake.

"Isn't she just like the ...," my companion began.

But my eyes were fixed on the bird and I didn't answer. It passed the wall of the enclosure and was circling one spot, descending slightly with each spiral. At last, it disappeared behind the wall of the house. The next moment, the bird rose again at the same point, fluttering its wings rapidly, then sank from view again. It re-emerged. It fluttered its wings for some time, rivetted to one spot. Again it descended slowly out of sight. We waited for it to rise again, but it didn't.

"What is it doing there?" my friend asked, staring fixedly at the wall.

There was a faint rumbling of thunder, and lightning bolts flashed and vanished at several points in the dark grey sky. The thought struck me at the same moment that my friend said, "That's where the tree by the well is."

We looked at each other and fell silent. Above, the sound of thunder shifted, descended, ricochetted across the earth, and then vanished into the sky. I grabbed my friend's hand. "Let's go and free her," I said.

"No," he said, tugging against my grip.

"Come on," I insisted.

"No," he repeated. "I'm not going over there."

"This one's not dead," I said, "however, if it rains ..."

But his hand had begun to grow cold in mine and he was staring blankly at me.

"Okay, as you like," I said and climbed down from the roof, leaving him there.

The heat still hung in the air and the tree's large leaves drooped, but their greenness struggled through the dust settled on their fuzzy surface. I walked halfway around the well and stood under the tree. There was no movement or noise in the branches above, but I believed the bird was hiding somewhere in the leaves, and I continued to peer into the treetop. At last I began to think it might have flown off before I had arrived. Just then I heard a faint noise which I could not identify but decided must be feathers rustling against the leaves. I looked up. The sound seemed to be coming from everywhere in the tree. I realized then that it had begun, quietly, to rain. I hesitated, then walked out into the open. After a short distance I turned back to look at the tree.

It was metamorphosing before my eyes. The raindrops were tracing green lines on the fuzzy leaves as they washed away the dust, and the wilted leaves were slowly regaining their freshness. Suddenly the rain began to fall more heavily and I turned toward the door in the wall. The faint smell of earth rose to my nostrils, then the sound of a rapid fluttering met my ears. I turned again to look back at the tree. The bird was fluttering about in a fixed spot just above it. As its swiftly flapping wings scattered fat drops of water, the bird appeared as if enveloped in a white fog. On all sides of this trembling tuft of fog the incessant rain drew white strings from sky to earth.

The whole yard was awash now. The familiar smell that rose from the mud at the first rain had abated, and now the fragrances buried in the deeper layers of the earth were beginning to emerge. These fragrances at my feet would rise from the ground and hover at a certain point for a while, before the rain dashed them back down, but I paid little heed to them: I was looking up at the tree, where the trembling fog and sound of feathers were no longer evident. Bathed in rain, the tree's leaves had turned dark green, its trunk, black. The entire tree blurred as the rain thickened. I realized that my clothes were soaked. I had hardly started for the door in the wall when the wind too began to blow harder. I shivered all over; the door seemed a great distance off. I turned and ran in the opposite direction until I stood under the verandah – a long, narrow, tin-roofed shelter that was attached to the back of the house. The water spilling from the roof of the shelter formed a curtain before me through which the driving rain looked like giant sheets of smoke, billowing and contracting in the gusts of wind.

The wind swept under the verandah roof, making the tin shudder. I felt the cold descend into my bones and my eyes cast about for some better protection from the downpour. Behind me were three doors whose top panels were set with round panes of blue glass. I had seen the house many times and knew that a living room with three fireplaces lay behind the three doors. As a child, whenever I went past these doors in the company of my family, I would insist that someone lift me up until I could look through the glass of the middle door, for the expanse of blue gave me a feeling of contentment.

Now I recalled the last family that had lived in this house. They were six or seven people who had sat for the most part in silence with their heads bowed. The women of the house would get up to do a piece of work, then return to their place and sit with their heads down. The men would return from work, go quietly to their rooms, re-emerge after changing their clothes and sit with their heads down. A girl would ask another something, be answered, and then both would fall silent and lower their heads. All of them seemed to be engulfed in a fog. In those days, I had to go to their house frequently on some errand or the other. Each time I would return irritated and angry, parody their way of sitting and ask not to be sent to the house again. My people would laugh at this, and two or three days later blithely send me back. Then, one day, the family left the house without informing anyone. The house had remained empty since then. The room with the fireplaces had never been opened again. And now I was standing outside it getting soaked in the downpour. The cold was unbearable, and I started pushing at each of the doors in turn. I soon realized that if the doors had not been bolted from the inside, the wind, which was growing steadily fiercer, would have flung them open a long time ago. The wind intensified and the water falling from the verandah roof sloshed on me. The filth that had collected on the tin roof slid off along with the water. I noticed several dark black stains on my clothes. Leaving the verandah, I dashed back under the tree. I thought again of the bird and, though I knew it was hopeless, tried to spot it among the branches, but water filled my eyes. At that very moment the tree creaked and I, taking it to be an ominous warning, leapt out from under it and dashed into the verandah once again.

That's about all I remember of that day.

That year it rained and rained, and the entire compound turned into a marsh. The ground inside the walls disappeared under a soggy carpet of weeds and grass. The front door of my house was closed off and everyone came and went through the back door, which opened on to the street. During this period I spent most of my free time inside my room. In view of my fondness for constructing things, I had been given new tools of high quality, with the aid of which the processes of chiselling wood, cutting everything from hard tin to thick glass, snipping and shaping heavy iron wire, and joining materials together had become much easier for me. I built tiny houses, and models of different kinds of transport. Most of what I made in my earlier endeavours would seem pale and ordinary to me after a few days, and I would toss them away or leave them lying about. However, a few of the things that I made during these rains I liked even better later. Indeed, when they were finally set up on the mantelpiece I would wonder how I had made them.

At one point, the main door of the house was opened so that the compound could be weeded of the plants that had sprung up during the rains. I noticed that the water had carved away a quarter of a small hillock to the left of the door, and a whitish, sticky mud had flowed off, spreading into a large puddle. When I went closer to have a look at the diminished mound, the mud clung to my feet. As I tried to gingerly tread on it my foot slipped so swiftly that, had the other one not been firmly stuck in the clay, I would have had a nasty fall. An elderly labourer who was helping to clear the field happened to be watching. He advised me to walk carefully, adding that this was a rare kind of soil from which delicate objects could be fashioned. He said that the soil had been brought from some other part of the country and that an old man who used to live nearby in this very compound, a long time ago, had used it to make models of small birds. As he mentioned the artisan, the old labourer pointed to the back door of the other house, beside which a crumbling wall was visible.

Immediately I became fascinated with the idea of working with clay, and at my request the labourer dug some dry soil from inside the mound and deposited a little pile of it inside my yard. He explained the method of wetting and preparing the clay. I set to work at once, and he turned back to his labours. I took a bit of mud, pressed it between my palms, and observed the result. There were no stones or sand in the clay, and the finest lines of my palm were visible on its surface. Suddenly, I felt the faintest whiff of kafoor leap up like a flame and vanish. I breathed deeply, bringing my palm up to my nostrils, but there was nothing but the cool smell of ordinary earth. I took another deep breath, then became aware of the silence extending in every direction, which the sound of a grinding stone inside the house enhanced rather than subdued. I scooped up a little mud in my hands and returned to my room.

Now I turned to making objects of clay. This did not require any tools. There was always a reserve of well-kneaded sticky clay in my room. I could not make animals and birds, but I could easily fashion little beads for jewellery and oddly-shaped pots. By the time the dry season arrived, I had made numerous small objects, and when the sun grew stronger I began drying, baking and painting them. I burnt my hands many times in the process, but worked on undeterred because the pain from the burns would vanish with the application of kafoor balm. However, as the fires I lit sometimes damaged various household items as well, I was finally prohibited from using fire inside the house, and I arranged to bake my wares outside, in a corner of the compound. The main door, which by now had been permanently closed, was reopened exclusively for me. The fierce rain had carved deep channels in the tender earth, making access to the main door difficult for vehicles, and for people in the dark. For this reason, and because the back door opened on to the street, the latter had come to be used as the principal entrance. Thus the field remained largely silent and empty and I could go about my work undisturbed.

One day, as I was dusting the ash off my baked pots I thought I heard a sound and turned to look. Two men I had never seen before were coming across the field, picking their way through the gullies. They reached the main door and hesitated. They did not knock. They appeared to be unable to decide whether to go up to the house or not. After observing them for a while, I began to clink my pots together – which was my way of determining whether they were properly baked. When they heard the sound, they noticed me and slowly drew near. They looked at my pots, I at them. Though their height, complexion, and facial features differed there was a strange resemblance between them that convinced me they were brothers. One of them pointed at the main door and asked, "Is this the house that's empty?"

"No, sir. That one is," I said, pointing at the other house. "It has a door that opens on to the street. The one you see is the door to my back-yard."

I noticed that new door panels had been put in to replace the old loose ones, and the door appeared to be firmly bolted from the inside.

"This house ...," He gestured again at my door. "Is this where you live?"

I nodded.

"Did you make these?" he asked, looking at my pots.

I nodded again.

"Very pretty toys."

"They're not toys."

"No?" he smiled. "What are they?"

"Pots."

"They're very beautiful pots. What else do you make?"

I reeled off a list.

"But none of them are toys?"

"No, sir."

"You seem to be a true craftsman. What do you do with the things you make?"

"They're for decoration," I said. "And I give them away."

"Are you going to give us something?"

"You're welcome to have any you like," I replied. "But I haven't painted them yet."

"Well then, later," said the man, and took another look around the field.

"Are you going to move into that house?" I asked.

"The two of us are always travelling," he replied, "but our families will be moving in."

"Are there any boys my age?"

He laughed: "No, sir. Just two or three women and the rest girls, all girls." He laughed again: "And all older than you. But," he added, pointing to the pots, "Mah Rukh Sultan is also very fond of this sort of thing."

He glanced around the area once more, then said:

"All right, we'll have a look at our new house now."

As they turned away, I raised my hand in salaam, ashamed that I had not thought of showing them this respect when they had first entered.

When they had left and I had returned to my work, I realized that only one of the men had conversed with me. At that moment I heard another sound and turned around. The fellow who had not spoken earlier was standing near me. Without meeting my eyes, he asked:

"Who is your local doctor?"

I gave him the name of our doctor.

"Does he live far from here?"

"No, he's nearby," I told him, and asked, "Is someone in your family ill?"

"No." He said something else, but I didn't understand it. Then he walked away silently.

When I told my family that some new people were moving into the house next door, I found that they already knew about it. I also learned that the repair of the house had been in progress for several days and that it was nearly finished. However, I was plied with questions about the men who had spoken to me. Of course, I could tell them no more than what had been said during the conversation. My family knew very little, only that the two were indeed brothers and that they came from another country, having left their home when still children. I remarked that they didn't look like foreigners, and retired to my room.

I arranged the things placed on the mantel with great care, changing their placement and order several times. Finally satisfied, I stepped back for a look. The most outstanding piece was still the kafoori sparrow. Days later, I found myself staring at it for a long time. It looked alive. Each time I looked at it I felt as though it were flying off the branch or swooping down. I still thought it must have been made fairly easily and wondered anew why I was unable to reproduce it. I also wondered why I hadn't thought of a good human name for it yet. My musings transformed into a light regret.

If it weren't for the fact that everyone called it the kafoori sparrow now, I thought sadly, I would have named it Mah Rukh Sultan.

I saw Mah Rukh Sultan that very week. That day, I had been tidying my room since the morning, putting all the objects I had left lying about in order. The articles I had made were all stacked on my bed and on the table that stood against the opposite wall. My tools were all over the floor and I was yanking more stuff out from under the bed when I realized that a crowd of guests had come into the living room. Leaning back from the bed a little, I peeped through the thin film of the curtain hanging over the half-open door. The living room was filled with masses of girls, all of them older than I was. I looked at their colourful dresses with interest, then set back to work, but their voices filtered in from the larger room. An older woman with a strident voice was holding forth at a great clip, as though afraid of forgetting her next sentence, recounting the difficulties of travelling with huge quantities of luggage, describing the floor plan of the house she had left behind, ticking off the advantages and disadvantages of her present abode. The women of my house showed sympathy but now and then one of her own girls would point out some exaggeration in the old lady's account and start to giggle. Then the old lady introduced the girls by name: Mah Rukh Sultan, Seem Tan Sultan, Dil Afza Sultan, Zar Taj Sultan, Pari Paikar Sultan and so on. My relatives remarked on the lovely names and the girls giggled and giggled. Then their laughter changed to sounds of wonderment and shrieks of joy. I guessed from their voices that they were standing by the kafoori sparrow. Its creator was mentioned and the voices grew momentarily subdued, then the cries of wonder and excitement rose once more. Now the objects displayed on the mantel were named one by one. At first, this made me feel good, but the thought that I might be called in and introduced to the crowd unsettled me. I rose slowly to close the half-opened door leading to the larger room, but realized I would surely be seen from behind the curtain as I did so. I hesitated, uncertain what to do, then noticed a twisted piece of sturdy wire on the floor and reached down for it. At that moment a voice came from the area of the fireplace:

"Mah Rukh Sultan! Do you see that? It looks like it's alive."

I pressed the crooked wire across my knees to straighten it, and had just lifted it to prod the door shut when a sudden silence descended on the living room. It was as though the room were empty. Listening attentively, I began to hear the rustling of dresses and the sound of whispering, but I couldn't make out what was being said. Barely had I extended the wire toward the door when the double doors were flung wide open and a woman relative of mine walked into the room. She took in the mess in a glance, then pointed to all the things piled on my bed and said, "Get this stuff off here, and hurry – then out you go!"

I had barely opened my mouth to protest when she silenced me with a wave of her hand. "Mah Rukh Sultan isn't feeling well," she said. "She needs to lie down."

My relative began moving the things off the bed herself and piling them up on the table. I was obliged to lend a hand. She launched into a lecture on the benefits of good housekeeping as she removed the objects. One leg of the bed was shorter than the others, and kept hitting the floor with a clunking sound. I was searching for a piece of wood to put under it when I heard the voice of another woman relative at the door: "Right here," she was saying, holding the curtain aside. "Bring her in."

I saw a cluster of women and girls at the door, but only one girl and an older woman came in. I couldn't tell who was supporting whom. The girl, however, kept her eyes lowered while the older woman craned her neck to examine everything in the room. With her help, the girl sat down on the bed, and the short leg hit the floor. The girl's head tilted back a little, but her eyes remained downcast. The old woman peered round the room again, her eyes lighting briefly on me. I was standing with my hand resting on the table. My relative tapped me lightly on the shoulder and asked me to leave, and I went out through the room's other door, the one which opened into a small yard enclosed by a low wall, beyond which lay the field. It was easy enough to get into the field from here, and I wandered around it for a while.

I hadn't been able to get a good look at Mah Rukh Sultan. I recalled only that she had one end of her white dupatta draped over her head while the other hung down to her feet, one of its corners wrapped around her hand. There was something else I couldn't quite place, but as I walked by the mound of oily earth it came back to me that I had felt a very light caress of kafoor when she had walked past me.

After a while I got bored wandering in the field and returned to the yard. I stood near the door of my room and strained my ears. There was no sound from inside. The door was not fully closed, and I pushed it open an inch farther. I saw at once that the bed was empty, then heard the sound of conversation in the living room, so I opened the door the whole way and walked into the bedroom.

Mah Rukh Sultan was standing there with one hand on the table. She was still holding one end of her dupatta. A clay necklace I had made but not yet painted was trembling gently in her other hand. Hearing me, she turned in my direction and with a motion of her head gestured for me to come near.

"Did you make this?" she asked, holding the necklace up to her face. "It's beautiful."

I just stood there, embarrassed.

"Truly lovely," she repeated, then asked, "Is this sort of clay found around here?"

"Oh no," I said. "Someone brought it here from far away and left it in the yard."

"Who?"

"I don't know," I said. "It was a long time ago."

"He doesn't bring it anymore?"

"I guess not," I said, and repeated, "it was a long time ago."

She continued to look at the necklace in silence. Its large round beads and flowers suddenly seemed dull, and I said, "I still have to paint it."

"It looks better the way it is," said Mah Rukh Sultan.

One by one, she lifted up the other things: pots, vehicles, houses. I was annoyed at my woman relative who, while counselling me to be tidy, had just piled everything up in a heap on the table. The thought that this disorder was due to Mah Rukh Sultan never entered my mind, but I did notice that Mah Rukh Sultan, after inspecting the items, was putting them down on the table in a new arrangement that was even nicer than the way I had set them. She picked up a little car, looked at its wheels, ran it across the table and then said:

"If you had a mind to, you could also make very fine toys."

I tried to say something, but could not; I opened my mouth again, hesitated once more, then said softly, "These *are* toys."

Mah Rukh Sultan smiled for the first time, looking perfectly healthy. She continued to pick up objects from the table and to put them down again, saying nothing. She picked up a wooden carving of an old-fashioned house, inspected the cut of its arch at length, and then said, "Don't you cut your hands doing this?"

"Sometimes," I said, and looked down at the marks on my hands. Mah Rukh Sultan looked at her own hands, but I didn't notice any marks there.

The voices from the big room grew louder for a moment. I realized that Mah Rukh Sultan must have been standing there for quite some time. Just then, she picked up a little square clock from the table and said, "This one's real."

"No, it's just ..."

"It's late," she said, peering at the hands of the clock, then turned toward the door and said, "They must be worried."

"How are you feeling now?" I asked, suddenly aware that I should have asked much sooner.

"You've been put to a lot of trouble on my account," she said as though delivering a rehearsed message.

I asked again, "Are you feeling better now?"

Lifting her eyes from the clock, she glanced at the door. I followed her eyes and once again felt the light embrace of kafoor. Mah Rukh Sultan was saying, "You must come visit us."

And I noticed that she was unwrapping the folds of her dupatta from her fist. I caught a glimpse of what looked like a little pot, even before all the folds had been unwound. I felt I should look away and did so. A few seconds later she said, "I brought this for you."

I looked. It was a short, square jar of white china. When she held out the jar to me, I noticed light marks on her hand. I took the jar from her and studied it closely. It wasn't as small as I had thought. I wondered how she had been able to hide it in her hand for so long.

"This is very nice," I said. "Did you make it?"

"I made it when I was your age."

I was about to ask her how one made such a thing when she noticed something on the table, picked it up and said, "This looks like the lid of a bottle."

I looked at the lid, then the table, then the floor. The bottle of kafoor balm lay open, tipped over on the floor near one of the table legs. A little of the ointment had spilled out on to the ground. I picked up the bottle and held it out to Mah Rukh Sultan without thinking, but she was handing the lid to me. Taking it, I screwed it on to the bottle.

"The cold balm," I told her.

She smiled again, and said, "You must cut your hands a lot." Then she said gravely, "Do come to our house, won't you?"

She stepped soundlessly toward the double door, opened one panel and went out. The voices in the big room paused momentarily, then came cries of happiness, audible kisses and the sound of Mah Rukh Sultan's name being called.

The family did not live in that house for long, and I never grew close to any of them except Mah Rukh Sultan – though I had more contact with her sisters. I could never get the count of the sisters straight, or their order of seniority. They all wore colourful clothes, talked loudly, and laughed boisterously. And their faces turned red with the slightest hint of mirth. When expressing wonder they would shriek, and when very happy they would cry. There were one or two women like this in my family as well and, whenever they visited, our house seemed to burst with their presence. But I was terrified of running into Mah Rukh Sultan's sisters and did my best to avoid them. Even Mah Rukh Sultan seemed to be lost among them, and sometimes when she escaped from the thicket of girls to talk to me, I was unable to hear her voice clearly for quite some time.

My first visit to their house was five or six days after they had come to ours. I was delivering an invitation to a religious ceremony at our home. An old woman, whether servant or family member I could not tell, ushered me into the room with the three fireplaces, where the strident-voiced woman was seated, putting tiny bottles inside a black box. After promising to come to the ceremony, she began interrogating me about my family members, near and distant, and then, volunteering information about herself, she spoke faster and faster. Soon I realized she was actually talking to herself, oblivious of my presence, and I allowed my eyes to wander. The three doors with the blue panes were open and the backyard was almost completely visible, but the corner with the well and the tree couldn't be seen. The ground had been levelled smoothly and cleared of twigs and rubbish. Opposite the verandah, in the distance, I could see the exterior wall with the double doors that opened on to the field. Both doors were open and, across the field, I could see the closed main door of my own house. Intense sunlight flooded the compound. Two or three days earlier I had made some more clay jewellery pieces, and today, as I had been about to put them in the sun to dry, I'd been sent to the old lady. I had come the long way around, via the street leading from the back door of my house to the front door of theirs, and was to return by the same route. Reflecting on this while looking straight across at my closed main door, my house seemed at once too close and too far.

The old woman's voice, which I had disliked at first, seemed even more repugnant now. She was recounting the difficulties she had faced in giving birth to her children, raising and training them, and in the telling, mentioned matters which were not spoken about to boys of my age in our family. Here and there she would touch on other matters, and I learned that one of the two brothers who had rented the house traded in perfumes and the other in chandeliers. At this she gestured expansively at the ceiling and I saw three large chandeliers suspended from a hook, their triangular glass lustres glinting from countless angles. In the centre of the chandelier, cut-glass balls dangled from the ends of chains. Even the links of the chains were made of glass. The balls swayed gently, shattering the light into a myriad colours.

All at once the sound of many footsteps was heard on the stairs. A large group of girls spilled down them, shouting and laughing, and a darkness of many colours filled the room. They all gathered in front of the central fireplace, talking among themselves, and I asked the old lady's permission to leave, but suddenly the cluster of girls came toward me and I found myself engulfed. They all began lauding the things I made, mentioning specific items. They peppered me with questions too, as they prattled on, but, mercifully, gave me little opportunity to answer. One of the things they did insist on knowing, however, was why I gave away the things I made. Before I could finish telling them, they started requesting the things they wanted. Two or three sisters would ask for the same thing, then laughingly shriek and paw one another. The chandeliers in the room seemed to tinkle with the sound of their voices. I began to feel a bit dizzy; the room full of melodious voices coming at me as in a dream.

My thoughts strayed to the people who had lived here before. It was my first visit to the room since they had left. For an instant, all of them appeared, sitting at their places with their heads bowed. My head spun once more, then different colours rose before my eyes and the band of girls was visible to me again. They were still asking for various objects I had made. Finally the old woman scolded them for bothering me and they all dispersed amid more giggling. The old woman told me to ignore their requests, but I promised to bring what they had asked for the following day. The dreamlike sensation had not abated. Maybe that was why I was unable to tell whether Mah Rukh Sultan was among the band of girls or not. Also why I had failed to notice that her sisters had requested objects that were still on my table and had never been displayed on the mantel. Among others, the unpainted necklace.

On my return, I learned that the old woman had, in her first encounter with them, already shared with my relatives everything she had divulged to me. All that and more. Not once but many times over. So, rather than reporting to them, I was informed of what they knew: that all the girls were the issue of one of the brothers, and that the other had adopted Mah Rukh Sultan. Just then I remembered that Mah Rukh Sultan had invited me to visit and I had returned without seeing her. I decided then and there that I would take my finest piece for her. I examined the objects on the mantel, then those on the table in my room. I put the things that had been requested in a basket and scrutinized the remainder of the collection. I noticed one or two defects in each of them; my mind grew muddled and I stood motionless before the fireplace for a long time. My eyes fixed on the kafoori sparrow; I regretted not having given it a good name. Then I thought of Mah Rukh Sultan standing at the table in my room and recalled the square clock that she had taken for real. I headed toward my room, but midway there remembered that I had given the clock to one of my relatives two days ago. This relative was very fond of me and always brought me some new tool when he came to visit. I had given him the clock on my own, and had even insisted that he take it when he refused. But now I was as angry, as if *he* had snatched it from me. I soon convinced myself that the clock was the best thing I had ever crafted, though the process of making it, while laborious, was not complicated. I decided I would make another one, and locked myself up in my room.

I worked on it straight through until midnight and the following day until noon. There were cuts all over my hands and the bottle of kafoor balm was almost empty but I did not stop. When it was finished I placed it on the table to view it, then moved it to the mantel to see how it looked there. This one was not as finely made as the original because the pain had stiffened my hands, but it was better than all my other pieces. I wrapped it in clean paper and put it in the basket underneath everything else.

I arrived at the house in the afternoon. The old lady was not at home. Another middle-aged woman brought me to the room with the fireplaces, and I took the articles out of the basket and set them randomly on the mantel. When the woman came over to have a look, I said; "They asked me for these."

"Who did?"

I felt uncomfortable repeating all the names, so I said, "All of them."

"Very well – I'll call them," she said, and was gone.

I was mentally rearranging the things on the mantel when Mah Rukh Sultan's sisters burst into the room en masse and made a beeline for the fireplace. Holding the clock in my hand, I stood wordlessly in the midst of the chaotic hum of girlish exclamations and squabblings over the articles. At last they calmed down, turned to me and spoke in seriousness, and I became aware again that they were all older than I was. Distressed, I stood there wondering how I might get to see Mah Rukh Sultan. My problem was solved when one of the sisters asked me, "Didn't you bring anything for Mah Rukh Sultan?"

"Where is she?" I asked.

Another sister, opening the blue-paned door in the centre, said, "She's in here. Come this way."

That is how, after so much time had gone by, I found myself once again in the tin-roofed verandah of the house. Mah Rukh Sultan was sitting on a takht that had been placed against the wall. Before her was a black box similar to the one I had seen the old lady filling with vials. Mah Rukh Sultan was taking the vials out of the box and arranging them on the takht. Smiling softly, she beckoned me to sit and, without preamble, I handed her the clock wrapped in paper. She looked at me, then unwrapped the paper, lifted out the clock and – with her eyes fixed on its hands – remarked:

"How beautifully made!"

I assumed she thought it was the same one she had seen in my room that day, but she asked, "Did you make this just today?"

"Yesterday and today," I said, a little disappointed. "I was in a hurry; it's not very polished."

"No," she said as she looked at it from different angles, and added, "This one is much nicer. The other one looked real."

She removed a few of the vials in front of the box and set the clock down in their place. The delicate gleam of the clock's colours became more pronounced against the black background of the box, and even I began to like it better than the first one. Mah Rukh Sultan picked it up

Takht: An all-purpose low wooden platform found in traditional homes. It can serve as a bed, a seat or a place to eat.

again. Holding it at arm's length, she brought it up to her face a few times, then put it down. "You like kafoor very much," she said.

I didn't understand right away.

"*Kafoor*?" I asked.

"You call that sculpture the kafoori sparrow, too."

"That ... that's because it's white," I said. "But I don't like that name, really."

"A lot of people are scared of it."

"Of the *kafoori* sparrow?" I asked, astonished.

"Of kafoor," said Mah Rukh Sultan. "It makes people think of death."

"Kafoor?" I repeated. "But kafoor is a cure for many pains."

"Death too is a cure for many pains."

There was a hint of teasing in her voice, so I glanced up at her with a laugh, but she wasn't smiling. She appeared to be lost in thought. She was tapping lightly on the black box behind the toy clock with the nail of her middle finger, making a faint, regular, clicking sound – as if the clock were ticking. Beneath this sound, I could hear her sisters talking and laughing in different parts of the house. One of the voices came nearer, reaching the door. One of the sisters came out on to the verandah, leaned over Mah Rukh Sultan, kissed her on the forehead, and went back in. Mah Rukh Sultan's eyes followed her for a moment, then she began to line up the little bottles again. She picked up the clock and, placing it alongside the box, asked me, "Who taught you all this?"

"Nobody."

"No one at all?"

I told her that I had always been fond of making things, even as a child, and had gradually accumulated a collection of tools. I described the sort of things I had made at first and those I had made later. As I spoke, one sister or another would come out from time to time, give her a kiss and return. Finally, when one of them leaned over and whispered something in her ear, I suddenly grew aware that I had been talking uninterruptedly for some time and got up to leave. Mah Rukh Sultan stopped me:

"Stay awhile longer," she said, and began to put the bottles back in the box. "Talking with you takes me back to my childhood."

Her words pleased me, but I didn't know what to say next, so I asked, "What's in the bottles?"

"Perfumes," said Mah Rukh Sultan, and placed the black box in front of me. At that moment I could sense all the fragrances under the verandah as they rose and sank. One fragrance would arise, then another would soar above it, pressing it down. At times many fragrances would merge into one, scatter, then unite. The scents brought to mind colours and voices, and the colours and voices brought to mind Mah Rukh Sultan's sisters, perhaps now gathered around the fireplace again. When I lifted the box it seemed to be tinkling with the scents inside. I asked, "What are these perfumes made of?"

Scarcely had Mah Rukh Sultan begun to list the various flowers than I sensed a pale, cold, silent, white smell caress all the other fragrances and flit away, then leap back, touch them all once more, and creep away again. Now I asked, "Is one of them kafoor perfume?"

Mah Rukh Sultan stopped and looked at me closely, and then she smiled with an effort.

"You can't make perfume of kafoor," she said. She took the box from me, touched each bottle in turn and named the kind of perfume it contained. Then she closed the lid of the box.

"The scent of kafoor is not among them," she said at last in answer to my question. Once again she made an effort to smile, placed her hand on the clock and said, "The smell of kafoor is in this."

"In the clock?" I asked in wonder, and picked up the little object.

"There was the same smell in your room that day."

"That was the kafoor balm," I replied, and now recalled the many times that I had cut my hands while working on this clock, smeared ointment on my wounds, and kept at my task. Now I felt the stiffness in my fingers and wondered whether I should mention any of this to Mah Rukh Sultan, but before I could decide she asked me:

"Do you really cut your hands a lot?"

Just then another of her sisters came out to hover over her. Mah Rukh Sultan stood up.

"Come here a moment," she said, motioning toward the door with the blue glass. I followed her back to the room with the fireplaces, where refreshments had been set out in lavish array, the aromas of the different foods filling the room. Every one of Mah Rukh Sultan's sisters insisted on feeding me a little of every single dish. Their attention began to make me feel uncomfortable, the more so since they had gone to all this extravagance on my account, and Mah Rukh Sultan was sitting next to me, eating nothing at all.

All I had managed to learn about Mah Rukh Sultan's illness was that at certain times she would suddenly feel suffocated, and wouldn't want anyone near her. She'd remain alone for a while and the attack would abate on its own. Sometimes I would go to visit, taking her something I had made, only to learn that she wasn't feeling well and was resting. I would leave the new item on the mantel of one of the fireplaces and go home after chatting briefly with her sisters. I'd venture there again two or three days later and there she would be, surrounded by her sisters, or sitting on the takht in the verandah. She always began the conversation with the question, "What are you making these days?"

Once I got started I gave her no chance to speak; she only put in a few questions here and there to let me know she was listening.

One day I made two houses so tiny I could hold them both in one hand. I was sure Mah Rukh Sultan would like them. And I was sure I'd be able to see her. I knew that she had had one of her spells just the day before. But on arriving I learned that she still hadn't recovered and was in her room, resting. I conversed with her sisters for a while, the little houses concealed in my hand, and at last got up to leave. Just then, the door to her room opened slowly, and Mah Rukh Sultan stood at the threshold. Her sisters leapt to greet her, shrieking with joy and calling her name, kissing and hugging her in turn. They wept, too, in their displays of affection. Mah Rukh Sultan patted each sister's cheeks with both hands and then moved them gently aside. In so doing her eyes fell on me, and she came over and asked, "Did you just arrive?"

I stood there in silence.

"Were you about to go back?" she asked again after a pause.

Again, I remained silent. In the meantime her sisters had disappeared; even the sound of their chattering had died away. I recalled the clamour of a few moments earlier and asked, "How are you feeling now?"

Her eyes fell on my hand, and instead of answering she asked, "What have you made?"

Then I remembered the little houses. Stretching out my hand, I opened my fist to display them to her. "How lovely!" she exclaimed.

"I made them for you."

Mah Rukh Sultan stared in marvel at the houses on my palm, then said, "I have something for you, too."

With slow steps, she walked back to her room. Reaching the door, she turned to me and said, "Please come in."

When I entered the room, she was already seated in the centre of the masehri. She motioned to me to sit on a cushioned chair near the bed. The room was sparsely furnished and decorated, but the finely woven curtains hanging before the alcoves built into the wall were quite beautiful, and at first glance looked like white carpets. One door opened to the large room with the fireplaces, and another led to the verandah. I could see some of the yard through the second door, but couldn't figure

---

Masehri: A bed with mosquito netting draped over it.

out which part I was looking at. I felt mildly confused as I turned this over in my mind, trying to orient myself by recalling the position of the yard. I shifted my attention back to Mah Rukh Sultan. She was lost in thought, her head bowed. After a while she raised her head, but her eyes were still downcast. I suspected that she had fallen asleep sitting upright, but my suspicions were proven wrong when, in the same absorbed state, she got up from under the masehri, walked to the almirah in the wall and returned with something in her hands. At first it looked like a handful of irregular pieces of clear glass. Sitting again on the canopied bed, she set the pieces down before her, stared at them for a second as though searching for something, then grasped a round piece between her thumb and forefinger and lifted her hand. I heard the light clink of little bottles and saw a tiny glass chandelier dangling from Mah Rukh Sultan's fingers, its faint reflections trembling on her face. Then she spoke: "Do you like things made of glass?"

"It's beautiful," I said. "Did you make it?"

"No, I don't know who made it," she said. "I've only altered it."

As she spun the chandelier slowly, holding it out toward me, I noticed that hanging from each of its dangling pieces was a delicate vial. All the vials were spinning in a circle as the chandelier rotated, thus I was unable to count them, but had the impression that there were at least ten. All of them were made of clear glass but were filled with different coloured liquids.

"Is there perfume in these bottles?" I asked.

"One is empty," Mah Rukh Sultan answered; then she smiled with some effort and went on, "You may fill it with whatever scent you like."

She handed me the chandelier and I examined it in the light coming through the open door. It was no bigger than the span between the tips of my little finger and thumb. Behind its transparent pendants I could see a portion of the yard. As my eyes played over the wall with the loosened bricks, I realized with a jolt that this was where the tree and well had been. The well had been filled in with earth and the site levelled over; a faint bump in the ground was all that remained of the tree.

Still holding the chandelier, I stepped through the doorway on to the verandah, then out into the yard. It looked a different yard entirely, and I returned to Mah Rukh Sultan's room. She must have gotten up again, I thought, for a colourful cardboard box had appeared on the cushioned chair.

"You can put it in here," she said, indicating the box, then fell silent.

Once again, I suspected that she had fallen asleep sitting up. I put the chandelier in the box and stood by the chair in silence for a long time, but she didn't invite me to sit down. At last I asked, "How are you feeling?"

"Not well," she answered faintly.

"You should call for someone."

"No," she said, more faintly still. Her head fell back a little and her eyes nearly closed. I hesitated, and finally tiptoed out to the large room.

The old lady stood facing one of the three fireplaces. She turned at the sound of my footsteps and came over to me to enquire after my family, but her eyes were rivetted on my hands. At last, pointing to the box, she asked, "What's in there?"

I handed her the box. Lifting the lid, she pulled out the chandelier a little way and, on recognizing it said, "Mah Rukh Sultan gave you this?"

I said nothing. She pulled the chandelier out a little further, looked at it carefully, then replaced it in the box and closed the lid.

"She's had this since she was a child," she said in a tone that mingled sadness and reproach. "She would never let anyone touch it."

Then she turned back to the fireplace and set to dusting again as though she were alone in the room. Her words were like an assault on my ears. The brightly coloured box was suddenly a heavy burden on my hands, and I wasn't sure what to do. Finally, I quietly placed the box on the mantel directly behind her and left.

For the next several days, I spent as much time as I could in my relatives' houses. I would return home only to sleep at night and leave as soon as I got up in the morning. The little chandelier twirled before my eyes, and everything I saw resembled some part or aspect of it. At length I decided to make a similar chandelier, and though I knew I had no way of moulding glass, I went ahead and bought a number of vials of ordinary scents from the bazaar.

On the third or fourth day, as I was leaving the house, it struck me that I could make the same chandelier in clay, and as this project seemed much easier, I returned to my room to attempt it. I started by trying to sketch the chandelier from memory, but I hadn't really looked at it for very long. Again and again I sketched it in my mind, but each time it appeared in my imagination suspended from Mah Rukh Sultan's hands, spinning slowly and steadily so that none of its parts could be firmly envisioned. I wasted sheet after sheet of paper, my mind in a muddle, and at last I got up and went into the living room. Nearly all my family members had gathered there. Two or three elderly women chided me for staying away from the house day after day. Then one of them ordered, "Now go and ask about Mah Rukh Sultan."

"What's happened to her?"

"She's taken a turn for the worse."

Then everyone began arguing about Mah Rukh Sultan's illness, and the oldest woman in my family declared, "The first day she set foot in this house I said there wasn't much left in her."

She began asking others to bear witness to this claim. I wondered what in the world they thought they were talking about, and was ready to dispute this prediction against any and all of them, but they sent me on, repeating their admonishment not to stay out all day.

The middle-aged woman escorted me to the large room with the fireplaces. There I found the two men I had spoken with that day by my house; they didn't acknowledge my presence, but only sat there with their heads bowed. The old lady was sitting slightly apart from them. I went over to her. She raised her head, saw me, and before I could ask, said, "Things don't look good."

Then she, too, lowered her head. I stood rooted to the spot. After some time, she raised her head again, pointed to Mah Rukh Sultan's room and said to me, "Go in and see her."

Reluctantly, I entered the room.

Mah Rukh Sultan was lying under the masehri with two of her sisters hovering over her. I leaned over her as well. Now and then her hand would rise, then fall back on the bed. The marks on her hand were apparent even in the dim light. The hand rose and dropped. I asked, "Is something wrong with her hand?"

"No," answered one of the sisters. "She's unconscious."

Just then Mah Rukh Sultan's hand rose a bit higher and halted in the air, just under my nostrils. I held my breath, but soon, suffocating, inhaled deeply. As though drawn up with my breath, Mah Rukh Sultan's hand rose a little higher, until it touched my nostrils. My eyes were half-closed; I could sense a sort of forsaken fragrance descend on the masehri. Again I held my breath, again felt suffocated and drew in a lungful of air. I experienced an immense forlornness. I took another breath, and began to see things in this forlornness. First, the kafoori sparrow, then the bird carcass and my hand swarming with ants, the bird with the white string and the rain flapping like sheets of white smoke above the yard, Mah Rukh Sultan standing by the table in my room, Mah Rukh Sultan sitting on the verandah, the chandelier spinning in her fingers, the dangling vials, one of them empty. I opened my eyes fully now. The reflection of the chandelier seemed to flit across her face, and her hand rested on the bed.

I went out to the large room, my head bowed, and left the house without saying a word to anyone.

I was sent over again in the afternoon with the message that all my female family members were coming to the house, but I had scarcely reached the door when I heard voices wailing the name of Mah Rukh Sultan, and turned back.

This story was first published as "Itr-e Kafur" in the volume of short stories *Itr-e Kafur*, Lucknow, Nizami Press, 1990.

interregnum

Then did I know how existence could be cherished,
Strengthened, and fed without the aid of joy.
– Emily Brontë

Guzashtim-o-guzashtim-o-budani hame bud
Shudim-o-shud sukhan-e ma fasana-e atfal
(We left it all behind, and off we went; what was fated,
came to pass.
We were done, and our doings became tales for the
children.)
– Kisa'i Marvazi

The insignia has been in our family for generations. Indeed, its existence dates back to the time that the earliest traces of our family history are to be found. Consequently, the history of the insignia runs parallel to that of our family.

Our family history is uninterrupted and almost complete, because my forebears were fond of preserving their accounts and the family tree. This is why its continuity, from its beginnings down to the present, has remained. But there have been interregnums in that history. Such as ...

translated by

muhammad umar memon

My father was an illiterate man and worked odd jobs. He was in command of many skills. As a child, I was convinced that he knew every craft there was. But he excelled in masonry, which was also his profession. Still, if because of bad weather or some other reason he couldn't find masonry work, he would do wood carving or something else instead.

I grew up at his knee and for a long time after I opened my eyes, his was the only face I knew. I have no real memory of my mother, although I do remember certain things from the time I was still at her breast. I used to cry a lot in those days. But my father, rather than amuse me, would just lay me flat in his lap and gaze silently at my face until, as I looked into his, I would quieten down on my own. Obviously, my father couldn't have cared for me all by himself; he had to work, after all. But from the memories of that time, which cannot be trusted anyway, my mind has preserved no other image than that of his face, and even of that image only this much: he is bent over me gazing at me silently in a verandah. Along with his face I see a part of a high ceiling, a few tattered red and green paper decorations hanging from its beams.

As I grew in awareness, I realized that my father stayed away from the house for fairly long stretches of time. This happened with such clockwork regularity that I soon knew instinctively when it was time for him to arrive and leave. At both these times, indeed slightly earlier, I would kick up quite a ruckus. As he would leave, I would pick up pieces of bricks from the rubble in the courtyard and hurl them at him, until some crone from the neighbourhood would come and pick me up. There were quite a few such women near our house, and a couple of them stayed with me while my father was out. Often they would be accompanied by filthy-looking children. My anger would subside after my father had left and I would be absorbed in either listening to the stories these women told me or playing with their children. But as the time of my father's arrival approached, I would start creating a fuss all over again. The moment he stepped into the courtyard I would rush at him and start hitting him with my small, weak hands.

Now he would kick up a ruckus even greater than mine. He would scream and flail in agony, as though I had crushed his bones to pieces. Finally, I would calm down and attend to him. He would baby-talk instructions like a child, and I would accordingly massage his body, stroke it gently or blow on it, wiping away pretend-blood from his pretend-wounds, pouring imaginary medicinal mixtures into his mouth from equally imaginary vials, while he – to indicate how awful they tasted – made such horrible faces that I would break into laughter.

At the time, and indeed until his last hour, I did not know that he was my real father. I used to think he was an old servant of my family who had loyally brought me up. He was more to blame for this misunderstanding than I was. He really treated me as though I were his master's son. Accordingly, I treated him badly. But I also loved him, in my own wild way, which meant there were always a few minor wounds somewhere on his body.

When I was a little older, his departures began to bother me even more. Now, sometimes, I would hide his tool bag, or replace a few tools with pieces of wood or brick, until he began to store the bag on a shelf high up on the wall. One day, when the shelf came within my reach, the bag disappeared. For the next several days, my father did not go out. Instead, he settled himself in the verandah under the red and green ceiling decorations and set to carving wood. He worked with such concentration that I was afraid to intrude on him. But I was even more afraid that he might soon give up his carving, grab his masonry tools, and go out to work. So I tried to come up with a way to get hold of the bag and make it disappear permanently.

I went searching for it throughout the house without telling him what I was after. Most of the doors opening into the inner halls remained closed and I did not know what lay behind them. Their corroded old-fashioned padlocks made one think that they hadn't been opened for ages, their keys most likely long since lost. The bag, I concluded, was not behind those doors. But the house also had many doors that were not locked. Behind them I discovered empty rooms and chambers. One could tell they had been repaired only recently after their furnishings had been moved out. Some still had water on the floors. That my father had also done masonry work in our home surprised me. Marvelling at this, I wandered off to a large door near the western wall of the house. It was a double door. The figure of a fish was engraved on each panel. Till then I had been unaware of its existence. I wondered what might lie behind it. I was certain this door did not lead to an empty room. To confirm this, I opened it ever so slightly and peeked inside.

My eyes first encountered a series of long wooden shelves. Then I saw many oversized books neatly arranged on them. Though my schooling had not yet begun, I felt somewhat drawn to the books, so I stepped inside to give them a closer look. I noticed that some books were also piled up on the ground near the wall directly across from me. I moved forward to have a look, but was distracted. Beyond the stack of books an old man was lying belly-up on a mat next to the wall, with his eyes closed. Engulfed in the musty odour of old papers he appeared no more than an old dog-eared book himself.

I stepped back. I could hear my father gently tapping with his hammer some distance away as I stood gawking at the old man. From his hair and clothing he looked like a beggar. I had just bent over, my hands on my knees, to take a better look at him when his eyes suddenly opened. He stared at me quietly for a moment, and then his lips moved.

"Come, Prince," he said. "Shall we begin the lesson?"

A lunatic! I thought, and ran to my father. But he remained engrossed in his work. A length of fine silver wire was coiled around the fingers of his left hand and he held a delicate little hammer in his right. He had used all his ingenuity to engrave patterns of curled leaves in various ways on an octagonal wooden platter, and was now pressing the silver wire into their extremely fine veins. Sensing my presence, he lifted his head and smiled softly.

"So," he said gently. "Where did you wander off to?"

"Over there ... Who's that old man?" I asked.

"I see, you have found your teacher," he said, and turned back to his inlay work.

"Teacher?" I asked.

"What exactly were you looking for?" He answered with a question of his own. And I remembered.

"The bag," I said, "the tool bag. Where is it?"

"You won't find it."

I started to get angry.

"Where *is* it?" I asked again.

"You won't find it."

I got even angrier. Just then he asked, "What day is it today?"

I told him, still angry, and then demanded, "Where is the bag?"

"Your lessons begin the day after tomorrow," he said with perfect equanimity.

I had just opened my mouth to yell something nasty at him when he suddenly extended his arms and drew me close to him. He gazed into my face for a very long time. The blend of hope and sadness in his eyes made me completely forget my anger. His powerful fingers were digging into my wrist and shoulder and his body was trembling gently. This image of my father is very special to me.

"Let go of me, you old coot!" I said, laughing, and feebly kicked at the wooden platter. This caused some of the silver inlay to come undone. My father quickly let go of me. The wire wrapped around his fingers had left a mesh-like imprint on my wrist. I held my wrist out to him. He rubbed it gently, blowing on it for a long time, and then said, "You start the day after tomorrow." And then again, "The day after tomorrow."

The thought of beginning my lessons did not please me. I remained put out with my father all the next day. By evening, though, curiosity about my teacher got the better of me. On the third day I followed my father eagerly into the room behind the door with the fish. The teacher was squatting on the mat. My father seated me in front of him and started to pick up the books piled up on the floor and arrange them on the high shelves, until only a single book remained.

"Be a good boy," he said, "and pick it up."

All this seemed amusing sport to me. The book was heavy but I managed to lift it and, at a prompting from my father, set it before the teacher. The teacher placed his hand on it and smiled softly, and I wondered why just the day before yesterday he had looked like such a beggar to me.

"Open it, Prince," he said.

Except for a few pages in the beginning, the book was entirely blank. That day, holding and guiding my hand, my teacher made me write on the first blank page. It pleased me greatly to see something from my own hand in so large a book. I wanted my teacher to have me write some more, but my father spread out his arms and drew me to him. His body trembled gently. Holding me, he spoke with my teacher for a while in hushed tones. God knows what symbolic language the two used, I couldn't understand a single word. Nestled in my father's arms, I let my eyes sweep over the rows of fat tomes on the high shelves. Finally, my father walked out with me in his arms.

From then on I spent the greater part of my time with the teacher and became all but oblivious to my father. So much so that for a good many days I didn't even notice that he had once again started going out to work, taking his tool bag with him. But the teacher was always there behind the fish-panelled door, surrounded by big, fat books. Perhaps he lived there. I would often see him lying belly-up near a pile of books on the floor, his eyes closed, looking like a beggar. Hearing me approach, he would open his eyes and say the same words:

"Come Prince, let's begin the lesson."

He never made me read, though he did teach me how to write fairly quickly. Every day, after a rigorous writing exercise, he would have me sit in front of him and would commence talking. Some days he would tell interesting stories of distant times and far away places, but mostly he talked about my own city. He would tell of the fortunes of families living in different quarters of the city: how such-and-such a family in such-and-such a quarter made its mark, then how it was ruined, which of its members survived and what condition they were in now. They were interesting stories, but the teacher narrated them without enthusiasm, so I remember them only as an assortment of disjointed pieces. However, he described the quarters of the city in such a way that each of them seemed like a living being, distinct from the other not only in disposition and character but also in appearance. He would become quite animated and go so far as to claim that by taking one look at a person he could tell which part of the city he came from, and could even trace the different areas he had lived in. I used to laugh at his claim at the time. Yet today I find something of this ability in myself.

Sometimes, as he talked, my teacher would stretch out belly-up on the mat and close his eyes, and I would start browsing through the books piled on the floor. During these browsings I discovered that I could read, but the massive handwritten manuscripts remained entirely inaccessible to me. Some of them were not in my language, and others were so convoluted in their verbal structure and script that I could manage only the vaguest grasp of their import after the greatest reflection. And even this never stayed with me longer than a fleeting moment. On such occasions, I would flare up with anger at my teacher. There were many times when I spoke to him very rudely.

Once, as he lay quietly, listening to me with his eyes shut, something flashed inside my head.

"Are you deaf, you bum?" I yelled and, picking up a heavy tome, hurled it at his chest. The very next day I was enrolled in a small school near my house.

I studied in different schools of the city. At first, my father walked me daily to and from school. When I came out after school, I would find him quietly leaning against one of the trees some distance from the gate. The moment he saw me, he would come forward and quickly take my books. And sometimes he'd even try to pick me up. But I would scratch and tear at him and rip myself away. On days when he was late, I would make my leisurely way home and insist the next day on going by myself. Eventually, I was going to and from school on my own. In time, I also started to go out on my own in my free time or on holidays and fell in with good company, and bad. I roamed all the different quarters of the city that my teacher had described to me: the dens of hypocrites, of cowards, of sycophants, of troublemakers.

During one of these forays, I spotted my father in the market.

He was standing in the section where day-labourers and artisans gathered every morning looking for work. He had placed his tool bag between his legs and was talking softly to some people nearby when his eyes fell on me. He left his bag on the ground and hurried over to me.

"What's wrong?" he asked.

"Nothing," I answered.

He looked at me with questioning eyes for a little while and then asked again, "Has something happened?"

"No, nothing," I answered again.

"You've come to see me?" he asked, then added, "In that case, you should see me at work." He laughed softly.

Just then a labourer called out his name and my father returned to his bag. A middle-aged man stood waiting for him. He asked my father a question, then explained something at length, repeatedly waving his hands through the air describing the shape of an arch or dome. He was wearing several rings studded with large precious stones on his fingers and kept twisting them nervously with his thumb. His loud, rasping voice stood out in the melange of voices, but I could not make out what he was saying. A little later my father picked up his bag and started off, following the man. I thought, At least I haven't replaced one of his tools with a piece of wood or brick. But far from making me satisfied the thought stirred a gentle sadness in me. And the sadness surprised me. I returned home immediately. Even though I busied myself the entire day arguing with my teacher over trifling matters, I missed my father. And the fact that I still hadn't seen him doing his masonry work nagged at me. I considered this a failing on my part, but it didn't occur to me to make up for it.

One afternoon while wandering around I found myself in front of one of my old schools which had been lodged for ages inside an old historic building. It was still there. The building had been in a state of dilapidation for a long time; when I'd been a student there, one of its roofs had caved in. My father had promptly withdrawn me from the school because I had been sitting under that very roof moments before it had come crashing down. Returning after such a long time I noticed that the broken-down wall around the school compound had been repaired. But the old outer wooden gate, with its flower-like iron studs and the small door in the lower portion of the left panel, had disappeared and been replaced with a steel grill-work gate behind which the high archway that gave access to the main building was clearly visible. People walked past the other side of the archway, even though it was a holiday. Thinking I might run into an acquaintance, I went in through the gate and proceeded toward the archway. When I came close to the arch I spotted, on its facade, the same pair of fish as on the door of my teacher's room at home. I was astonished that I had never noticed the fish on all my earlier visits to the school. I looked at them closely. The arch's decaying facade was being restored. The fish were chipped here and there. The tail of the one on the right was missing, and the empty space had been roughly filled in with orange-coloured putty which my father, leaning against a couple of diagonally mounted poles, was now carving into the shape of a tail. He had a piece of cloth wrapped around his head, so I didn't see who it was at first. I realized it was him from his bag, which was resting against the right-hand base of the arch, a few tools peeping out from its mouth. I observed him for a while, lost in his work, then picked up a wad of the putty from the ground and tossed it at him. It struck the pole near his foot and fell back. He looked down, laughed softly, and said, "So you've found me out."

His voice seemed to me to be coming from the gaping mouth of the broken fish. Then he turned back and worked silently for a long while.

Finally I asked, "How long are you going to stay perched up there, you old coot?"

"You're right, it's time to go," he said. "But I still have a little work left to do. It won't take long."

In a little while he climbed down. He held an assortment of small tools in his hand, and washed some of them in a nearby water tank. He removed the cloth from his head and used it to wipe them dry, then looked at me and smiled an exhausted smile. I took the tools from him and returned them to the bag, and the two of us started walking toward the gate. About midway he stopped, looked over his shoulder and examined his day's work, then started off again toward the gate.

Four or five days later, when I saw him leave the house with his bag once again, I asked, "Where will you be working today?"

"The same place," he said. "And I'll be late again."

But shortly before noon that day, a fight broke out among some students; the scaffolding on the arch was jostled in the fray. My father lost his balance and fell from where he was working, on to the school's stone floor.

I was at home arguing some trifling matter with my teacher at the time. My father was carried home by some labourers. They gave a vague account of the accident in their peasant dialect and returned to work. His body bore no mark of injury, but his eyes showed that he was in pain. The teacher and I laid him down on the bed.

My father lay there quietly for several days and my teacher sat silently at his bedside. A couple of old women from the neighbourhood looked after both of them. During this time I ventured out several times but returned after going only a short distance.

One day on my way home I thought of the arch and the broken fish on its facade. I turned around and headed for the school. It was a holiday on this day too. I went and stood before the arch. One of the fish had been restored. The network of scales carved on its back looked as though every single scale had been cast individually and then set into the fish's body. Each scale was raised slightly in the centre, tapered off around the edges, and then intertwined with the neighbouring scales. There was a small round hole in the spot where the fish's eye was located. I felt as if the fish were staring at me with its mouth agape. I turned my eyes away.

On the upper portion of the other fish, the putty had been completely removed, revealing a semicircle of thin bricks underneath. Even the crude, protruding bricks described the outline of a fish. The outline contrasted sharply with the finished fish on the right and made the facade look crooked and furrowed. The scaffolding was still in place. I grabbed one of its poles and gave it a slight push; the diagonally-mounted pole at the upper end collided with the arch, making a light tapping sound. The sound seemed to me to be coming from the fish's gaping mouth. Then the sound turned into a human voice which in its peasant dialect was inquiring after my father's condition.

My eyes fell on a man standing under the arch. He was one of the labourers who had carried my father home. I answered briefly when he inquired after my father and then praised his skills at length. He used a variety of masonry terms with which I was unfamiliar. He mentioned a number of famous historical buildings in the city and said he had collaborated with my father in restoring and repairing them. He even told me his name and insisted that I let my father know that a labourer by that name had been asking after him. He then asked me to wait while he went into a nearby chamber and emerged with my father's tool bag. He heaved a deep sigh as he placed the bag in my hands. He looked considerably older than my father. He heaved another deep sigh and was about to say something when somebody called him from inside the school. I saw him step into the arch and turn left.

The tools clinked softly inside the bag, and even though I was looking down I once again felt that the fish on the right was peering at me through the hole in its eye, its mouth agape. I arranged the tools in the bag and went out on to the street through the school's grill-work gate. When I got home I put the bag on top of a pile of books in the teacher's room and went out.

My father was still lying quietly in the verandah with my teacher sitting by his side.

My father couldn't go back to work after his fall; in fact, he couldn't even get out of bed. For several days he lay there so perfectly still and quiet that one suspected he had sustained a brain injury and was lying comatose. But once when I tried to move his bed to the book room, he indicated with his eyes that he did not wish to leave the verandah where he had spent every season up until then. Gradually he resumed talking, but in a faint voice.

One day he beckoned me to come near him. And my teacher, still perched at my father's bedside, got up and withdrew to the book room.

"My work is done," said my father, motioning me to sit down on the bed.

I remembered how he had stopped and turned to inspect his day's work; I sat down on the bed and placed his head on my knees.

"There's still a fish left," I said, lowering my head to look at him.

He looked at me wordlessly. I saw the reflection of my face along with the decorations hanging from the beams of the ceiling in his eyes. Perhaps, I merely imagined it. Then he turned his face away and said, "Help me sit up."

After he was seated, supported by several pillows, he became absorbed in thought. Never before had he seemed to me to be a thinking individual. But now, as he sat propped up against a pile of pillows, dressed in clean and proper clothes, he was in deep thought. And, for the first time I considered the possibility that he might be my real father.

"When only this house and you were left," he began, gazing at the ceiling, "I realized I had to do something."

I was certain that he was about to narrate his life story, but he continued to stare silently at the ceiling, lost in thought. Then he turned his face aside and said, "Go. Go take a stroll."

"I don't feel like it," I said.

He took my shoulder and drew me gently toward him. His grasp was frail and his hand tremulous.

"Only a few possessions were left," he said, almost in a whisper, "I made sure they didn't dwindle any further. It will seem like a lot to you."

I remembered the closed doors with the rusted padlocks. I said, "I don't need possessions."

"I've also added a little," he said, again in a whisper.

"I don't need anything."

"It's there somewhere, amidst it all," he said. "I didn't look for it, you do it." He paused.

"It" – he emphasized the word – "could be in the books too."

With that he grew visibly weaker. I ran to my teacher's room. He got up as soon as he saw me. I grabbed his hand and dragged him to my father's bed. My father turned his face to look at my teacher, and then at me. As he looked at me, he gained control over his halting breath and said, "Don't ever lose it, it is our insignia."

I looked at the teacher questioningly to find out what my father might be referring to, but he sat deathly still as though he had heard and seen nothing. My father's eyes, however, their brilliance faded, seemed fixed on something.

"What is it?" I asked, bending over him.

"It has led to bloodshed," he said in a faint voice, and his hands tightened into fists. His breathing grew irregular again.

The teacher sat still, sunk in a voiceless immobility, and I was at a total loss what to do. I was fully convinced now that I was my father's real son. At the same time I was confused about what to call him. So I just held his shoulders and quietly watched as his face took on different colours. Soon he began to look much better and said in a perfectly lucid and composed voice, "Go, take a stroll."

I could not say no this time. I let go of his shoulders and walked out of the house.

My father didn't last long. He spent his last days lying quietly in bed; he would groan softly now and then, but if asked what ailed him, he would not say. Once when I insisted, appearing irritated at his reticence, he said only this: "Who can say?"

Two, maybe three days later, the teacher shook me awake from my afternoon nap, and no sooner had I opened my eyes than I was sure that my father had died. But when I rushed to his bedside I found him alive. The minute he saw me he extended his hand, seized my shoulder and began to speak quickly. His voice was terribly faint. I bent over him to hear him clearly, but still I could not understand what he was saying. When I leaned closer, I could only make out that he was whispering something in baby-talk. Then he lapsed into a coma, and at some point, breathed his last.

For a while after my father's death I remained perfectly calm. I consulted the teacher with great care about the last rites and personally decided on every detail. But when the arrangements got underway, something went off inside my head and I became very upset. In my agitation I concluded that it was not my father but I myself who had died, and further concluded that it was I who was the father. Soon the two conclusions began to merge. I started doing all kinds of absurd things. I picked up broken pieces of brick from the rubble in the courtyard, throwing them on to the verandah. I lapsed into a dialogue with myself which I conducted in baby-talk. I took the water which had been prepared for the ritual cleansing of my father's body and poured most of it on myself, then dumped garbage into the remainder. I unfolded the length of white cloth which had been sent for to wrap his body and draped it around myself. And when they started off with the bier I created such hindrances that several times the body nearly fell to the ground. I made such a fuss that people even forgot to offer their customary condolences. In the end, I was seized, brought home forcibly, and locked up inside the house where the comforting words of the weeping old women so enraged me that I forgot all about my father's death. But I didn't show my anger to the old women and, quite unexpectedly, fell asleep.

I slept into the next day. I had a few dreams, but they had nothing to do with my father or his death.

For three days I remained in a daze. Several times during the day my teacher came to check on me. He would gaze at me silently for some time and then leave. On the fourth day I recalled that my father had asked me to look for something and I started rummaging for it madly throughout the house. My search took me to the fish-engraved door. I entered the room and began grabbing the books from their neat rows on the shelves and throwing them down on the floor. I rifled through them without reading. A cloud of dust settled on the floor and book worms, like silvery fish, slithered out of the books and began crawling every which way. Meanwhile my eyes fell on the tool bag lying on the pile of books by the mat. I sat near the bag and lingered there for a long time.

When night came, I fell asleep where I was.

That night I saw my father in a dream. He was standing in front of the arch, his head turned back to look at it and his eyes peering up at the fish he had restored. The fish returned my father's look with one shining eye.

The next day I picked up the tool bag, strode out of the house and went to the same spot in the market where my father used to stand. It was late and the labourers had already left. Still I stood at that spot for a long time. Nobody paid me any attention. Finally, my teacher came along looking for me. He grabbed my hand and led me back home. When he tried to reason with me on the way, I ripped his clothes.

My wrangling with my teacher continued unabated for several days. In the end, he stopped coming to my house, but saw to it that I was sent my meals regularly. Filthy young vagrant girls and bad-postured twittering old hags would knock at the main door, stuff a bundle of food in my hands, and silently withdraw. Then one day I saw my teacher standing behind the girl who had brought my food, his hands resting on her shoulder. When he saw me, he stepped forward. He gazed at me silently for a few moments and then, pointing at his chest, said, "Now it's all over for me."

That day, for the first time, I looked at him carefully in the daylight. His face was a web of wrinkles and he looked more of a beggar that day than ever before. We stood facing each other silently for a long time as the girl went on scratching her head with both her hands. Her long nails made a rasping sound as she raked her matted hair, reminding me of the man with the slew of rings on his fingers, who had hired my father in the marketplace. I thought again of the time I had picked up my father's tool bag and gone to the marketplace, and how my teacher had brought me home.

"I haven't treated you well," I said in a low voice.

Either he didn't hear my words or chose to ignore them, instead looking at me fixedly as though expecting something. He had looked at me in much the same way on earlier occasions and it had always provoked an involuntary anger in me. This time, too, I was irritated and lowered my eyes. I wanted to say something, but before I could, he turned around and placed his hand on the girl's shoulder.

"Now for Tahira Bibi," he said to the girl and retreated, taking small, slow steps behind her.

Only after they had both disappeared from view did I realize that I had failed to ask my teacher in.

I didn't even know where he lived. The old women of the neighbourhood could only speculate and suggest different addresses. But when I went to those addresses, I didn't find anyone who knew him. I wasted several days in this pursuit, but it afforded me the opportunity to go through practically the whole city once again. In my wanderings I paid particular attention to the historical buildings of my city. I inspected the sections that had been restored and easily detected many examples of my father's handiwork. The fish carvings never failed to show up on some door or gate of these buildings. Even the doors of the city's old crumbling houses bore them. Each of the fish appeared to me to be the work of my father, and each broken fish reminded me of the one he had restored on the school archway.

During these walks I became firmly convinced that the fish was the insignia of my city. I felt as if I had solved an obscure puzzle. At the same time, I sensed that the solution was more obscure than the puzzle. Thoughts of my father assailed me, until during one such walk, as I was approaching the ruins of a little-known historical building, I abruptly turned back. On arriving home I picked up the mat from my teacher's room and spread it out in the verandah in place of the bed where my father had last slept. The red and green decorations hung directly above the mat, from the beams of the ceiling. I noticed that this verandah too had seen some repairs, as had the ceiling, where applications of plaster were clearly visible everywhere, except for the section with the decorations. No repairs here, and the old sagging plaster looked as though it would crumble any day. I wished it would crumble then and there, and lay down on the mat with my eyes closed.

Just then someone rapped on the main door.

The girl who had accompanied the teacher on his last visit to the house was standing in front of the door. She was scratching her head with one hand and in the other held a large piece of fruit of a sort in season then, which she kept attacking with her teeth.

"What's the matter?" I asked.

After groping a while for a suitable spot to bite into the fruit, she said, "Tahira Bibi has sent word that your teacher is no more."

For a fleeting moment I imagined that the teacher was standing with his hand on her shoulder. I stared at the girl for so long that it made her blush.

"When?" I finally asked.

"Days and days ago. I've come here three times to let you know, but you weren't home."

"Who all are in his house?"

"In the teacher's house? Nobody."

"Who looked after him?"

"Tahira Bibi. She would come over."

"Who is she to him?"

"I don't know."

"Where does she live?"

"Tahira Bibi? Don't know."

Thereupon she turned around and left. After a moment I closed the main door, but just as I was turning away, I heard another knock at the door. I opened it. The girl was standing there again. This time she held a balled-up piece of red cloth in her hand.

"I forgot this," she said, as soon as she saw me, and handed the bundle to me. "Here, take them. They're keys."

"What sort of keys?"

"I don't know. Tahira Bibi sent them."

I closed the main door.

Standing on the mat in the verandah I unwrapped the cloth. It was a scrap of some thick but exceedingly soft fabric with a bunch of old-fashioned keys tied in one corner.

The cloth reeked of the fruit the girl had been eating so I hurriedly untied the keys and, dropping the cloth on the floor at the foot of the mat, began counting them. The rust had recently been scraped off some of them.

The largest key, with minuscule digits engraved all the way around the eyelet, bore a resemblance to the teacher's face, but why this should be so eluded me. I put the keys under the mat, lay down once again and closed my eyes.

I remembered my father's death in the very same spot, held my body rigid, and stretched out my legs. I felt the softness of the fabric against my heel. With my eyes closed, I arched my body and picking up the red rag, rolled it into a ball.

I was about to throw it away when I noticed that the smell of fruit had entirely vanished from it. As I drew it closer to my nostrils I smelt the faintest suggestion of an entirely different odour. My eyes opened involuntarily.

I unfolded the scrap fully and smoothed it out on my palms. It was a large handkerchief with a green silk fish embroidered in the centre. The web of scales had been embroidered with tiny stitches that had come undone here and there. But at this point my attention was focused more on the faint smell which seemed to emanate from the handkerchief than on the fish. I rolled the handkerchief back into a ball and smelled it several times, inhaling deeply. The scent rose slowly and then subsided, like the breathing of someone asleep. I was interested in scents and was quite a connoisseur of perfumes, but I was unable to isolate a single element of this compound smell. I kept inhaling it with great concentration for a long time. I felt the odour slowly leave the handkerchief and descend into my chest. I could not recognize the smell, but I was quite sure that, had it been the slightest bit more pungent, I would have suffocated there and then.

When my eyes began to grow heavy with sleep, it vaguely occurred to me that I was lying in the same spot where my father had breathed his last, and that I had just heard the news of my teacher's death. But before the thought could produce any effect, I drifted into sleep.

I saw my teacher, but in my dream he appeared in the form of a young girl, and I, as often happens in dreams, wasn't a bit surprised.

This story was first published as "Vaqfa" in the volume of short stories *Itr-e Kafur*, Lucknow, Nizami Press, 1990.

obscure domains of fear and desire

Ba kuja sar niham keh chun zanjir
Har dari halqa-e dari digar-ast
(Hide – but where?
Each door I close opens another.)
–Anonymous (found in a ghazal by Mir Taqi Mir)

Thou holdest mine eyes waking;
I am so troubled that I cannot speak.
I have considered the days of old,
The years of ancient times.
– Psalm 77

"We kept looking at each other, in silence, for the longest time ever. Our faces didn't betray any kind of curiosity. His eyes had an intensity, a brightness, but throughout this time, never for a moment did they seem to be devoid of feeling. I could not understand if his eyes were trying to say something or were merely observing me, but I felt we were coming to some silent understanding. All of a sudden a terrible feeling

translated by
javaid qazi and muhammad umar memon

of despair came over me. It was the first time I'd felt like this since I'd come to this house.

"Just then his nurse placed her hand on my arm and led me out of the room.

"Outside, as I spoke with his nurse, I realized that my speech was a shortcoming and that the patient was travelling far ahead of me on a road I knew nothing about."

I have given up talking, not looking. It isn't easy to stop looking if one happens to possess a pair of eyes. Keeping quiet, even though one has a tongue, is relatively easy. At times I do get the urge to close my eyes. But as of now they are still open.

This may be due to the presence of the person looking after me. She is my last link with the old house in which I first opened my eyes and learned to talk. When I lived in that house, she was just a little doll, only a year-and-a-half old. And so affectionate toward me. I would call for her as soon as I entered the house and she would cling to me the whole time I was there.

Now she has no memory of those days. All she has been told is that I am the last representative of her family. She does not know much else about me. In spite of this, she is very fond of me. She thinks this is the very first time she has seen me. She does not remember that I used to call her my "Little Bride." I started calling her that because she would refer to me as her bridegroom whenever someone in the family asked her who I was. This amused everyone. They would all laugh and then, just to tease her, someone would claim me as their "bridegroom." When she heard this she would throw a regular little tantrum. Among those who teased her were several older relatives, both male and female.

In those days, her small world was crowded with rivals. But even then, the ranks of her rivals did not include the person for whom she had the warmest feelings, beside her mother or myself. And in return, this woman cared more deeply for the little girl than for anyone else. She was at least two years older than me. Twelve years prior to the time I'm talking about, I had seen her at my elder brother's wedding. She was the younger sister of my brother's wife. But due to a complicated pattern of kinship, she also happened to be my khala, my aunt.

At the time of my brother's marriage, she was a mature young woman and I was a mere boy – a shy, awkward stripling. We often chatted, shared jokes, and teased each other. But despite all this informality, she maintained the air of an elder toward me. However, I never detected any affectation in that attitude, which perhaps would have irritated me. She treated me not as though she were much older than I, but as though I were quite a bit younger than she. And I liked that.

There were times, however, when I got the distinct impression that I was, after all, just her young nephew. This happened when she compared her hometown with mine, insisting hers was a much better place. I would immediately leap to the defence of my town and argue with her endlessly in a rather childish manner.

During those years, she visited us once in a while – staying for long periods of time. During this particular visit she had been with us for three or four days.

I came into the house and, as usual, called out to my Little Bride as soon as I'd stepped into the courtyard. But the house was silent. No one seemed to be home. But Khala. She had just emerged from the bathroom after her bath and had sat down in a sunlit spot to dry her hair. I asked her where everyone was and she said they had all gone to a wedding. Not knowing what else to say, I asked her about my Little Bride even though I had a hunch that she might have gone to the wedding too.

I went and sat next to Khala and we started talking about this and that. Most of the time we talked about my Little Bride and chuckled over her antics. After a while her hair was dry and she stood up to tie it in a knot. Attempting to arrange her hair, she raised both arms and placed her hands at the back of her head. Her bare waist arched slightly backward and her bust rose and then fell back a little, causing her locks to fall away from her. I noticed this in a flash of a second but it had no particular effect on me. She continued to put her hair up in a neat litttle bun as we went on talking.

Suddenly one of her earrings fell off and landed near her foot. I bent quickly to retrieve it for her. As I knelt at her feet, my eyes fell upon the pale curve of her instep and I was reminded once again that she had just taken a bath. I picked up the earring and tried to put it back in her ear, keeping up a rapid patter of conversation the while. I could smell the musky odour which arose from her moist body. She continued to fiddle with her hair and I kept trying to put her earring back on. But for some reason I couldn't get it to stay, and her earlobe began to turn red – I must have jabbed her with the post of the earring. A little cry came from her throat and she chided me mildly. But she quickly smiled as she took the earring from me and put it on herself. A little while later, she went up to her room and I to mine.

But soon I was upstairs again, looking for a book. On the way back, I glanced at Khala's room. She was standing in front of the bamboo chik. Her hair hung loosely about her shoulders and her eyes looked as though she had just woken up. I went into her room and we were soon talking about this and that. She started to tie her hair up all over again, and again I saw what I had seen earlier. But this time, seeing her waist bend backwards, I felt a bit uneasy. I chattered on about the wedding the family had gone to and, exaggerating rather wildly, I insisted that the bride barely came up to the waist of the groom.

Khala laughed at this. "Anyway, at least she's a little taller than your bride."

We started talking once again about my Little Bride, whose absence made the house seem quite empty. I was about to introduce some other topic when Khala got off the bed and came toward me.

"Let's see if you're taller than I am," she said with a smile.

Grinning we came and stood facing each other. She moved closer to me. And once again I became aware of the fragrance which arose from her body – a warm, moist odour which reminded me that she had just bathed.

We drew still closer and her forehead almost touched my lips.

"You're much shorter than me," I said.

"I'm not," she retorted and stood up on her toes. Then she giggled, "How about now?"

I grabbed her waist with both hands and tried to push her down.

"You're cheating," I said and, bending, grabbed her heels and tried to plant them back on the floor. When I stood up again, she wasn't laughing any more. I clasped her waist firmly with both hands once again.

"You're unfair," I said, my grip on her waist tightening.

Her arms rose, moved toward my neck, then stopped. I felt as though I were standing in a vast pool of silence that stretched all around us. My hold on her waist tightened further.

"The door," she said in a faint whisper.

I pulled her close to the door without letting go of her waist. Then I let go of her reluctantly till I bolted the door and turned toward her again.

I remembered how she had always behaved like an older relative toward me and I was angry with her for the first time, but just as suddenly the anger melted into an awareness of her tremendous physical appeal. I bent over and held her legs. Even as my grip around her legs tightened I felt her fingers twist in my hair. She pulled me up with a violent intensity and my head bumped against her chest. Then, with her fingers still locked in my hair, she moved back toward the bed. When we got to its edge, I eased her on to it, lifting her feet on to the bed with my hands. But she suddenly broke free and stood up.

I looked at her.

She murmured, "The door that leads up the stairs ... it's open."

"But there's no one in the house."

"Someone will come."

We went down the stairs silently and bolted the door at the bottom. Then we came back up together, went into her room and bolted the door behind us. Apart from the tremors running through our bodies we seemed fairly calm, exactly the way we were when we talked to each other under normal circumstances. She paused near the bed, adjusted her hair once again, and taking off her earrings put them next to the pillow. In a flash, I remembered all those stories I'd heard of love affairs that started after the lovers stood together and compared their heights. But I decided at once that these stories were all imaginary, wishful tales and the only true Reality was this experience I was having with this woman, who was a distant aunt – but an aunt who also happened to be the younger sister of my brother's wife.

I picked her up gently and placed her on the bed, thinking that just a while earlier I had entered the house calling for my Little Bride. Maybe the same thought crossed her mind. I had just begun to lean toward her when she suddenly sat up straight. Fear flickered in her eyes.

"Someone is watching," she said softly and pointed to the door. I turned my head to look and also got the impression that someone was peeking through the crack between the double doors. The person appeared to move away and then return to look again. This went on for a few minutes. Both of us continued to stare in silence. Finally, I got up and opened the door. The chik which hung in front of it was swaying gently. I pushed at it with my hands and then closed the door once again. The sunlight streaming in through the crack created a pattern of shifting light and shade as the chik moved in the breeze.

I turned back toward Khala. A weak smile flickered around her lips but I could hear her heart throbbing loudly in her chest, and her hands and feet were cold as ice. I sat down in a chair next to her bed and began telling her tall tales of strange optical illusions. She told me a few similar stories and soon we were chatting away the way we always did. Not one word was exchanged about what had transpired only a few minutes earlier. At last she said to me, "The others should be coming home soon."

I remembered that the door leading up the stairs had been bolted from the inside. And just at that moment, we began to hear the voices of my family members. I got up, opened wide the door of the room and went out, Khala right behind me. I unbolted the door that led up the stairs and then we came back to her room and continued to make small talk.

Soon, I heard a noise and saw my Little Bride at the door, looking really like a bride. Khala uttered a joyful shout, grabbed her, pulled her on to her lap and started to kiss her over and over again with a passionate intensity. The little girl shrieked with laughter and struggled to escape from the embrace. Apparently, in the house where the wedding had taken place, some over-enthusiastic girls had made her up like a bride and decked her out with garlands. By the time her mother came into the room with some other children, she was on my lap. I was asking her about the fancy food she'd had at the wedding and she, able to pronounce the names of a few dishes, kept repeating them over and over. And when her mother tried to pick her up she refused to budge from my lap.

"Oh, she is such a shameless bride," Khala said, and everyone burst out laughing.

At some point we all came down to the verandah where the other members of the family had gathered. Khala kept showing my Little Bride how to act shy, and every now and then bursts of laughter rose up from the assembled throng.

By the time the sun had gone down, I'd made many attempts to catch her alone. But she sat imprisoned in a circle of women, listening to talk about the wedding. That night, I tried thrice to open the door that led up the stairs but it seemed to be bolted from the inside. I knew that a couple of women – unmarried women, perpetual hangers-on in the household – also slept in her room, but even so I wanted to go upstairs.

Next day, from morning till noon, I saw her sitting with the women once again. I never did like spending much time with women, so I muttered some inane remarks to her and did my best to stay away.

By late afternoon all my family members had retired to their rooms and most of the doors that opened on to the courtyard were now bolted from within. I went up the stairs and lifted the chik in front of Khala's door. She was fast asleep. I stood staring at her for a long long time. I was sure that she was merely pretending. Her head was tilted backwards on the pillow, her hands clenched tightly into fists. She had removed her earrings and placed them next to her pillow. The scenes which had taken place in this very room just the day before flashed through my mind, but I drew a complete blank when I tried to remember what had happened during the moments that followed. It seemed to me that I had just picked her up in my arms and placed her on the bed. Quickly I stepped inside the room and was turning to close the door when I noticed an extraneous woman, one of those fazul women, sitting with her back against the balcony, winding woollen yarn into a ball. She greeted me enthusiastically with the utterly superfluous bit of information that Khala was sleeping. I pretended I was looking for a book and then, complaining that I couldn't find it, I left the room. But while searching, I had looked at Khala several times. She seemed to be fast asleep after all.

Late in the afternoon, I saw the fazul woman come downstairs and once again I went up and peered into Khala's room. She was standing in front of a mirror combing her hair with her back toward me, while another extraneous woman recited a woeful account of the first time she had been beaten by her husband. I'd heard this story many times before; in fact, it had been a source of entertainment in our house for quite some time. Khala laughed and then, noticing me in the mirror, asked me to come in and sit down. But I merely asked her about the imaginary book I was searching for and went back downstairs.

I was away from the house for most of the evening on a family matter, but I botched the whole business and returned home late at night. The doors of all the rooms were closed from within, including the one that led up the stairs. I went into my room and closed the door. For a while I tried to summon the image of Khala. I failed, but did manage to evoke her scent very briefly. As I slipped into sleep, I felt sure I would see her in my dreams. But the first phase of my sleep remained blank. Then, toward midnight, I dreamt that the extraneous women were dressed up as brides and were making obscene gestures at each other. I was wide awake now. I managed to get back to sleep toward dawn, only to wake up at daybreak from a dreamless sleep.

My head felt foggy and confused. I decided to go and take a shower. In the bathroom, I felt as if Khala had just been there, and I shook my head again and again to clear it.

When I emerged from the bathroom I saw Khala sitting in the sun drying her hair. One of my elders went up to her and began a lengthy discourse on the various ancient branches of our family. In the verandah, the same two extraneous women I had seen the previous day were quarrelling over something, but the presence of the old gentleman forced them to keep their voices low. Three other women soon join'ed them and contributed their halfwitted views, to reconcile the two or perhaps add fuel to the fire. Khala listened to the elderly relative very attentively, her head respectfully covered. I left her to this gentleman and went upstairs, but came to a dead stop outside her room. Another extraneous woman was standing outside the chik. She asked me if Khala had taken her bath. I told the old hag that I wasn't responsible for bathing Khala and stomped downstairs again. Up till now, I'd had no idea we had so many extraneous women crawling about our house. Their only practical use seemed to be to help out with domestic chores, whether exacting or easy.

Downstairs, the elderly gentleman was still pacing in front of Khala. He had finished dealing with the past history of the family and was starting on the present.

Late in the afternoon, I was sent out once again. But the situation I'd been trying to deal with since the previous day deteriorated further and I returned without accomplishing anything.

That night I woke up many times. It occurred to me that Khala's customary visit was almost at an end and the hour of her return was drawing near. In the morning, I felt as though my head were full of fog once again and, in spite of a cold shower, I couldn't get rid of the heavy-headed feeling. I was sure if I found Khala alone somewhere, I would kill her. And I didn't much care how I'd do this either. I decided that I'd better stay away from her that day.

Much later, I saw her just as I emerged from my room. She sat talking with some women and motioned with her hand for me to come over. The verandah was unusually quiet. The little girl slept in her mother's lap. Clearly she was ill. I took her on my lap and started talking to her mother about her condition. Then the old gentleman came on to the verandah. The atmosphere became even more sombre. He made an effort to moderate his loud voice and asked about the child. But it woke up Little Bride nonetheless. She looked as though she had almost recovered. The old gentleman began to tease her about her bridegroom. From the way the child responded, it became clear to us that she had not realized she was in my lap. The old gentleman then asked her where I was. Her answer made everyone laugh. Finally I tickled her lightly. She realized who I was and began to giggle in embarrassment. The elderly relative picked her up and took her away. She was quite fond of him also, and had woken up several times during the night calling for him.

As soon as the old gentleman left, the atmosphere of the room changed and peals of laughter rang out again and again. While they were all talking, Khala and I began to argue about what the date was that day. We debated back and forth, as the others looked on with keen interest. Khala simply wouldn't take my word.

From where we sat, I could see the corner of a calendar that hung in a room next to the verandah. Long ago a relative had drawn it up for us. With it you could tell the date of any day in any year. But this took a long time and you had to do several lengthy calculations. Eager to prove our cases, we both got up to examine this calendar. We entered the room together. But as soon as we were behind the door we clung to each other convulsively and almost sank to the floor. Then just as abruptly we stood up and went out. The little girl's mother asked us if we had decided who was right, but just then there was some laughter, and then some more. Khala turned pale.

Anyone coming in on us at that moment would undoubtedly have assumed that we had just emerged from the room after spending quite a long time together.

That day I successfully finished the task I had mishandled twice before, and returned home even later than the previous night. Everyone was in bed. I, too, went in and lay down. From the moment Khala had slipped off her bed and come toward me to compare heights, to the time we entered the room with the millennium calendar, I had not given much thought to how she might be feeling, whether she might be totally unaffected by it all. All the same, I did seriously consider killing her. All night long, I was assaulted in turn by remorse, the allure of her physical charms, and the longing to meet her alone again.

In the morning, when I emerged from my room after a sleepless night, I was in the throes of remorse. So when an extraneous woman, the first one to rise, told me that Khala's brother had arrived late the previous night with some bad news and that they had both gone away together, the only thought that came to my fogged brain was, I wish I'd been able to apologize to her.

None of the elders in my family could believe it when I told them that I had grown tired of my sheltered life and wanted to be on my own. And when they showed reluctance, I was quite unable to assuage their doubts and concerns. I succeeded in making them give in to my demands only because they cared a great deal for me.

They made elaborate arrangements for my journey. It was seeing this that I realized how comfortable and secure I had been in my house and felt rather fed up with myself. A few days before my departure they gave me a small stone amulet inscribed with sacred names to wear around my neck. It was a family heirloom. This increased my annoyance. Quietly I took the amulet off and stuffed it back into the chest full of old clothes where it had always been kept.

My elders said goodbye to me in a subdued manner, and as I walked away from my home the voices that followed me the longest were those of the extraneous women. They were praying for my safe return.

I faced great hardships as I struggled to make myself independent. And finally, it was the good name of the family elders that helped me. And, without moving a finger, indeed without even being aware of it, they helped me become self-reliant.

The work that I had undertaken involved inspecting houses. Initially, I felt I would fail in this profession because aside from my own house, all others looked like heaps of dung or half-dead vegetation to me. Sometimes I felt a vague hostility toward them. Sometimes they looked like cheerless toys to me, and sometimes I stared at them for a long time as though they were foolish children, trying to hide something from me. Perhaps, this is why – though I cannot pinpoint exactly when – houses began to assume a life of their own for me.

To start with, I had no interest in the people who inhabited these houses. I could, however, make an estimate of how old a house was, how and when certain improvements had been made over the years, as well as the speed with which Time passed inside it, merely by looking at it. I was sure that the speed of Time within a house was not the same as on the outside. I also believed that the speed of Time varied from one part of a house to the next. Therefore, when I calculated the rate of a home's deterioration and the years still left in the structure, the estimate usually bore no relation with its outward appearance. Still, none of my calculations ever proved to be right or wrong, because even the smallest estimate of the years left in the life of a house was always larger than the years that remained in mine.

One day, as I was standing in front of a house, something about its closed front door gave me the distinct impression that it had covered its face – either out of fear or to shield itself from something, or perhaps out of a sense of shame. I was unable to assess the house. When I went in, I examined every nook and cranny, every ceiling, wall and floor very carefully. I wasted an entire day without coming to any conclusion and came home only to spend most of the night thinking about it. I reconsidered my assessment strategy and tried to remember all the details. At some point, it occurred to me that there was a part of the house that aroused fear and another where I felt that an unknown desire was about to be fulfilled.

The next day I found myself in front of another house. The front door was closed, but it seemed that the house was staring at me with fearless, wide-open eyes. A short while later I was wandering inside it. When I entered a certain part of it, I became apprehensive. I awaited the second sensation. Sure enough, in another part of the house, I felt as though a significant but unexpressed wish of mine was about to come true.

I was surprised at myself for having overlooked this fact until then. I returned to the houses I had seen before and located the domains of fear and desire in each of them. No house, whether old or new, nor one among many of the same basic design, was without these domains. Looking for these domains of fear and desire became an obsession and, ultimately, this obsession proved harmful to my business. I was convinced, without the least bit of proof, that it was impossible to assess the life-span of these homes when they contained the domains of fear and desire. After suffering tremendous losses, I felt I was becoming an idiot or was losing my mind altogether, and I decided to give up my profession. But inspecting houses was my job and even if I did not consciously look for these domains of fear and desire, I instinctively knew where they were. I resolved to cut down my interest in them.

Then one day I discovered a house where fear and desire existed in the same domain.

I stood there for a while, trying to decide whether I was experiencing fear or desire but I could not separate the two. In this house fear was desire and desire, fear. I stood there for a very long time. The lady who owned the house wondered if I was in a state of shock. She was a young woman and at the time there was no one else in the house except the two of us. She came close, to examine me carefully, and I realized that the domain of fear and desire was affecting her as well. She grabbed both my hands and then, with a strange, cautious boldness she advised me to rest for a short while in the front room. I told her that I was quite well and, after talking to her a while, I left the house. Perhaps it was after this day that I started taking an interest in the people who lived in these houses.

Eventually I could not imagine one without the other. In fact, at times I felt both were one and the same. For they both intrigued me equally.

This interest increased my involvement. Now I could look at a house in the most cursory manner and yet discover passageways that were secret or wide open, in use or abandoned. I could tell whether voices rising from one part of the house could reach the other parts of the house. I'd examine each room very carefully to ascertain which parts of the room were visible from the crack between the door panels, or from the windows, or the skylights, and which parts could not be seen. In every room, I found an area which was not visible from the crack between the door panels nor from any window, nor from any skylight. In order to isolate this area, I would stand in the middle of the room and mentally paint the whole place black. Then, using only my eyes, I would spread white paint on all the parts visible from the cracks or windows. In this manner, the parts which remained black were found to be the truly invisible parts of the room. Apart from the rooms meant for children, I never found a single room in which the invisible part could not provide a hiding place for at least one man and one woman.

Around this time, I began to concentrate on the shapes these invisible parts formed. They shaped the outlines of different images which, at times, had a truly amazing resemblance to certain objects. But I never found a complete picture of anything. Everything appeared incomplete or fragmented, even though I examined countless such "invisible" parts. Some of these images had familiar shapes – of a lion, for instance, or a crab, or a pair of scales – but they were always unfinished. Other images resembled unknown objects and even though unfamiliar, still gave a sense of being incomplete. They left a strange effect on the mind which was impossible to articulate.

One day I was in the outer room of a new house, looking at an image of the invisible part of the room. The image had an unfamiliar shape. As I examined it, it occurred to me that, long ago, I had seen a decrepit old house in which the domain of desire had exactly the same shape.

Until then I had only ascertained the boundaries of the domains of fear and desire in these houses. I had not thought about the shapes their outlines formed. Now I began to recall many – or perhaps all – of these shapes, and it occurred to me once again, that either I was turning into an idiot or I was losing my mind altogether. Anyway, I was now convinced that no one else could look at houses the way I did. I was also quite overwhelmed by the thought that no one else had the kind of power that I had over the people who lived in these houses.

I didn't stay in any one place. I wandered through many cities and moved in and out of many homes. It began to seem, to me at least, as though the cities were crowded with houses, that each house was filled with women, and that every woman was within easy reach. Many women made advances at me, and I made advances at many, too. I also committed many blunders.

For instance, some women whom I thought to be empty of, or unfamiliar with, or even full of hate for desires, turned out to be saturated with them and more than willing to do the utmost to fulfil them. In fact, at times they made such bold overtures that they frightened me. Other women who seemed to me to be oozing with desire, and just waiting for the slightest sign from me, turned out to be so naïve that when I made a pass at them they were unable to understand my intentions altogether. Some were overcome by depression, others were terrified. In fact, one got so worked up that she abandoned her calm and tranquil domestic life and actually ran away from home.

She was in the habit of arranging and rearranging her lustrous black hair. I thought she wanted to draw my attention to it. But she just disappeared one day. I was taken aback. I set out looking for her. I just wanted to tell her that her black hair had misled me, but she kept running away from me. Perhaps she thought I was pursuing her like some lascivious animal. I never found her and I suspect that the fear I induced in her may have been the cause of her death. But I often console myself with the thought that her falling into the river was an accident. That she hadn't drowned; she'd been rescued.

After that, I gave up making passes at women. Instead, I took to waiting, wanting them to make the first move. At times, the wait became rather protracted. During one such lengthy interval, I went to a new city where no one knew me. One morning, as I was wandering around the main bazaar of the city, a woman standing in front of some shops smiled at me and beckoned me with her hand. She wanted me to come closer. At first, I thought she was a professional and I kept on walking. But then she called out my name. I stopped and turned toward her and she hurried over. "Don't you know who I am?" she said with a smile.

I finally recognized her. Many years ago she and I had been very close. She hadn't changed much except for the fact that she looked a little older. I was surprised that I had not been able to recognize her. But I was also pleased to run into someone familiar in a strange town.

"What are you doing here?" I asked.

"I live here," she said.

In a few minutes we were chatting away with the greatest informality. Again and again, I got the feeling that she had become a prostitute. I had no experience with professionals. I couldn't even tell them apart from ordinary women. Then why did I suspect she was a professional? As I stood there staring at her, I became more and more suspicious. She noticed that I was examining her and a smug sort of look came over her face, confirming my suspicions. She had been making a play for me for quite some time – with words, eyes, even body language. In the past, I had been the one to make the advances. Years ago, when I had known her, she had already been a woman of some maturity. And now there she stood, acting coquettish and coy like a teenage girl. This saddened me. I examined her closely once again. She was still attractive. But she had also changed a great deal. As I stood talking to her, I sensed Time speeding – right there, in that bazaar.

"Where do you live?" I asked her.

She pointed to a colony behind the shops.

"Come, I'll show you my house," she said. "If you have the time."

Our relationship had begun in much the same manner. She had shown me the house where she'd lived by herself. We walked side by side through the busy street. She stopped at a shop and bought a big padlock. She placed the lock and one key that went with it in her bag, and dangled the other key casually between her thumb and forefinger as she discussed the merits of a certain type of lock with the locksmith. Then, in an absent-minded way, she handed me the key she held in her hand and we walked on.

She wants everything the way it used to be, I thought to myself, and once again it seemed to me that Time was running out in that bazaar.

"How much farther?" I asked.

"We're almost there," she said, and turned into a broad side street.

Presently we found ourselves standing in front of an ancient wooden door that had just been given a fresh coat of paint. She removed the padlock that hung on this door, put it in her bag and went inside. I stayed where I was. Then a smaller side door, adjacent to the main door, opened and she stepped out. She now had the new lock in her hand.

"You haven't forgotten, have you?" she asked, and flashed a bold smile at me.

"I remember," I said.

I took the lock from her and she went back into the house through the small side door. I bolted the main door and locked it with my key and went into the house through the small side door, bolting it behind me.

Now I found myself in a large room which contained many niches and alcoves but nothing in the way of furniture. I stepped out of the room into a spacious courtyard enclosed by a wall. I noticed that a tall window made of weathered wood had been built into this wall. I started walking toward it when I heard a voice to my right:

"No, not there. Over here."

I turned and saw that, adjacent to one corner of the wall and behind several small trees, was a verandah. The woman stood there, under an arch. I went and sat on a divan placed there. Behind me was a door. She opened the door and we went into a room. The neatly arranged room contained a bed and other domestic odds and ends. She fell on the bed heavily as though she were very tired and I took a chair.

"So do you live here alone?" I asked her.

"Alone ... well, you could think of it as living alone. Actually, I live here with an old acquaintance – an elderly woman."

"Where is she now?"

"I really don't know. A few days ago she suddenly burst into tears and cried quietly all night long. In the morning she said, with the greatest reluctance, that she missed a certain home. All of a sudden, she longed to be back in the house where she'd spent her childhood. Soon afterwards she packed up all her things and left. I'll introduce you to her when she returns."

"Why would I want to meet a melancholy crone?"

"No, no. You don't understand. She can be very amusing. One minute she'll be telling you what a marvellous man her husband was. And the very next, she launches into a story about how he used to beat her up. She can be murderously funny."

"I have no desire to be murdered by the anecdotes of some old hag," I said, and walked out of the room.

She came after me.

"What's the matter?" she asked.

"I'd like to see the house," I said, and went down into the courtyard.

"There isn't much to see," she said. "There is this verandah and this room, and that outer chamber. The rest of the structure has collapsed."

We were standing some distance away from the window which had been built into the courtyard wall. I examined the wall carefully. It was apparent that the house had earlier consisted of one large structure and the wall had been put up to divide it into two halves.

"Who lives on the other side?"

"I don't know," she said. "Perhaps no one."

Now we were standing near the window. The window had been haphazardly constructed out of rough planks. A board had been nailed diagonally across the two panels in order to seal it permanently. I was drumming softly on this board when I felt the ground under my feet shift. I placed my hands around the woman's waist and pulled her close to me. She looked a little surprised. I was also amazed at myself. I took a few steps back and then let her go. So the domain of desire is right here, I said to myself and then, stepping close to the window, I turned toward the woman again. She looked up at me and smiled.

"You've become rather aggressive," she said.

Once more the ground shifted under my feet and I shuddered.

And the domain of fear also, I thought with a causeless melancholy.

The woman stood in front of me, smiling. Somehow, she had succeeded in simulating a look of arousal. I lingered near the window for quite a while. It was a strip of ground barely two feet wide adjoining the window. The rest of the domain lay on the other side of that window.

"Who lives on the other side?" I asked.

"I told you, Mr Impatient, no one."

"Come on, let's go," I said, moving close to her. We proceeded toward the verandah. Now she had begun to really feel aroused and she put her arms around my shoulders.

"It's very close and oppressive in there," she whispered, and we stopped where we were. I remembered our old encounters, when passion used to sweep her off her feet like a wind storm, and now, here in this house, she was either overwhelmed by a storm of desire once again or leading me to believe that she was.

In this house, or at least in this particular part of the house, Time moved faster than it did in the bazaar. A kind of affection for this woman, who happened to be the only person I knew in this strange city, began to stir in me.

"You haven't changed at all," she said softly.

"Well, along with Time ..." I began and then suddenly, glancing upward at the window, I saw something shiny in the crack between the frame and the upper edge of the panels. At exactly that moment, the woman began to slip away from my grasp. She had closed her eyes, the way she used to. I took her in my arms and looked at the window once again. A pair of dark eyes was looking at us through the crack. As I bent over the woman in my arms, I caught a fleeting glimpse of a red dress through the chinks between the boards. Slyly I looked up once again. The bright black eyes were locked on us. They were not looking into my eyes. They were focused on our bodies. The idea that we were being watched by an unknown woman who was under the impression that I was unaware of her presence excited me and I averted my face.

At this point we were standing very near the window. Slowly, very slowly, I bent over this strip of ground until my head reached the bottom of the window. I had only the vaguest sensation that there was a woman with me, and that I was holding on to her with both my hands. I fixed my eyes on the lowest chink in the window. Looking down through the aperture, I saw a bare foot. Had the toe of this bare foot not twitched again and again, I would have thought that it had been moulded in pure white wax. Behind the foot, at a distance which I could not determine, I saw an ancient arch of dark wood and the lower portion of a column. The foot took on a red glow from the shade of the dress, and I sensed the fragrance of a body in which another, more ancient odour was also implicated.

The toe rose from the ground and I saw that a long black string had been tied around it. I couldn't tell where the string led. If I'd wanted to, I could have reached in and grabbed the string, and perhaps I had decided to do just that. But the woman with me gripped my hands. Then she opened her eyes briefly and closed them tight again. She may have suspected that I wasn't concentrating on her. So I became attentive to her. After a while, she rearranged her hair and said, "You haven't changed at all."

I looked at the window once again. There was no one on the other side. It was then that a question welled up inside me. Had this woman wanted to stage a show for a girlfriend? I kept on staring at the window for a considerable time and then abruptly, I turned toward the woman again and examined her face intently. A vacant look of satiation had settled over her expressionless face.

"You haven't changed either," I said to her, and went on to the verandah.

I went to see this woman nearly every day.

"Until the old lady returns," she had told me on the very first day, "this house is yours."

And, frankly, I did begin to think of it as my own house, and went there whenever I felt the urge. If the main door happened to be closed from the inside, I would knock and she would open it. I would sit and talk with her for a little while and then I'd go away. If the main door had a lock on it, I would produce my key, open the lock and enter the house. Then I'd come back out through the side door, put the lock on the main door, re-enter through the side door and bolt it behind me. She would meet me either on the verandah or in the room and I would end up returning late that day. But lately it seemed that almost every time I went to see her, I found the main door locked from the inside. I'd have to knock to be let in. She'd open the door and we would spend some time laughing and joking and then I would leave her.

One day I knocked on the door for a long time before realizing that it was locked from outside. It dawned on me that I had become used to knocking. I unlocked the door and went in. Then I came back out from the side door, put the lock on the main door, re-entered the house through the side door, bolted it behind me and walked toward the verandah. The woman was not in the verandah and the door to her room was closed from outside. A couple of times earlier, she'd come home only after I had arrived. I opened the door to her room and lay down on her bed. I must have stayed there for a long time, in between sleeping and waking. Eventually, I left the room and went out on to the verandah. The afternoon was fading into evening. I was somewhat surprised at myself for having waited so long for her. Anyway, I waited a little longer and then went out through the side door, unlocked the main door and went into the house again. I bolted the side door from the inside and was about to go out of the main door when I stopped suddenly and turned back toward the verandah. I walked across the verandah into her room and changed the position of the bed.

She should know I've been here, I thought, and came back out into the courtyard. I was going toward the main door when something made me stop in my tracks. I turned around slowly and looked at the window in the wall. A pair of dark eyes was looking straight into mine through the chink between the top of the window and the frame. I turned back toward the main door.

I should have known, I thought with groundless melancholy, and slowly turned and walked back toward the verandah. I went into the woman's room once again and pushed the bed back to its original position. Then I came out into the courtyard and crept along the wall that ran at an angle to the verandah. Staying close to the wall, I slowly inched forward in the direction of the window. When I drew close to it, I bent down so low that my head almost touched the ground. Through the aperture at the bottom I could see the waxen foot with the black string still attached to the big toe. At first it remained perfectly still, but then it looked as though it had started to pull back. I reached under the crack suddenly, grabbed the black string and gave it several quick turns around two of my fingers. The foot struggled to retreat, but I pulled it back with equal force. Now, between my eyes and this foot was my intervening hand with the black string wrapped around my fingers. The string, apparently of silk, was very strong and clearly my fingers were about to be sliced off. I gave it several more turns around my fingers and then suddenly my hand came into contact with the toe.

The pull of the string was making it impossible for me to think clearly. When I had moved from the verandah toward the window, I had made up my mind to reach out to her but now I couldn't figure out what to do and my fingers were just about ready to drop off. The evening gloom fell over my eyes like a heavy blanket of darkness. I felt a cutting pain, but at the same time it became possible for me to think. The very first thing that occurred to me was that I was not the only one in pain. In contrast to my tough and masculine hand, the delicate feminine foot was very soft and the thread that was cutting into my fingers was also tied to that foot. I pressed the toe gently and caressed the foot with my two untied fingers. It felt even softer than I had imagined it to be, but it was also cold as ice. Yet I could feel the warm current of blood surging under the delicate skin.

By now the blackness of night had spread everywhere and I could barely see the silhouettes of the small trees. I am hurting her, I thought. Suddenly it occurred to me that up until then I had pulled the string toward me only once. I loosened the string around my fingers by a few turns and groped about the window with the other hand. I grasped the board which had been nailed obliquely across the window and tried to get up. But the board came loose and, precisely at that moment, the string unwound from my fingers. I placed both hands on the window to keep my balance, but the window fell open since there was nothing to keep it closed now. Suddenly, I found myself on the other side of the window. In the dark, I could just barely see the dim outline of the dark wooden arch and a shadow moving slowly toward it.

I followed the shadow into a region of dense gloom beneath the arch and soon lost sight of myself.

This was my first experience with total darkness. I passed through the arch and went on for a short distance. But then I found myself stopping. I tried to move north, east, south, west, in all four directions, but the darkness made it impossible for me to advance. I lost all sense of my whereabouts. Neither could I determine the position of the arch any more. All I knew was that I was with an unknown woman in an unknown house and that – I was sure of this – we were alone. My long association with women and houses had given me the keen instincts of an animal. And now as I stood in the dark, I peered about as keenly as one. I took a deep breath. I was certain that the characteristic perfume emitted by ancient houses, which I'd begun to smell outside the door, would soon assail my nostrils. But this did not happen. And even though I knew it was futile, I squinted into the dark with an intensity that, I am sure, must have made my face look truly frightening. In spite of this, I could not cut through the darkness. As far as the sounds of voices were concerned, I had ceased to be conscious of them from the moment I first twisted the black string around my fingers. Still, I made an unsuccessful effort to listen. I felt as though I had been standing there straining my senses for a very long time. Then I sensed that I had just passed under the arch. Soon afterwards I felt two soft hands brush against mine. I grasped them firmly and pulled them toward me.

After a long interval, I relaxed my grip, and my hands – exploring the elbows, arms, and shoulders – began to move toward the face. I tried to get a sense of individual features. But apart from a hint of long, thick eyelashes, I could not fathom any other feature. My hands wandered across her body, along her legs and down to her feet until my head touched the ground. I tugged at the string gently and then stood up. Now, once again, I felt soft hands clutching my own. Her palms pressed against mine. And then in the dark, my hands became aware of colour for the first time. Two white palms, a pattern traced upon them with red henna, moved from my palms to my wrists, then to my elbows, and from there to my shoulders and then further up until they cupped my face. Her fingers, which had red rings on them, passed over my cheeks and came to a stop at my neck. She tapped my neck three times and then her palms came to rest on my shoulders and stayed there for a long time. Then, groping slowly across my clothes, they reached down to my feet. They then vanished from that darkened scene for a few seconds and came to rest on my shoulders again. I remembered that ancient scent which had wafted toward me once, mingled with the odour of femininity. This odour is among those smells that are as old as the earth and were around long before flowers came into existence. It was an odour that brought to mind half-forgotten memories. However, at this moment it did not remind me of anything. In fact, I was fast forgetting what little I did remember.

The pressure of her hands on my shoulders increased and then relaxed. And now, all at once, I became aware of the fulsome, palpable presence of a female body. It occurred to me that I was with a woman who had seen me with another woman – at least once – in broad daylight. I also realized that it was useless to try and see in the dark. I closed my eyes. I knew that closing them would not make any difference. And, truthfully, there was no difference, not for a while at least. But just when I'd forgotten the physical limitations of my eyes, I saw that I was slowly sinking into a lake of clear water. At the bottom of this lake I could see the ruins of ancient temples. I opened my eyes and was relieved to see only darkness all around. I recalled that there was a woman with me in this gloom. My breath felt the heat that was rising from her body. She is being swept along by a storm, I thought. Once more my eyes began to close and I could not keep them open no matter how hard I tried. Once again I saw the same clear water lake. The ruins of ancient temples drifted up toward me until they hit my feet. But I couldn't feel them. Then, even as I watched, the clear water of the lake turned dark and the ruins disappeared.

I don't know how long it was before I woke up. It was still pitch dark all around me. But on one side I saw the outline of the arch and beyond it the beginnings of dawn. I turned to the body lying motionless in the dark and let my hands wander all over it, touching everything. I placed my palms on hers, waiting a long while for them to become moist with warmth. But they remained cold and dry. However, my hands did feel once again the bright red pattern on one of the palms. The shape of this pattern represented something unfamiliar. I stared hard at this shape and it became clear to me that the same shape resembled the domain of fear in a certain house, the domain of desire in another, and the invisible part of yet another room. I tried to remember all the places where I had seen this shape. It occurred to me that even though the shape was unfamiliar, it was, nevertheless, quite complete. For this reason, I had to struggle to convince myself I had never seen this shape anywhere before. I made a futile attempt to pick up this shape from the palm of her hand. Then I touched it with my forehead and, walking through the wooden arch, went outside. The window resembled a dark stain. I went through it and emerged on the other side.

When I crossed the courtyard and made my way toward the main door, the morning birds were chirping in the small trees directly across from the verandah and some old woman there was coughing away.

I did not stop speaking suddenly. In fact, at first, I didn't even realize that I had given up speech. This because I never *have* been very talkative. The fact is, I just started devoting more time to thinking. After I came away from that house, I slept for two days straight. I caught myself thinking even in my dreams and I continued to think after I woke up.

The first thing that occurred to me was that I had got through that night with only the sense of touch to guide me. I had experienced everything by touch alone. Rather, all that I had experienced was merely a transformed reflection of my sense of touch. Even so, I had missed nothing and, except for the first few minutes, I imagined that all five senses of mine were being fully satisfied.

I was never curious about that woman. This surprised me and I tried to force myself to think about her. But my mind rejected every image of her I conjured up. I struggled with myself for many days but was eventually forced to accept defeat. In the fierce long debate in my mind, I came to a realization: I wouldn't be able to recognize her even if I saw her from up close. But she would recognize me instantly, whenever and wherever she saw me. This thought did not disturb me that much, but then neither did it put me at ease. I accepted it like some worn-out, exhausted truth and gave up thinking about it. At about this time I realized I had, more or less, also given up talking.

I have not sworn an oath of silence. It's just that I do not need to speak. This has been made possible for me by the kind people who live in this house. They spotted me somewhere, recognized me, and told me that for many generations our families had been very close. They brought me to this spacious house and graciously urged me to pick any room I wished to live in. I looked over the whole house and chose for myself – who knows, this might have pleased them – a section which had been unoccupied for a long time.

My bed is positioned exactly in the domain of fear. I have not been able to discover the domain of desire in this house. But that cannot be. So I have now become convinced that fear and desire converge here in exactly the same spot. And that I have dominion over it.

Once I was walking about my room in the middle of the night, when I happened to see this spot. It had assumed a black shape. This shape had an unfamiliar but complete outline. I kept on staring at this image for a long time. Then I examined the entire room carefully, looking into each and every crevice, every window, every skylight. I stained the room white with my eyes, but the black shape remained untouched by the whiteness.

The shape of the invisible part, I thought, was ... Right at that moment, I heard the chirping of the morning birds outside. I was absolutely sure that if I tried even a little, I would remember where I had seen the shape before. But I had made a kind of pact with myself never to make the effort. From that moment on, I gave up talking.

The same day that I was introduced to my nurse, I shifted my bed partly out of the domain of fear and desire. She sits on this part of my bed and I just look at her. I believe that in this way I'm protecting her. And also myself.

This story was first published as "Ojhal" in the literary journal *Shab-Khun*, Allahabad, later anthologized in the volume of short stories *Seemiya*, Lucknow, Kitabnagar, Nusrat Publishers, 1984.

sheesha ghat

Sad mauj ra ze raftan-e khud muztarib kunad
Mauji keh bar-kinar ravad az miyan-e ma
(Each wave that strikes out to embrace the shore
Rolls up a hundred more when it departs.)

– Nazeeri Neeshapuri

And with such luck and loss
I shall content myself
Till tides of turning time may toss
Such fishers on the shelf

– George Gascoigne

After keeping me with him with the greatest of love for eight years, my father, my moohbola baap, was finally forced to find another place for me. It was not his fault, nor was it mine.

He had believed, as had I, that my stuttering would stop after a few relaxed days with him. Neither he nor I had expected that the people here would turn me into a sideshow, the way they do a madman. In the bazaars, people listened to my words with a curiosity greater than that

translated by

moazzam sheikh and elizabeth bell

displayed toward others, and whether what I said was funny or not, they always laughed. Within just a few days my condition worsened so much that when I tried to say anything at all, not only in the bazaar but even at home, the words collided with my teeth and lips and palate and bounced back the way waves retreat on touching shore. I would get so tongue-tied that the veins in my neck would swell and a terrible pressure would invade my throat and chest, leaving me breathless and threatening to suffocate me. Beginning to pant I would be forced to leave my sentence incomplete, and then start all over again after I had recovered my breath. At this my father would say, "You've said that. I heard you. Now go on." If he ever scolded me, it was for this. But my problem was that I just couldn't resume my account from where I had left off, I had to start all over again. Sometimes he would listen to me patiently and at others he would lift his hand and say, "All right, you may stop."

But if I couldn't begin my account from the middle, I couldn't leave it unfinished either. I would grow agitated. Finally, he would walk away, leaving me still stuttering, talking to myself. Had anyone seen me then, I would have been thought insane.

I was fond of wandering through the bazaars, and enjoyed sitting there among the groups of people. Though I could not comprehensibly put thoughts into words, I made up for this by listening closely to what others said and silently repeating it to myself. Sometimes I felt uncomfortable, yet I was happy enough. The people here did not dislike me, and above all, my father held me dear and looked after my every need.

For some days, though, he had seemed worried. He had begun talking

---

Sheesha Ghat: The name of the place. Literally, the glass wharf.

Moohbola baap: Literally, "by-word-of-mouth father," these words have been retained here - where they appear for the first time - since neither "foster father" nor "adoptive father" conveys the sense of the original adequately.

to me for long stretches of time, a new development. He would come up with questions that required long answers, and then listen attentively without interrupting me. When I would grow tired and begin to pant, he would wait for me to resume my account, listening all the while with the same concentration. I'd think he was about to scold me, and my tongue would start to tie itself in knots, but he would just gaze at me, saying nothing.

In only three days my tongue began to feel as if it were unknotting a little. It was as if a weight were being lifted off my chest, and I began to dream of the day when I would be able to speak as others did, with ease and clarity. I started to collect in my heart all the things I had wanted to share with others. But on the fourth day, my father called me over and had me sit very close to him. For a long time his talk rambled aimlessly, then he fell silent. I waited for him to pose one of his questions, but he said abruptly, "Your new mother is arriving the day after tomorrow."

Seeing the joy dawning on my face, he grew troubled, then said slowly, "She'll go crazy if she hears you speak. She'll die."

The next day my luggage was all packed. Before I could ask any questions, my father took my hand and said, "Let's go."

He didn't say a word to me during the journey. But on our way, he told a man who chanced to inquire, "Jahaaz has asked for him." Then they both started talking about Jahaaz.

I knew Jahaaz, too. When I had first come to live with my father, Jahaaz earned his livelihood by performing clownish imitations at fairs and bazaars. He would wear a small pink sail tied to his back. Perhaps that's why he was called Jahaaz, a ship. Or perhaps he wore the sail because his name was Jahaaz. The pink sail would billow when the wind blew hard and Jahaaz would look like he was moving forward under its power. He could mimic to perfection a ship caught in a storm, convincing you that angry winds, raging waves, and fast-spinning whirlpools were bent on sinking the ship. The sounds of the wind howling, the waves slapping, the whirlpool's ringing emptiness, even the sails fluttering, would emerge distinctly from the mimic's mouth. Finally, the ship would sink. This routine was very popular with children and older boys, but was performed only when the wind was high. If the wind halted, however, the young spectators were even more delighted, and called out: "Tobacco, tobacco!"

I had never seen anyone smoke tobacco the way Jahaaz did. He used every kind of tobacco, in every way it was possible to smoke it, and when the air was still he would perform such astounding tricks with clouds of smoke that the spectators couldn't believe their eyes. After producing several smoke rings, he would take a step back, then twist his hands and wrists in the air as though sculpting a figure in soft clay. And sure enough, the rings would take on a shape, just like a sculpture, and stand suspended in the air for some time. The boys were not allowed to watch some of his mimic acts. For these he would hide inside a rapidly closing circle, two or three spectators deep, and the only way those standing at a distance knew that Jahaaz was performing was by a glimpse of the fluttering sail and the sound of the spectators' laughter.

A year after I had come to my father's, Jahaaz almost lost his voice. He also acquired a severe cough. For his acts he had used many different voices, but now if he opened his mouth a coughing fit would seize him, and at times it took him nearly as long to finish his sentence as it would have taken me. Not only did he cease to perform his mimic routines, he stopped coming to our village altogether, and after the first year I did not see him again.

We passed many settlements and ghats on our way. Everywhere we went, there were people who knew my father, and he would tell them that Jahaaz had asked for me. I didn't understand what this meant, but asked no questions. In my heart I was angry with my father. I wasn't the least bit happy about living apart from him. But my father didn't seem happy either. At least he didn't look like someone who was about to bring home a new wife.

Finally we arrived at a grimy settlement. The people here were glass-workers. There were few houses, but each one had a glass furnace, and ugly chimneys belching smoke protruded from the straw thatch of the roofs. Layers of soot had settled on the walls, the lanes, the trees. People's clothes and the coats of stray dogs and cats were black from the smoke. Here, too, a few people knew my father. One of them asked us to eat and drink with him.

An oppressive feeling stole over me. My father looked at my face carefully, then he spoke to me for the first time on that journey.

"People don't get old here," he said.

I didn't understand him. I looked at the people strolling by and, indeed, none among them was elderly. "The smoke eats them away," he said.

"Then why do they live here?" I wanted to ask, but the question seemed futile, so I simply stared in my father's direction.

"Jahaaz knows glassworking, too," he said after a while. "This is his home."

I stood up with a start. My tongue was in many knots all at once, but I couldn't stay silent now. Would I have to live with a smoke-belching bazaari clown like Jahaaz, in this settlement where a dark barbarity seemed to pour over everything? This question had to be asked, no matter how long it took. However, with a reassuring gesture, my father beckoned me over to sit by him, and said, "But Jahaaz moved away long ago."

I was relieved. As long as Jahaaz doesn't live in this settlement, I said to myself, I can live with him anywhere. Then my father said:

"He lives on the ghat now." He pointed in its direction. "On Sheesha Ghat."

The oppressive feeling returned. My father did not know perhaps that I had already heard of Sheesha Ghat from visitors to his house. I knew that it was the most widely known and least inhabited ghat of the big lake, and that a terrifying woman by the name of Bibi was its sole owner. She had been the lover of a notorious dacoit – or maybe he was a rebel – and she later became his wife. In fact, it was during one of his visits to Sheesha Ghat that his whereabouts had been betrayed by informers to the government people and he had died, at their hands, on this very ghat. A strange development altered the situation completely; the entire ghat was given over to Bibi. She had made her home in a huge boat that now lay anchored in the lake. She ran some sort of business, in connection with which people were allowed to come to the ghat now and then. Otherwise it was forbidden to go there. Nor had anyone the courage to do so. Everyone was frightened of Bibi.

How had Jahaaz come to live on Sheesha Ghat? Would I have to meet Bibi as well? Would she speak to me? Would I have to answer her questions? Would she lose her temper when she heard me speak? I had grown so absorbed in these questions and their imagined answers that I didn't even realize we had left the settlement of the glassworkers. I was startled when I heard father's voice in my ear, "We're here."

This was perhaps the most deserted area around the big lake. An expanse of muddy water began at the end of the barren plain, its far shore invisible in the distance. On our left, set back from the water, a big boat obscured the view of the lake. Perhaps at one time it had been used to transport logs. Some of those logs seemed to have been used later to build many rooms on the deck, quite a few of them – large and small. The planks on the boat were all loose, and a light creaking sound issued from them, as of some giant object slowly breaking apart. On the shore of the lake a low, long retaining wall lay face down on the ground. Near it stood four or five rickety platforms with huge cracks in them, and close by was a mouldy length of bamboo, nearly claimed by the soil.

I sensed that this must have been a bustling place once. It was called a ghat, but all that was left now was a roofed shelter extending from a building toward the shore, the front of it overhanging a little pool of lake water that had sloughed over into a depression in the ground. At the rear of the shelter, on a little rise, sat a shapeless building of logs and clay which looked as though its builder had been unable to decide whether to construct it of wood or earth and, during these contemplations, the building had reached its completion. The roof, however, was all of wood. A small pink sail, perched on a projection in the centre of the roof, was fluttering in the wind.

My father must have been here before. Grabbing my hand, he quickly walked down the slope and up the five earthen steps that led to the doorway of the building. There was Jahaaz, sitting on the floor, smoking. We went in and sat down too.

"So you're here, are you?" he asked my father, and began coughing.

He seemed to have aged quite a bit in eight years. The extreme paleness of his eyes and darkness of his lips made it seem as though they had been dyed in different vats. From time to time his head would move as if he were admitting something. During one of these motions he caught a glimpse of me with his pale eyes and said, "He's grown up!"

"It's been eight years," my father told him.

We sat silently for a long time. I would have suspected that the two were talking in signals, but they weren't looking at each other. Suddenly my father stood up. I rose with him. Jahaaz raised his head, looked up at him, and asked, "Won't you stay a little?"

"There's a lot to be done," my father said. "Nothing's ready yet."

Jahaaz nodded his head, as though agreeing. My father walked out and was down the earthen steps before he turned, came over and took me in his arms.

We stood there silently for a long time, then he said, "If you don't like it here, tell Jahaaz. I'll come and get you."

Jahaaz's head moved in that way of his, and my father went down the steps and away.

I heard Jahaaz cough and turned toward him. He took a few quick drags of his tobacco, made an effort to even out his breathing, then got up, took my hand and walked out under the shelter. We just stood there quietly, Jahaaz running his eyes over the lake. Then we returned to the earthen steps, but Jahaaz stopped at the first step. "No," he said. "First, Bibi."

We walked along the shore of the lake until we came to the big boat. Carefully balancing on the gangplank made by joining two boards, we reached the ladder at the other end, then climbed on to the boat. There was a curtain of coarse cloth over the door of the small front room. The two-coloured cat dozing before it peered at us through half-open eyes. Jahaaz halted as he neared the curtain. I stopped many steps behind him.

At Jahaaz's first cough the curtain slid aside and Bibi appeared. The sight of her filled me with fear, but more than that with amazement at the thought that this shapeless woman had once been someone's lover. She looked at Jahaaz, then at me.

"Your son's here?" she asked him.

"Just got here," Jahaaz replied.

Bibi looked me up and down a few times, then said, "He looks sad."

Jahaaz didn't say anything. Neither did I. The silence lingered for some time. I kept looking at Bibi. "Do you know how to swim?" she asked.

I shook my head.

"Afraid of the water?"

I nodded.

"A lot?"

"Yes, a lot," I indicated.

"You should be," she replied, as if I had said what was in her heart.

I viewed the expanse of the lake. In the still air, the muddy water seemed completely at rest; the lake could have been mistaken for a deserted plain. I shifted my gaze to Bibi. She was still looking at me. Then she turned toward Jahaaz, who was handing her the tobacco-smoking paraphernalia. For some time they smoked and discussed something to do with finances. Meanwhile, a brown dog appeared from somewhere, sniffed at me and went away. The cat, which had been dozing all this time, raised its tail on seeing the dog, arched its back, then retreated behind the curtain.

I peeked at Bibi from time to time. She was a strongly built woman and seemed bigger than her boat, but it also seemed as if she, like her boat, were slowly disintegrating. At least, that was my impression from looking at her, and from her words, which I couldn't hear very well. Suddenly she stopped in the middle of what she was saying, raised her head and called loudly, "Parya!"

The sound of a girl's laughter came toward us, as though floating on water. Jahaaz took my hand and led me back to the gangplank. I heard Bibi's voice, "Take good care of him, Jahaaz." And she repeated, "He looks so sad."

The way she said this, even I began to think I was sad.

Yet there was no reason for me to be sad. When Jahaaz showed me my quarters, I couldn't believe this was part of the shapeless house on the deserted ghat, between the muddy lake water and the barren plain. All efforts had been made to ensure my comfort. The rooms were lavishly decorated, mostly with glass objects. Glass was also inlaid in the doors and the vents in the walls. I was surprised that Jahaaz could create a

---

Parya: Given Urdu orthography, it is significant that although the most likely reading of this name is "Priya" (beloved), it can also be read as "Pariya" (fairies).

place like this. He must have had help from someone, or else had been trained in the art of decoration, I thought. A lot of the items seemed to have been brought there that very day. I suspected that other things had been removed, and that before me, perhaps long ago, someone else had lived here.

After I had seen the place where I was to live, I thought I had seen the whole of Sheesha Ghat. But on the second day I saw Parya.

I am amazed to this day that during the many times people at my father's house spoke about Sheesha Ghat, no one had ever mentioned Bibi's daughter. I first heard her name the day I arrived at Sheesha Ghat, when Bibi called her from the boat. I was so overwhelmed by the day's confusion, it didn't even occur to me to wonder who Parya was. The next morning, I heard the sound of someone laughing. Then a voice said, "Jahaaz, let's see your son."

Jahaaz jumped up and grabbed my hand.

"Bibi's daughter," he told me as he led me out to the shelter.

About twenty five yards away I saw Parya, standing tall and perfectly erect at the far end of a narrow, slowly swaying boat in the lake. With a light shimmy of her body she advanced the boat toward the shelter. Another little twist brought the boat nearer. Advancing and stopping, she pulled right up to the shelter.

"Him?" she asked, with a questioning glance at Jahaaz.

I was as wonderstruck that this girl was Bibi's daughter as I had been at the thought that Bibi had once been someone's lover. I tried to look at her closely, but now she was inspecting me from head to toe.

"He doesn't look so sad," she said to Jahaaz.

Then turning to me, she said, "You don't look sad."

"When did I say I looked sad?" I tried to say, feeling a little irritated. But all I could do was stutter.

Parya laughed and said, "Jahaaz, he's really ..." Then she began laughing louder and louder, until Bibi's voice boomed from the boat,

"Parya, don't bother him."

"Why," Parya asked loudly, "because he's sad?"

"Parya," Jahaaz said encouragingly, "you'll have fun with him."

"Who needs fun?" she said and started to laugh again.

I began to feel uneasy, as though trapped, but then she asked, "Have you seen your new mother?"

"No, I haven't," I told her with a shake of my head.

"Don't you want to?"

I didn't answer and looked the other way.

"You don't?" she asked again.

This time my head moved in a way that could mean yes or no. It occurred to me that my new mother was to arrive at my former house today, or perhaps had already arrived.

My father had said that she would go crazy if she heard me speak. I tried to envision myself talking and her slowly going crazy. I tried to imagine what it would be like to live with a woman who would go crazy because of me. I also reflected that at this time yesterday I had been at my old house, and the memory seemed to come from the distant past. I re-lived my eight years there in eight seconds. Then I thought of my father's embrace before leaving me in Jahaaz's custody. I believed now, even more than before, that he loved me deeply.

"Jahaaz will love you deeply, too." Parya's voice startled me.

I had forgotten about her, but she had been watching me all this time. She moved to the other end of the boat, balancing herself as she walked. With a little spin of her body, her back was toward the shelter. A light swing of her torso nudged the boat forward and slowly she slid away from us. I felt as if a wonder had taken place before my eyes.

"If Bibi had not called to her," I said to myself, "I would have thought she was the spirit of the lake." If not the spirit of the lake, she was indeed a wonder, because she had been born underwater, and her feet had never touched the earth.

Bibi had received her boat from her forefathers, Jahaaz told me that day after Parya left. No one could say how long it had been in the big lake. But Bibi had lived far away from the lake where her husband, the dacoit, or whatever he was, came to meet her clandestinely. When Parya was about to be born, her husband had Bibi sent to the boat along with a midwife. One day, Jahaaz had heard Bibi crying in pain. Suddenly, the voices changed. Some government people had arrived and were questioning Bibi as to the whereabouts of her husband. Bibi would not tell them anything at all, so they took to repeatedly holding her underwater and in the midst of one of the longer episodes, Parya was born.

"I could clearly see bubbles coming from Bibi under the water," Jahaaz said, "then amid the bubbles Parya's little head emerged. And you could hear her cry."

The government people realized that Bibi hadn't been lying about the pain. They left, but continued their surveillance. And one day, Parya's father came to the ghat, just as they had thought he would. They surrounded him on the boat. He tried to escape, but was injured, fell into the lake and drowned.

Since that day Bibi had made the boat an abode for Parya and herself. She sometimes ventured out, but never let Parya set foot on land. She would roam around the lake in her small craft, or would return to her mother on the big boat. Why? Had Bibi made a vow of some kind? Was it the condition of some pact? No one knew how long Parya would continue circling the lake, and whether her feet would ever touch earth.

I spent a year at Sheesha Ghat, and during that year I witnessed the passing of every season, and in each season I watched Parya's boat roam the waters. She was my only means of diversion. The outer door of my abode opened on to the barren field, which led only to the fishing settlements at its nearest outskirts, past the smoky dwellings of the glassworkers. I stayed away from these habitats because of the drying fish. The fishermen were always immersed in their work and were of no use to me, just as I was of no use to them.

There were many ghats at the far ends of the field, including some large fishing settlements. A few ghats were alive with activity, but once or twice when I went to them I realized that the news of Jahaaz's foster son had preceded me. So, except for roaming the abandoned field and amusing myself with a few stray objects, I mostly sat underneath the shelter. Jahaaz, too, after running around all over to complete his errands, would come and sit here with his tobacco supplies and recount all sorts of tales. They were tales worth remembering, but I forgot them anyhow. But, I do remember that when a story of his failed to hold my attention, he would become agitated, even frenzied, and narrate it the way he used to perform his imitations. He would then suffer a bout of coughing and ruin what little interest there had been in the story.

In the beginning, I thought that Sheesha Ghat was completely cut off from the rest of the world, and that this part of the lake had always been a wasteland. That was not the case. It was true, however, as I had heard before, that no one could set foot here without Bibi's consent. I had assumed that Bibi never let anyone come here, but once, at Jahaaz's, I noticed that on certain special days the fishermen gathered here, bringing their nets and boats. Sometimes, they came in such large numbers that the scene looked like a little fair set up on the water. Sitting at my post under the shelter, I would hear the fishermen calling to each other and shouting directions. Filtering through their voices here and there came the sound of Parya's laughter. At times they seemed to be forbidding Parya from doing something. Occasionally, the voice of one of the older fishermen would be heard scolding Parya, yet laughing heartily at the same time. Then Bibi's voice would come from the boat: "Parya, let them work!" Parya would laugh in reply, and the fishermen would tell Bibi not to say anything to Parya.

On those days, and other days too, Parya would come to the ghat early in the morning. Standing in front of the shelter in her boat, she'd chat with Jahaaz for some time, then call me out to the shelter as well. If Jahaaz went away, she would talk to me. Her conversations were a bit childish. She would tell me stories about her dogs and cats, or why Bibi had scolded her the day before.

Sometimes she would ask me a question so suddenly that I'd start to answer with my tongue instead of the bobbings of my head. She would laugh wildly at these attempts only to get a scolding from Bibi that made her push out to the far reaches of the lake. In the afternoon, Bibi would call out to her in a loud voice and Parya's tiny craft would be seen advancing toward the boat. Then the sounds of Parya laughing and Bibi getting angry would emanate from the boat. Late in the afternoon, she would set out again and stop in front of the ghat. If Jahaaz were not there, she would talk to me about him. She found something to laugh at in everything about Jahaaz, whether it was his smoking, his disorderly dress or the sail on top of his house.

As she was talking to me one day, I began to suspect, and was soon convinced, that she had never seen the clown routines Jahaaz used to perform in the bazaars years before, and neither did she know about them. That day, for the first time, I tried to speak somewhat calmly, so that I could tell her about Jahaaz's mimic routines. She listened to me very attentively for a long while, without laughing, the way my father had begun to listen to me in the end.

Then Jahaaz walked out underneath the shelter, smoking, and relieved me of my efforts by telling Parya all that I had been trying to recount. He even performed two or three of his minor routines. To me they seemed pathetic imitations of his old ones, but Parya laughed so hard her boat began to rock. She wanted more, but Jahaaz was overcome with a coughing fit. Parya waited for it to stop, but he gestured to her to go away. As she turned her boat around she said, "Jahaaz, Jahaaz, you would make even Bibi laugh."

The next morning she arrived at the shelter earlier than ever, but Jahaaz had slipped away somewhere. She began talking to me about Jahaaz and described the mimicking as though I hadn't seen Jahaaz performing his routines the day before, indeed, as though I'd never known about them. I listened to her for a while, then tried to tell her that Jahaaz used to walk through the bazaars with the sail tied on his back, and mimic sinking ships before the crowds. But I could not tell her, by tongue or by gesture. Finally, I fell silent.

"Tomorrow," I said in my heart, "somehow, I will tell you."

I watched her as she retreated from sight.

"Tomorrow," I said again in my heart, "somehow."

My father arrived at the ghat the same evening. In one year he seemed to have aged more than Jahaaz had in the eight-year period before my arrival. His step was halting. Jahaaz walked by his side, supporting him, almost carrying him.

As soon as my father saw me he drew me into his arms. Finally, Jahaaz separated him from me, and made him sit down.

Turning to me, Jahaaz said,"Your new mother has died," before the coughing overtook him again.

There was no conversation between my father and me. Shortly after he arrived, Jahaaz took him off somewhere and returned late at night, alone. I had just lain down. Jahaaz fell asleep after smoking his nightly tobacco, but I kept wondering how my father could have grown so old so quickly. I thought of my new mother who had died without seeing me, and perhaps without going crazy. Then I went over the year I had spent at Sheesha Ghat, remembering how I had been bored at first by the extended, nearly unbreakable silence. Now I felt that the place was always full of sounds. Faint calls would come from the glassworkers, fishermen and the other ghats. Water birds would call over the lake. But I had never paid attention to them. Now, when I tuned my ears a little, I heard the halting sound of waves coming in and turning back after touching shore, and the faint creaking of the planks of Bibi's boat.

I decided that Sheesha Ghat was the only place for me, and that I had been born to live here.

"Tomorrow morning, I'll tell Jahaaz," I told myself, and fell asleep.

In the morning my eyes opened, as usual, to the sound of Jahaaz's coughing. Then I heard Parya's voice, too. They were talking, as on any other day. Jahaaz was inside and since he was unable to see Parya's boat from where he sat, he spoke loudly, coughing again and again.

I got up and went out to the shelter. There was Parya, standing in the middle of her boat. After chatting with Jahaaz a little more, partly about Bibi, she walked to the other end of the boat. The boat made a half-circle from the light movement of her feet and then Parya's back was toward the shelter.

For the first time I took a good look at Parya, and found myself more amazed than ever that a woman like Bibi could be her mother. At that instant Parya's body twirled and the boat moved away from the shelter. It swayed a moment and stopped. Parya scanned the expanse of lake before her. Again the boat rocked lightly but Parya, straightening her body, adjusted its balance. She made another barely perceptible motion with her feet. The boat made a very slow half-circle.

I viewed Parya from head to foot as she stood in the bow. I was afraid she might not like the way I was staring at her, but she wasn't looking in my direction. She was gazing intently at the ghat's still water, as if seeing it for the first time. Then, measuring her steps, she walked to the end of the boat nearer the shelter. Leaning over the water, she looked into it once again, stood up, shook her body into alignment, and very calmly placed a foot on the water's surface as one steps on dry earth. Then her other foot left the boat. She took one step forward, then another.

"She's walking on the water!" I exclaimed to myself, my surprise tinged with fear. I turned my head toward Jahaaz, who was smoking a little distance away, then looked back to the lake. Between Parya's empty boat and the shelter there was only water, concentric circles of waves spreading on its surface. A few moments later Parya's head emerged from the circles. She slapped the water with her palms over and over as though trying to clutch the surface of the lake. The water splashed and I heard Jahaaz's voice, "Parya, don't fool around with water."

Then a noose of smoke tightened at his throat and he doubled up, coughing wildly. My eyes turned to him for an instant. He was having a fit and needed help. I looked back at the lake. New circles were spreading on the bare water.

Parya rose again, then began to sink. My eyes met hers.

I jumped up shouting, "Jahaaz!" my tongue beginning to knot.

I leapt toward the old man. His coughing had stopped, but his breath was gurgling. He was rubbing his chest with one hand and his eyes with the other. Dashing up the steps, I grabbed both his hands and shook him with force.

"Parya ...," my mouth said.

He looked into my eyes with his pale irises, then lightning flashed in his eyes and I felt as though a bird of prey had escaped from my grip. Dust was dancing on the steps to the shelter and Jahaaz was standing at the shore.

Parya's boat completed a full circle. Jahaaz looked at the boat, then at the water. Then, with full force, he let out a call in a strange language. I heard Bibi match his cry from her boat. Then from far, far away the same voice returned. Bibi's asked, "The sad one?"

"Parya!" Jahaaz said with such force that the water before him trembled.

Other voices, far and near, repeated Jahaaz's cries over and over. Fishermen, some with nets, some empty handed, began running toward the ghat from all directions. Even before they got to the shelter, some of them had plunged into the water. Jahaaz was signalling to them with his hands when a splashing sound came from the left. I saw a barking dog running helter-skelter on the big boat and the two-coloured cat, its back raised, looking at the dog from a corner of the roof. Then I saw Bibi, almost naked, like some prickly man-eating fish, as she cut through the water. Her body collided with Parya's boat, sending it spinning like a top. Bibi dived and came up on the other side of the boat. She signalled to some of the fishermen and dived again.

Fishermen from other ghats were seen rowing toward us. Some had jumped overboard and were swimming in front of their boats.

Heads bobbed everywhere in the water between the shelter and Parya's boat. The crowd grew, collecting along the shore as well. There was din and commotion everywhere. Everyone was talking, but it was hard to tell what was being said by whom. The loudest noise, of splashing water, obscured all sense of the passage of time. Finally, a loud voice rang out. The clatter peaked and suddenly died to nothing. The bodies in the water, swimming soundlessly, slowly gathered at one spot. All were silent now except for the dog barking from the boat. At that moment I felt my hand clamped as though in a vise. Jahaaz was standing next to me.

"Go," he said, giving my hand a shake.

I couldn't understand where Jahaaz wanted me to go. Now he was pulling me into the house. Turning back, I tried to look toward the lake, but he tugged my hand. I looked at him. His eyes were glued to my face. "Go," he said again.

We had come to the back door of the house. Jahaaz opened it. In front was the barren plain. "They've found her," he told me, then pointed off across the plain and said hurriedly, "You'll reach the glassworkers' settlement in a short time. There you'll find someone to take you out of here. If not, just mention my name to anyone."

He put some money, tied in a handkerchief, in my pocket. I wanted to ask him many things and didn't want to leave, but he said, "Only you saw her drown. Everyone will ask you questions. Bibi more than anyone. Will you be able to answer?"

The scene rose before my eyes – the people, fishermen with rings in their ears, rowers with bangles on their wrists, visitors from different ghats – all forming a ring around me, two or three deep, questions flying from every direction, Bibi fixing me with her intent stare. They all fall silent as Bibi approaches me ...

Jahaaz noticed me trembling and said, "Tell me what happened. Anything ... Did she fall into the water?"

"No ..." I managed somehow.

"How did it happen, then?" Jahaaz asked. "Did she jump?"

"No," I said, and followed it with a shake of my head.

Jahaaz shook me, "Say something, hurry!"

I knew I wouldn't be able to say anything with my tongue, so I tried to communicate through hand gestures that she had been trying to walk on the water. Yet my hands halted again and again. I felt that even my signals were beginning to stutter, and that they too were incomprehensible.

Jahaaz asked in a constricted voice, "Was she walking on the water?"

"Yes," I said again with some difficulty.

"And she went under?"

"Yes."

"She was heading toward Bibi?"

"No."

"Where then?" he asked. "Was she coming toward us?"

"Yes," I gestured with my head.

Jahaaz lowered his head and grew a bit older before my eyes.

"I've seen her every day," he said at last, "from the day her tiny head popped out of the water," – he was nearly coughing the words – "but I hadn't noticed how grownup she'd come to look."

I stood silently, watching him grow even older.

"All right, go!" he said, putting his hand on my shoulder. "I'll find something to tell them. Don't you tell anybody anything."

What could *I* tell anybody? I thought. And my attention, which had meanwhile strayed from the ghat, returned to it. But Jahaaz gently turned me around and nudged me in the direction of the open field.

When I reached the edge of the field, I turned toward him and he said, "Your father came to take you back yesterday. I told him to wait a few days."

Again he coughed a little. He grabbed both panels of the door and slowly began to back away.

Before the door closed, I had already started on my journey. But I'd only gone some fifteen steps when Jahaaz called out to me. I turned around and saw him walk toward me haltingly. He looked as though he were imitating a ship whose sails had been torn off by the winds. He came up to me and embraced me. He held me to him for a long time. Then he released me and stepped back.

"Jahaaz!" Bibi's wail was heard from the ghat.

The pale eyes of the old clown looked at me for the last time. He nodded, as though in affirmation, and I turned and walked on.

This story was first published as "Sheesha-Ghat" in the journal *Saughat,* Bangalore, 10th March, 1996. It won the Katha Award in 1997.

ba'i's mourners

Few people know – perhaps none – that for a long time in my boyhood I used to be mortally afraid of brides. My fear sprang from a story about a bride in our family, many generations ago.

Before I had heard the story, I, like my peers, used to feel a certain attraction toward brides. If I attended a wedding, I tried to find a spot as close to the bride as I could. I would touch her henna-dyed hands, her dazzling red clothes, her jewels, over and over again. The varied scents emanating from her body – of flowers, attars, and those other things that remained unrecognized – would draw me to her, and the gentle tinkling of her jewellery seemed to me sweeter than the sweetest melodies. I also noticed that every woman, on becoming a bride, turned into something soft and beautiful. So I was smitten by love – albeit short-lived – for just about every bride, and after she left with her groom I'd feel crushed, at least for a time, like the lover whose love has been cruelly taken from him.

But one evening, when the rain was coming down hard, I got to hear the story of that bride in our family. After the nikah she had been sent off in the customary way from her parental home. But as she was about to be helped out of the carriage at her husband's house, it was discovered

translated by

muhammad umar memon

that she had died en route. She had bitten her lower lip until it bled. Her body had started to turn stiff. And an old centipede was found burrowed deep in her calf. It is said that a centipede sets its fish hook legs into the victim's skin and, little by little, enters the flesh all the way down to the bone. Eventually the victim dies, partly from the spreading poison, but mostly from the unbearable pain. This particular bride, it would seem, had died from the pain. She could have been saved, if only she had let someone know. But in those days speaking up in such a manner was considered forward and immodest in a bride, so she hadn't opened her mouth, had endured her pain and quietly perished.

"If the poor woman had only so much as let someone know that a centipede had dug into her calf," the female relative who was narrating the story added, "the centipede could have been extracted with a pair of heated tongs or, if not, someone could have tossed a fistful of sugar on it and it would have dissolved then and there."

The sugar remedy was something even I could understand. In those days whenever one of those gigantic centipedes appeared anywhere in the house, we would quickly throw some sugar on it. It would thrash and writhe for a while, then begin to melt, and turn to water in no time.

My heart went out to the silent bride. I even felt a certain love for her, in spite of the intervening generations. But her story did not end there. The narrator went on to say that her death caused weeping and wailing to break out in the festive houses. Both families decided to bury her as she was – fully bedecked in bridal attire and jewellery. That very day the bride, her "skin a vibrant yellow-orange from the sheen of her jewellery," as the expression goes, was lowered into her grave.

Peace escaped her even here. A man stole into the cemetery the same night, opened the freshly dug grave, and descended into it. His screams brought the people in the vicinity scrambling to the scene, whereupon they saw him lying unconscious beside the bride, the marks of her jewellery imprinted on his hands and face. The members of the two bereaved families also hurried to the cemetery upon hearing the news only to discover that the offending individual was none other than the groom himself. As he was being pulled from the grave the bride's body, which was stuck to his, also rose part of the way, before coming unstuck and falling back.

Certain funeral rites were quickly repeated and the grave was closed again. Now they attended to the husband. He was raving from the instant he came to. First he said that the bride's ornaments had grabbed him and dug into his body; then he said that the bride herself had grabbed him; and then he claimed that the bride's entire body had stuck to his. Why had he descended into the grave in the first place? Initially he gave no answer. Later, when his senses returned somewhat, he began by saying that he had opened the grave only to have one last look at his bride. Still later he revealed that he had been removing the bride's jewels.

For several days the groom wandered around as though demented. Eventually, he was found dead at his wife's gravesite. From that day on, despite the knowledge that the bride's grave had a substantial treasure in it, no grave robber dared so much as look in its direction. Slowly, with the passage of time, all trace of the grave was lost.

The story made me feel, for the first time in my life, that a bride was something to be feared. I began to hear the muffled tinkle of jewellery in the falling rain. Just then one of my elder brothers spoke up: "The bride wasn't really dead. People just took her for dead and buried her alive. The poor thing, out of sheer modesty, couldn't say she was alive."

Some people laughed at this, but the narrator admonished my brother for making fun of such matters. The thought that the bride was buried alive frightened me even more, and when I somehow convinced myself that she lay dead in her grave, she appeared even more frightening.

She haunted my thoughts for several days. Sometimes I imagined her alive, sometimes dead, each seeming by turns scarier than the other, and her jewellery scarier still. At weddings, I felt nervous going near the bride; indeed I was frightened of weddings altogether. After a while, my fear began to slowly subside, but my former attraction toward brides had left me altogether.

Right about that time, in the house across from ours, a wedding, which I was obliged to attend, took place.

It went by the name of "balcony house," because a balcony, spanning the length of its two top-floor rooms, jutted out over the street. We knew the people who lived there. I was friendly with the two younger brothers of the girl who was getting married. She was playful and talkative. She used to tease me all the time, with or without provocation, and said things now and then that made me feel both a bit nervous and a bit shy around her. All the same, her teasing pleased me, as did she herself.

I too got busy with my friends, taking care of the wedding chores inside the house and out. Several times the desire to step close to the bride and touch her surged up in me like a flame, only to subside just as quickly. After the nikah, when it was time for the ceremony that marked the bride's departure from her parental home, I tried to slip away, but my friends grabbed me. There was a crush of women in the long devrhi below. I took my place quietly by a wall.

Some time later the bride was escorted down from the room upstairs. Outside in the street the carriage stood waiting. In the devrhi, women were saying their farewells to the bride one by one. They hugged her by turns and wept loudly. It was as if a death had occurred in the house, rather than a wedding, and the mourners were engaged in a weeping tournament, each trying to outdo the other. Some faces were so contorted they made me laugh; I was busy silently mimicking their assorted weeping styles to preserve, and later draw on this repertoire, to amuse others. Just then a male voice rang out from the entrance door, sternly ordering

---

Devrhi: entrance hall

the womenfolk to shut up and to let the bride into the carriage immediately, or they would miss the train at the station. Silence swept over the entire hall. The bride, surrounded by the crowd of women, began to pick her way slowly toward the outer door to the soft sound of her jewellery – leaning on the shoulders of both her younger brothers. Two women gathered the lower part of the bride's costume and held it slightly off the ground. The red wedding dress and long veil allowed nothing of the bride to be seen, except a portion of the white of her calf just above her heavy ankle ornament, which seemed to be touching her embroidered slippers.

As she walked past me I wondered why, as a bride, she looked so diminutive. I craned my neck between two women standing directly in front of me, to take a better look. I don't know how she managed it, but she was able to glance at me from behind both her double veil and the screen of strung-flowers and ornamental gold and silver streamers cascading down her face.

A tremor swept her entire body, and it was as if the two women in front of me dissolved quickly into a big red blur. I heard the sharp clink of jewellery and saw the bride pulled to her full height standing straight in front of me. She bent over, hugged me, and began to cry loudly. The mingled scent of flowers, attars, and her body assaulted my senses in unison. I felt her jewel-studded bracelets dig into my shoulders, the pain obliterating the pleasurable softness of her touch. The women tore her away from me, but a link of her gold necklace was caught in a button of my open collar. The efforts to release it managed only to tangle it further.

The bride was now standing, fully bent over, a couple of steps from me – with the gold necklace flashing between us – as several women tried to wrench the offending button off my shirt. The sound of crying got louder in the devrhi. Instantly, I recalled the bride whose jewellery had grabbed a man. I felt as if that very bride was standing before me;

why, I could even see her dust-coloured face behind the veil and floral strings. I saw her advance toward me without taking a step. Soon her body would be stuck to mine, or mine to hers. In those few moments I felt also that there wasn't a soul in the devrhi except the two of us – indeed, it wasn't even the devrhi but a freshly dug grave, with the branches of a crooked tree drooping over its open mouth.

I twisted backward swiftly and bumped into the wall, then tore through the crowd and ran out into the open. With the gold link from the bride's necklace still stuck to my shirt button, I sprinted across the street and into my house.

Though I didn't tell my family anything about this incident, it had an adverse effect on me. Whenever I walked into an empty part of our house, I was seized by the fear that a bride was about to come out at me from behind something. Vague sounds awakened me at night, and my sense of smell was flooded with a mix of pleasing odours that hovered around me for some time after I had woken up. Behind the rain or any other continuous noise I heard the sound of crying and the soft, muted sound of jewellery. It became difficult for me to walk past an unused room whose door was ajar – for, on several occasions, I had glimpsed the white calf of a leg, a centipede digging into its flesh, receding slowly into the room.

The family that used to live in the balcony house moved out shortly after the wedding and an elderly couple moved in. During the time the house remained vacant, my steps faltered every time I passed by the devrhi. If the door appeared open, even a crack, I imagined seeing the glitter of jewellery in the dark and believed that if I were to peer through the opening I would surely see the bride there, not the loquacious bride of the balcony house, but the one in our family who had quietly died, many generations ago.

I knew all these were mere illusions. But imagined sights appeared truer than real sights to me, and fancies more real than facts.

I was convinced that I would pass my life, all of it, haunted by this fear, but as I got older the fear faded, along with many other boyhood feelings. The bride progressively lost her hold on me.

Now whenever she came up in a family discussion, I would detect various inconsistencies in the story and wonder with amazement that I once could have been so frightened of her. The demise of this fear sometimes evoked a vague sadness in me. Perhaps, I told myself, the time is not far off when both the lifeless memory of the bride and the equally lifeless fear of that memory will fade from my mind forever.

But only days ago both briefly came back to life.

There had been a death among our relatives that day. When we arrived at the cemetery with the bier, the grave wasn't ready. The gravedigger had thrice dug halfway down only to discover the remnants of earlier graves. Shovelling the earth from the fourth site, he assured us that no previous grave was likely to be found there.

The people who had accompanied the bier wandered off into the cemetery to while away the time. I too joined one of the groups and looked around the place with growing interest and attention, for I was visiting it after quite some time. Besides, this happened to be our family graveyard, though most of the graves belonged to other people. Actually, anybody could be buried here, but since my ancestors had donated the land, they had to take our permission first. This provided a sort of income which, considering that the graveyard was quite large, still amounted to very little. At that moment the others in our party were talking about just this financial aspect, but in a legalese which entirely escaped me.

I turned my attention away from their discussion and noticed that the trees appeared far fewer than before, and even among these most looked withered and dead. In the increasing heat of the sun, I felt the absence of the trees even more keenly. The branches of the misshapen tree near us looked twisted and cracked. With its bare black branches, the tree looked positively funereal. Except for a single branch. Sprouting from the dry trunk, this branch was surprisingly green, covered with bright leaves and shading a patch of earth.

In a few days it too will dry up, I speculated, standing under the branch looking at it. "This tree has always been like that – dry as a bone; and this branch too – always lush green," one of our party members remarked.

He was a poor, decrepit man. Noticing how attentively we were listening to him, he added, "Perhaps a bride is buried here. Under this very branch."

"People say if a bride dies before reaching her groom's house, the branches shading her grave never wither," he offered again, noticing our growing attention. For a moment my boyhood – a boyhood pervaded by that bride – returned to me.

Meanwhile the party had moved on ahead, chattering away, and I could not stop them. I knew in my bones that I was standing near the unmarked grave of that very bride. I felt the dry earth shift under my feet, and one of the cracks in the ground widen.

Is it starting all over again? I wondered. But I wasn't frightened. Waves of melancholy surged up from the ground. When I tried to escape them, I felt the old fear return. I defiantly quelled the desire to bolt. Instead, I sat down firmly on the hot desiccated earth.

The spell lasted no more than a few seconds. Then things were back to normal.

It was announced that the grave was ready and the people wandering around in the cemetery began to gather at the spot. I got up and made my way to the assemblage, pondering throughout how the whole thing had begun and ended so quickly.

Although it escaped me at the time, the thought occurs to me now that perhaps the reason it had happened was that I knew that Ba'i too had been laid to rest in this very cemetery.

The old couple had moved quietly into the balcony house, growing older with the passage of time, unbeknownst to the world. I don't recall when or how I first became aware of their presence, but sometimes, through the wide-open outer door of their house, I would often notice an elderly man seated on a takht in the devrhi. Usually, a few rattan chairs would be placed beside the takht, occupied occasionally by a couple of old men from the neighbourhood. Often I saw them quietly absorbed in a game of chess. To concentrate more fully on my studies I had, in those days, moved into the secluded rooftop room of our house. I could easily see the door to the devrhi across the street as well as the two top-floor rooms from this vantage point. A row of flowerless potted ornamental plants ran along the front edge of the overhanging balcony and a little girl, decked out in rustic silver jewellery, appeared every second or third day to water them with a tin-coated copper can. Our two houses were separated not just by the street but also by our garden; from that distance, she really looked like a little girl.

Later – exactly when I cannot tell – I came to know that she was in fact the couple's maidservant and went by the name of Khanam. All the neighbours and shopkeepers of the area were familiar enough with Khanam to joke around with her. She was a pahaaran – a mountain woman – and perhaps even older than the couple she served, but she was no taller than a girl of eight or ten. Perhaps that's why people talked to her as one talks to children. She walked as if propelled by a series of pushes. And her speech imitated her gait: as if every word got stuck in her mouth and waited to be ejected by a kick from the word following it. The neighbourhood brats, as well as some of the shopkeepers, mimicked her, which sometimes annoyed her, prompting her to threaten, "I'll report you to the police!" But by now everyone knew that, if anything, she was more afraid of the police than they were. Mischievous boys of our locality would sneak up behind her and shout, "Police!" in her ear causing her to jump up and take off in a panic, stopping a few steps later to snap, "I'll report you to the police!" She came and went freely to all the neighbourhood houses – mostly to talk with the domestics – and was our chief source of information about the old couple.

She called her mistress Ba'i and her master, Sahib. It is from her that we learned that the couple was childless. Ba'i had no family. Sahib did have quite a few distant relatives, some of whom lived in this very city, but social interaction between them and Sahib had ceased a long time ago. When one of them fell ill or there was a death among them, only Sahib went to visit. Ba'i never stepped out of the house. She suffered from rheumatism in her knees, which made it difficult to move around; climbing up or down stairs was practically impossible.

Once when Khanam mentioned Ba'i's chronic ailment to my mother, she gave her a simple recipe for a rubbing-oil, but was uncertain of the exact proportion of one of the ingredients. After Khanam had left and my father had come in, Mother asked him about the right proportion of the ingredient, which led them to talk about Ba'i and Sahib. It turned out that Father knew something about the couple. He told Mother that in her youth Ba'i was a well-known singer in the city. He also revealed the name by which Ba'i went back in those days – a name known to every music enthusiast. Sahib was the scion of an old, noble family, but time had turned against him. All the same, he was the greatest admirer of Ba'i's art. He had married Ba'i in those days and the two had left the city shortly thereafter.

"And you – you didn't go to hear her sing?" Mother asked, laughing.

Father also began to laugh. "I was neither an enthusiast nor the son of a nobleman," he said. "I was a student in those days. All that frantic running around, just to scrape together enough money for the fees, left me no time. I didn't hear her sing, but it was impossible not to hear of her fame as a singer."

Most times when I saw Sahib he would be sitting inside the devrhi, which made it difficult to see his features clearly. Every now and then, though, I would spot him either as he emerged from the house to go out or when he returned. He held a carved, ebony-coloured walking stick in his hands. His clothes, of an eastern cut, conformed to the garb of the city's old, venerable dignitaries. But he never failed to appear wearing an English huntsman's hat. He would walk very slowly, tapping the ground with his cane. But even on these occasions I only saw him from afar. I spotted him a couple of times some distance away in the bazaar, and recognized him only by his walking stick and hat.

As for Ba'i, I saw even less of her. The door to one of their two rooms, visible from my room, remained permanently closed. The door to the other room was usually opened when Khanam watered the plants, although once in a while they also opened it when it felt stuffy and sultry or when a fine cool breeze started to blow. On these occasions Ba'i appeared seated on her bed inside the room. Several times I saw Khanam combing her hair, and once Ba'i was combing Khanam's. In her case, too, it was not possible to observe her features clearly from such a distance; I could only tell that she was a portly woman, well along in years.

Initially I suspected that Sahib had set up his quarters permanently on the ground floor. But one day Ba'i's door was left open and I saw him sitting on her bed, bending forward every so often, while Khanam walked up to the couple, then withdrew, only to approach them yet again. I figured the two were eating together. I was to witness this scene many times over. Once I even saw him trying to feed her something forcibly; the old lady repeatedly refused, pulling her face away this way and that, but laughing heartily all the same. Just then Khanam arrived with the water. Ba'i clapped her on the back and she exited, shaking her shoulders with suppressed laughter.

Perhaps my family would know, but I cannot even guess, how long Sahib and Ba'i lived in the balcony house. They held no real interest for me. The couple was part of the colourless landscape around me, and whether I looked at them or not hardly mattered. Which perhaps explains why I failed to notice that the door to the upper-storey room hadn't opened for days, nor had the door to the devrhi below, which remained bolted from inside. Only the day Khanam showed up at our house to borrow the hot-water bottle did we find out that Ba'i had been gravely ill for the past several days and Sahib had been out of town. When asked who was looking after the old lady, she informed us that Ba'i had sent for two of Sahib's female relatives who had arrived just that day.

In the evening I found the doors to Ba'i's two rooms wide open and a couple of new women moving about in the rooms. The next morning a fresh contingent of some half a dozen women materialized, and by the afternoon of the third day their numbers had grown further. On the fourth day, shortly after sunrise, crying was heard from the house.

I looked on for a while and then came down to inform my family. I found Khanam sitting in our courtyard, crying. She had already broken the news. Ba'i had passed away a short while ago. The attending ladies had sent Khanam out for some incense to burn near the deceased, but the shops hadn't opened yet. My mother was rummaging inside a cupboard in the verandah wall for a small packet of incense and, at the same time, asking Khanam about the details of Ba'i's illness. Khanam told us everything in due course. She also mentioned that Sahib still hadn't returned, that Ba'i had been perfectly well when he'd left, and that he never told anyone but Ba'i where he was going.

I went back up to my room. The sound of crying at Ba'i's place had nearly died out by the time it was fully morning. But carriages kept arriving at short intervals, dropping off women passengers in front of the devrhi. Their male escorts, who didn't look like the men of our locality, would stand in the devrhi, while loud wails erupted and quickly died down upstairs. At one point, though, the wails peaked and did not subside; they grew progressively louder and finally reached full-fledged pandemonium. I walked over to my door. Ba'i's quarters looked like a riot scene: there was no crying, only screaming, with Khanam's voice rising above everyone else's. Women were jabbering and springing on each other, overcome by grief. A terrible restlessness had gripped them and Khanam, like a bat caught in a sudden avalanche of light, was flailing about inside the room, bumping madly into everybody. Shortly afterwards, male voices rose from the street. I peered into the space under the balcony. The contingent of men was having a heated argument in front of the devrhi, while a couple of neighbourhood people were trying to calm them down. Finally, after watching the tumult raging both upstairs and down, I saw the women file out of the devrhi and depart with their men. They were talking loudly, as their men – just as loudly – tried to shush them. I could not make out what they were saying. I looked at the balcony again. The doors to the two rooms were closed. And it was so quiet, as if nothing had happened at all, though I did smell the incense carried by the breeze.

I went downstairs to let the family know about the commotion. But Khanam was already there and had apparently told them the whole story, which our own women were repeating now.

According to Khanam, Ba'i had spent most of the past few days in a semiconscious state during which, now and then, she would suddenly become alert and ask for Sahib, only to drift back into a stupor again. But a day ago she had become fully conscious and looked quite all right. She had asked for something to eat, then had Khanam bring her her jewellery boxes. She put on the jewellery, every single ornament, and emphatically told Khanam to leave the devrhi door open for Sahib. All night long she sat in her bed fully awake. In the morning, she inquired about Sahib again, had Khanam comb her hair, and asked for her kajal box. As Khanam was returning with the box, life departed from Ba'i.

Sahib's female relatives, a whole host of them, arrived. The lamentation got underway. After some time, the women began to throw themselves on Ba'i's hands, feet, and face as they wept and wailed. While this was going on one of the women, still crying, pulled away from Ba'i's face. Another noticed that one of Ba'i's earrings was missing. She asked where it had gone. "Where the ring did," the first woman said, pointing to a third woman in the group. A ring was also missing from Ba'i's finger. This was the beginning of the riot. Before long, everyone was accusing each other of stealing, all the while trying to establish her own close relationship to Ba'i and laying claim to her jewellery. It got to the point where they pounced on Ba'i, picking her corpse clean of every last bit of jewellery. In the words of the womenfolk, she was left "naked."

I thought Khanam's account was somewhat exaggerated. I said that I had watched the entire incident myself and hadn't noticed any such plunder. I then recounted the incident exactly as I had witnessed it from my rooftop. Khanam listened indifferently, even with faint contempt, and responded that she, at least, had been present at the scene. Then she said that the women relatives had all left in a huff, and she, entrusting Ba'i's body to some neighbourhood women, had come here specifically to ask us to somehow find Sahib and let him know. Father was called in. He had no idea where Sahib might be, but he nonetheless scribbled a few words and had the servant hand-carry them to some of the old, knowledgeable people in the city who he thought might have been acquainted with Sahib. It was only at this point that we noticed the trickle of blood running down Khanam's nose and ears, and that the crude, heavy silver jewellery which never left her was missing from her hands and feet as well as from her face. Mother screamed: "What? Did they plunder your jewellery too?"

No, Khanam said. What had happened was that as she had grabbed at the women one by one and searched them in order to retrieve Ba'i's jewellery, each woman had fended her off. So she herself tore off every piece of her own jewellery and hurled it at them, saying, Here, take these as well.

"After all, they were my Ba'i's too," she said and started to wail.

It was only after a long time and with the greatest difficulty that she could be quietened. She let us apply medicine to her wounds to stop the bleeding, and then sat down to wait for the servant to return. She was given food; she didn't refuse it and ate with her head bowed.

Meanwhile, the servant returned. Nobody could say where Sahib had gone; they didn't even know if he was back in the city.

As Khanam was about to leave, the servants who took care of the outdoor chores brought fresh news. Somebody had reported to the police that Ba'i had been murdered in broad daylight and robbed of her jewellery. The police had just arrived, taken the body into custody, and were now looking for Khanam to record her statement. How much she dreaded the police became apparent to us now. Her face, desolate enough without its jewellery, looked positively deathly. She looked with glassy, lifeless eyes at each one of my people as they expressed their views on the latest incidents.

To top it all, one of my maternal uncles, an expert in legal matters who had, in fact, arrived from Kanpur in connection with a lawsuit, scared her even more by saying that the matter would likely drag on and that as a witness she would be repeatedly subjected to interrogations by both the police and the attorneys. When finally asked to go and give her statement, she threw herself down and began to flail and writhe. She wouldn't listen to anybody and scurried from room to room trying somehow to hide herself. Finally, we had to hand her over to the servants outside who were told that under the circumstances it was hardly appropriate to let her stay here.

As Khanam – screaming and frantically throwing her tiny legs every which way in resistance – was being literally carried out, I noticed that my maternal uncle had taken Father and Mother aside and was telling them something in hushed tones. He gestured for me to come over to him and announced that he was taking me to Kanpur that very minute.

"And remember," he said emphatically, "don't tell anybody here or in

Kanpur that you have witnessed anything, or they will drag you into the court to testify too."

Mother quickly packed my bags for the trip. We left the house through the door that opened into the back alley, crossed over to another street, and set out for the train station.

In less than a week I was called back from Kanpur. On my return I found out only three things: one, that Khanam had gone into hiding with one of our servant's kinsfolk and had disappeared the very next day; two, that Ba'i had been interred in our family graveyard with my father's permission, indeed at his suggestion; and three, that there was still no news of Sahib.

I went upstairs and looked over at the house. Most of the plants on the balcony had withered, and all the doors, both upstairs and downstairs, were shut. It appeared as if they hadn't been opened for years.

On the afternoon of the fourth day Sahib showed up at our house, wearing his huntsman's hat and tapping his walking stick as usual. I was preparing a flowerbed in our front garden, while Father stood nearby giving instructions. Sahib came over to us. Father stepped forward to greet him, then offered his condolences. Sahib thanked him for allowing Ba'i a plot in our family graveyard. He made to leave immediately, but Father asked him to stay a while longer.

They moved to the adjacent terrace and sat in the chairs under the mulberry tree and started to talk while I continued with my work. Sahib stayed longer than expected. He was given to speaking softly, so I could not hear him clearly, but I could guess that he was recounting Ba'i's virtues, in the way that the dead are praised, narrating incidents to substantiate them.

Finally he got up. Father gestured to me to escort him to the gate that opened on to the street and he himself accompanied Sahib to the edge of the terrace adjacent to the garden. Sahib stopped at the outer steps of the terrace, shook hands with Father, climbed down the stairs and walked a step or two, then stopped and – leaning his entire weight on to the walking stick – abruptly turned around.

"Just tell me this, please ...," he began in a loud voice; then fell silent.

Father said a few words by way of consolation and Sahib turned around and strode away, tapping his stick. At the gate, he said without looking at me, "This is far enough, son. May you live long," and walked out of the gate into the street.

Later, that week, when I opened the street-side door of my room, I saw a couple of horse-drawn carriages, packed with household stuff, standing in front of Sahib's devrhi. Some neighbourhood people stood nearby talking amongst themselves. I also saw that the row of potted plants had disappeared from the balcony. I stayed where I was. After a while Sahib emerged from the devrhi, closed the door behind him, fastened the chain, put a large copper padlock on it, and placed the key in the hand of a neighbourhood elder. Then he embraced everyone in turn. This caused his hat to slip from his head, but he secured it each time before embracing the next person. The first carriage began to move. Sahib climbed aboard his carriage and took his place next to the coachman on the front seat. The carriage lurched forward, then halted. Sahib got off and said something to the coachman, who climbed down from the other side, walked to the back seat, took out a footlocker and a clay water pot with its wooden stand, and moved them to the front seat. Sahib settled in at the back. He looked at the people standing in front of him and raised his hand in farewell. The reins jerked a little and the carriage started off behind the one in front. At the end of the street both the carriages turned toward the railway station.

This story was first published as "Ba'i ke Matam-Dar" in the journal *Quarterly Aaj*, Karachi.

sultan muzaffar's chronicler of events

At least, not in this continuum ...

– H Beam Piper

Didim, tapidim, nah didim, tapidim
(We saw, we were in agony; we did not see, we were in agony)

– Iqbal

Now that Sultan Muzaffar's tomb has become so famous in his own lifetime that people come from far away to see it, I have been ordered to write an account of how it was built.

This order puts an end to my days of staying at home.

I found out from the Sultan himself that his tomb had been built. And when the Sultan told me that his tomb had not been constructed in the valley, where his ancestors were buried, I understood that the tomb was in the desert because I had been the chronicler of his desert campaign. And when he told me that the mausoleum was unique I understood that it would be roofless – also because I was the chronicler of his desert campaign. That was my last chronicle.

translated by

aditya behl

After it began a period of staying at home. I have forgotten many things about that time, but I remember my first day of staying at home so well I can write on it like an authoritative chronicler.

On my morning walk that day, I saw many small plants lying by the edge of the valley of the tombs. These had, perhaps, been uprooted only a short while ago. They were shoots of the big umbrella-shaped trees, rows of which grew all around the valley. I did not know the name of these trees, but had rested beneath them sometimes. Their trunks were whitish, with thick, dense branches, and one felt sleepy in their shade. I carefully inspected the shoots which lay on the ground. Two of them still had their roots intact. I picked them up and plastered some of the wet earth from below the big trees around their roots. Then I began walking home. By the time I reached I had decided where to plant them in my garden. I hadn't stopped on the way, though, when I passed by a small lake, I had bent to take some water in my hand and sprinkled the plants' leaves with it.

I estimate that the Sultan's envoy must have started for my house at precisely that moment.

I had finished planting the two shoots in my garden and was planning how to shelter them from the sun. The children of my house had gathered around one of the plants. They had tried to shade it with their toys and playthings. They were so happy with this new game that they were fighting for their turns. I was sprinkling the leaves of the other plants with water when the shadow of the Sultan's envoy fell across it. I saw the shadow first, and then the envoy. The children left the plant and gathered around him, but after looking carefully at his uniform they grew frightened and ran away to hide in the house.

I, too, examined his uniform with care. Imperial envoys bear no written or oral message aside from their uniforms. The purpose of their visit is apparent from the uniform they wear. This envoy's uniform meant that the Sultan demanded some service of me and I was to wait at home for his order. This envoy, or an envoy wearing this uniform, had come to my house frequently in the past. But when I saw him this time I was surprised as it had only been a few days since the Sultan's desert campaign had ended. I didn't expect the Sultan to start so soon on another venture that needed chronicling. But the unpredictability of the Sultan's behaviour was not a thing to be surprised at for long. To me, therefore, the most remarkable thing about that day was that one of the two shoots I had planted was crushed underfoot by the imperial envoy. The other shoot was safe, however, and I could rest in its shade when it grew.

I was resting under that very tree when I noticed a shadow move and one of the Sultan's envoys came and stood before me. It is not difficult to recognize imperial envoys even though their uniforms differ. I examined every inch of this one's uniform many times, from top to bottom, down to the last thread, and racked my brains. The envoy watched me silently, and his growing surprise was reflected in his eyes. Finally, I was forced to speak.

"My vision isn't very good any more," I said.

"Obviously," he said, coming very close to me, "because even after seeing me you are still where you were."

And then I remembered.

"An imperial summons," I said immediately.

The envoy turned around swiftly and tripped over a root of the tree which was sticking out. Perhaps he hurt himself, for when he was going back he limped slightly. Perhaps that was why I preceded him on the way out. When we had gone a little way I stopped and let him walk on ahead, following him after he had gained a few steps.

After receiving my orders from the Sultan I returned, as was my habit, via the bazaar road. After lingering at many small shops and observing the buying and selling there, I entered the main bazaar. The market was almost the same as when I had last seen it, although there seemed to be more of a crowd now. The places fixed for the vendors had not changed either, so my eyes fell first on the gardeners who sold flowers and plants, spreading them out on the ground in front of them. However, I could not see the old gardener from whom I always used to buy plants—sometimes without needing any at all. He used to sit with the others but, unlike them, would always arrange his wares as if it were a small garden. Like the others he, too, was employed in the imperial gardens, and sold off those unwanted plants which, because they interfered with the aesthetic arrangement of the Sultan's gardens, were uprooted.

This green and flourishing part of the market had only one customer besides me. When the gardeners saw us, they began to call out the names of different flowers and plants as was their practice. The old gardener had remained silent on such occasions. Even now, among the crowd of noisy gardeners, I could see one man sitting silently. When I paused in front of him, he quietly began rearranging the plants he had set out. I sat on the ground and casually picked up some, saying, "There used to be an old man who sat here, with plants arranged around him."

He nodded. I noticed the other customer sit down near me and pick at the petals of a large yellow flower. Then I looked back at the young gardener, searching for a likeness of the old man.

"Who was he to you?"

"My grandfather," he said.

"Do you also work in the Sultan's gardens?"

He nodded his head once again.

"In your grandfather's place?"

"In my father's place," he said.

I looked around the entire market. And felt again that, apart from getting more crowded, there had been no great change in the bazaar. Then again, the platform on my right, where public shows took place, appeared somewhat higher and its edges more worn. The crowd on the platform was thicker than in other parts of the market, but then this had been the case earlier too. I turned my attention back to the gardener.

"Don't you have shoots of large trees?"

He picked out some plants and set them before me. I glanced at them cursorily, turning them over in my hands. The other customer was still fussing with the yellow flower, and two of its petals now hung loose. But instead of looking at the flower he was looking at me.

"You are spoiling it," I pointed out to him.

"I have bought this one," he told the gardener, and pulled the plant out completely.

He continued to sit there even after that. It occurred to me that perhaps he wished to stay with me for a reason. I looked at him once, intently, but his wasn't a face I recognized. I strained my memory and stared at him, but could not trace the likeness of any familiar person in him. Still he continued looking at me. Confused, I put my hands on my knees and began to get up. But then my eyes fell on a small heap of green plants beside the gardener. I sat down. Then I got up again and came around to the gardener's side. I picked up one plant and, looking at it, asked the gardener, "These don't have roots?"

"These are not for planting."

"Then?" the other customer asked.

"People take them away," said the gardener, "to feed *them.*" And he indicated the platform where the public shows were held.

The other customer now stood beside me. He bent down, picked up two or three of the plants, and asked the gardener, "What's so special about these?"

"The poison."

And I understood who the people staging the shows on the platform were. I asked the gardener, or perhaps I asked myself, "Have they started to come again?"

"Did they come here before?" he asked me.

They did. The desert was their home, and every year, in the show season, they would make a trip into town. They would stage their show from afternoon till the setting of the sun. When they were on stage no one would look at the other performers. Sometimes fights broke out between them and the other artistes, which the spectators would have to resolve.

And the marvel they staged was that they would eat anything and everything. The crowd searched far and wide to bring them things they thought no human, or animal, could eat. But these desert-dwellers would eat everything, and then collect money from the spectators in return. Sometimes people would look at their show and collapse laughing, sometimes they would be frightened and move back, and sometimes they would turn their faces away in disgust. Some spectators felt so sick during the show that their companions took them away. But the crowd at the platform didn't thin from afternoon till the setting of the sun.

Many seasons before the Sultan's desert campaign began, these people had stopped coming to town. They did not come even after the desert campaign ended. I was certain that we would never see their show in town again. But they were staging their show now, and the crowd on the platform of the main market was larger than ever. Two or three men from this throng jumped off the platform and, laughing and joking amongst themselves, came toward us.

"Give them to me," said one of them to the gardener, extending his hand toward the plants.

The other customer put the plants he held on the ground, and the spectators gathered them up with the rest of the plants.

After they had gone back, I was very angry. I heard the voice of the gardener: "There is no remedy for their poison," he said, "and they are not planted within the town."

I moved on toward the platform where the shows were held.

There was still some time before sunset. I stopped near the platform.

The other customer walked past me and clambered on to it. I saw him merge with the crowd of spectators. But when I left the market and turned into the desert road, he was walking behind me. I walked silently until I reached the outskirts of the town, and the margins of the desert could be seen in the distance. I stopped and sat on a stone to rest. In a little while he was standing in front of me. I raised my head to look at him. He, too, regarded me silently. Finally I asked, "Do you know me?"

He sat down on a nearby stone and stretched slightly.

"Do you?" I asked again.

"Sultan Muzaffar's chronicler," he declared as if making a public announcement, "going to write an account of the making of a tomb whose construction he has never seen."

After that he was silent – as if he had never spoken.

The Sultan's servant, I thought, and asked him, "Have you been appointed to torture me?"

But he seemed to be struggling with some torment of his own. I felt a vague sense of sympathy for him.

"I have been appointed to observe you observing the tomb," he said.

"Only to observe?"

"And also, when you finish writing the chronicle of its construction, to write its history."

I was surprised, because the man did not appear to be very old.

"You are the Sultan's official historian?" I asked. "What about the one before you?"

"There were many before me."

"The one who was there at the time of the desert campaign?"

"He had to die."

Just then a group of people coming from the desert passed by us. They appeared to be inhabitants of other towns. Then some more groups of people went by. I saw no one go toward the desert. For some time there was complete silence around us, and then the vendors who had set up makeshift shops along the road could be seen coming toward us with rapid steps, carrying their wares with them. When they drew near us, one or two hesitated hopefully, but, seeing we paid them no heed, went on. Only then did I experience, sitting there, the complete silence of the desert. At that point my companion stood up.

"It's time," he said, and began walking toward the desert.

I saw the sun beginning to set and started walking beside him. We walked silently and reached the edge of the desert. Far off, we could see the outline of a building. A long straight road had been built to reach it. This road was paved with small slabs of stone with two, low ridges – also made of stone – on either side of it. The road sloped so much on both sides that the sand that gathered on it continually spilled out, like water spilling from the town's drains during the rains. We continued to traverse the road in silence. The tomb was not visible now. Soon the road climbed higher and higher, until it ended at the steps of an elevated platform. We climbed the steps to the platform. On the other side of it a similar road descended into the desert. On that straight road, far off in the distance where its two boundary walls appeared to meet, stood the tomb, right in the middle of the path. The road made it seem like the sharp point of a knife had cleaved straight through to the heart of the desert.

I was growing tired. Hot gusts of desert wind, in which the cool of the approaching evening had only just begun to mingle, increased my fatigue. I decided to rest on the platform for a while. The white stone floor of the platform was still hot, but I could sit on it. From this distance the architecture of the tomb did not seem unique in any way. The rays of the setting sun fell on its round serrated roof. I said, "Its roof ..."

"Doesn't exist," said my companion, "but can only be seen from a distance."

"Shall we go near it and see?"

"No," he said, "not until the custodian arrives."

I had to sit on the stone floor a little longer, waiting for the custodian.

I thought he would come along the same road we had traversed, but he appeared from around the tomb. Walking rapidly, he climbed up on to the platform, bowed before us perfunctorily and, slowly turning around, began leading us up the road. The distance between the platform and the tomb was less than I had estimated. Soon we stood in front of its gate. Once we arrived, the custodian began to speak. He recounted every step of its construction – from the measuring of the ground to the laying of the last stone slab – as if he were showing me the tomb being built. I got the feeling I was not listening to what he was saying, but reading what I had written myself.

After finishing his account the custodian advanced toward the platform, but I put a restraining hand on his chest.

"You have told us everything," I said, "but I want to see it as well."

I entered through the doorway. On all sides I saw walls and more walls. Walls all around, high and low, intersecting each other at angles and then drawing far away from each other. The highest walls were at the very back. These had been erected in the shape of a semicircle, and were the walls which gave the illusion of a roof from a distance. Because of the proliferation of walls, and because the sun was setting, it was somewhat dark inside the tomb and one did not feel the absence of a ceiling. The walls ranged far and wide, making a labyrinth whose centre was impossible to locate. When I wanted to come out, I could not find my way. Perhaps this was why people came from great distances to see the tomb. I wandered through the labyrinth for a long time, until the custodian came to find me.

In a little while we were on the stone platform again. I spoke to the custodian:

"I have to find out something else."

He seemed somewhat anxious.

"I have told you everything, from the beginning to the end," he said slowly.

"Did you see the tomb being built from beginning to end?"

He remained silent.

"Were only the people of the town employed to construct it?" I asked.

"Eventually, the desert-dwellers were as well."

"Who oversaw them?"

"I did."

"Did they know they were building a mausoleum?"

"They knew. They were told before they started."

"That they were building the Sultan's mausoleum?"

He fell silent again and seemed even more upset.

"Who chose the site for the tomb?"

"The Sultan."

"Where did the stone come from?"

"I have already told you. The mountain range on the far side of the valley of the tombs ..."

"It was brought from there, but for which building?"

"It has been used for the tomb."

"The tomb is exactly where the fort for the desert campaign used to be. Which stone was used for the fort?"

Somewhat astonished, he looked at me and said, "I have been ordered to tell you about the tomb. I have not seen the fort."

"The fort was demolished," I told him.

The custodian stood there silently. I looked first at the road going toward the tomb, then at the road coming into the desert. Both roads were exactly the same. Had the stone platform not been there, it would have been one road.

"This platform ...," I asked, bending over the intricately carved white stone of the platform, "why has this platform been built?"

"In order to rest," he replied.

"On it?"

"Obviously."

"What is underneath it?" I asked.

"Sand."

"Did the Sultan choose the place for this platform too?"

"No, one of the imperial servants did," he said, "but on the orders of the Sultan."

"Obviously," I said.

The custodian kept glancing at the sun, so I asked him my last question: "Why was it not necessary to tell me that the stone from the fort was used to build the tomb?"

"I have told you everything I was ordered to," he said, and I sensed a slight touch of fear mix with the irritation in his voice. "Whatever you write besides this will not be what I have told you."

He turned toward my companion. "And you will have to bear witness to this," he fumed.

He descended from the platform and, leaning against the left boundary wall, proceeded along the road to the town. His feet scattered the sand gathered in the declivity of the road, so that it poured with even greater rapidity from the lowest shelves of the wall. I could see sand particles flaring like sparks in the rays of the setting sun.

The custodian's last sentence had reminded me of the existence of my companion. I looked toward him. He was truly very young. I asked him, "Who taught you how to write history?"

"No one did," he said, "I have studied it on my own."

"What have you studied?"

He listed many disciplines of knowledge.

"And histories?"

"Just one. The history of the desert campaign."

The historian of the period of the desert campaign came to mind. He was my only enemy. I remembered his voice, and also that when he laughed his eyes would close of their own volition.

"You said he had to die?" I asked.

"Yes. The Sultan did not like his history of the desert campaign."

"But he was a very good historian."

"He had written all those things in his history that the chronicler of the desert campaign had written," he said. He paused a bit, then spoke again, "He said so in his defence as well."

"In his defence?" I asked. "And what was the charge against him?"

"This was it. That he had written all those things in his history that the chronicler of the desert campaign had written."

"How was he made to die?"

"By eating the poisonous fruit of a tree."

"By order of the Sultan?"

He did not respond. I asked again, "By order of the Sultan?"

"By order of the Sultan I am now writing that history."

"Is it with you now?"

He nodded his head.

"And the account of the chronicler?"

"And the account of the chronicler."

"It wasn't destroyed?"

"It will be. When I finish the history and present it to the Sultan. I have been assured of this."

"Up to where have you written?"

"The arrival of the Sultan in the desert ..."

" ... And into the fort ..."

"There was no fort there."

I looked at him in astonishment, and he spoke emphasizing every word, "There was no fort, and in the fort there was no woman."

I looked at him with even greater astonishment.

"You have written this," he said in a sharp voice. "I will not write it. I have been given the right."

"That's why it is also your duty," I said quietly.

"But why are we talking about it, about the campaign?" he said.

Then, seeing me sitting on the stone floor of the platform he came toward me and said, "In a little while it will be dark."

"I will stay here for now," I said. "Perhaps till morning."

"Will you start writing today?"

"No. I will get paper tomorrow," I said. Then I told him, "Chronicling has to be done on imperial paper. You will get paper too, but without the imperial seal, and not in numbered quantities."

I forgot that he had a chronicle of events with him, and that he himself had started writing a history. He listened to me disinterestedly and then, even though he had seemed annoyed with me until then, sat beside me. Putting his hand on my shoulder, he said conspiratorially, "The building of this tomb ... can't we write an account of its construction together?"

"Then you too will have to say in your defence that you have only written what the chronicler of the building of the tomb had written."

He sat there lost in thought for a while. Finally, pressing down hard on my shoulder, he raised himself up and said, "It's getting late for me."

"Your work will start after mine," I said. "You can rest now."

"And you ... will you stay here?" he said with some distress. "It gets very cold here at night."

"I will be able to bear it. Otherwise I can take shelter inside the tomb."

At that moment neither I, nor perhaps he, remembered that the tomb was made only of walls.

As soon as he left, darkness spread through the desert and the tomb began to be obscured from my sight. I tossed and turned many times to get comfortable, then settled down to rest. At first, I felt safe in the building and the desert didn't bother me. But then the building turned into a large black stain, to which imagination could give any shape it chose. I imagined a fort with tower and ramparts. I heard the susurration of the wings of desert birds returning from the town's lakes – as they flapped over me and then flew far away – and I began to remember the

Sultan's desert campaign. I tried to forget, but the effort proved futile ...

I had been made to sit in the eastern tower of the fort. A bundle of counted imperial paper lay in front of me. A beautifully carved weight of white stone lay on the papers so that the wind, which always blows quicker around towers, could not fly away with them. At the top of each sheet of paper the golden seal of the Sultan – a crown, two swords and, shading them from above, a royal parasol – shone in the light of the rising sun.

I had been brought to sit in the tower some time before sunrise, so that I would not see the people who had conducted me into the tower and then left silently. I rested one hand on the white stone weight and was waiting for the sun to rise so I could watch its light run across the waves of sand, flowing in every direction. After that my pen was to commit to paper everything my eyes saw. This was easy for me, because I did not have the responsibility of explaining what I saw and wrote. And I had not even been told anything about the desert campaign. I had only heard in the bazaars of the town that the campaign had started and that the Sultan himself was in the desert. Then I was suddenly summoned at midnight and made to sit in the dark in the eastern tower with a bundle of imperial paper. At the time I did not even know that I was in the tower of a fort, or that a temporary observation post had been set up for me to sit in and clearly see all that was happening far away in the desert. This was why my mind was completely tranquil and I was waiting for the light.

But when the light spread I saw the rampart of the fort in front of me. Behind it nothing but the silent sky. Between my tower and the rampart stretched a flat roof and on it I saw the Sultan bending over a bundle of clothes. He remained bent over like that until the first rays of the sun. Then he rose and walked slowly to the rampart, which was slightly shorter than he was. He raised himself up on his toes and looked outside, then turned around toward the flat roof. Above his waist he wore battle armour, and the rays of the sun made the iron links of his mail shine like stars.

"On all sides, only the desert," he said. His loud heavy voice sounded hollow in the open air, and I could hear him only with difficulty.

"Only the desert," he said again, and I imagined he was addressing me. But then I saw the bundle of clothes move, and a woman standing there. Her face was hidden by her hair. I could not see what she looked like, but when she walked toward the Sultan I had the impression that she was not a woman of our town. Layers of clothing covered most of her body, but even so I could discern the gleam of jewellery on her hands and neck.

"Let me see," she said, moving closer to the Sultan. Then she put both hands on the rampart as if she wanted to pull it toward her rather than glance over it.

The Sultan watched her efforts for a while. Then he grabbed the woman's shoulders and hoisted her up. The sound of the woman's screams crashed against my tower and appeared to resound from far away in the desert. The Sultan set her down on the ground. The woman's hair had become entangled with the links of his mail, and she was in pain. The Sultan slowly, and with some difficulty, disentangled her hair, and then grabbed her shoulders once again.

"Look," he said, trying to raise the woman higher, but she thrashed about and twisted out of his grip.

"I don't want to see," she said, spitting hatred, and went to sit in the opposite corner of the roof. After a while the Sultan came and sat next to her, and stayed there for some time.

Watching this alien scene, I quite forgot I was sitting in the tower to chronicle the campaign. I watched them quietly for a long time, until the sunlight turned fierce and the Sultan's face grew red.

"The sun is getting strong again," he said to the woman. Then he gestured toward the tower and said in imperious tones, "Let's go over there, underneath the roof."

"No, not under the roof," she replied flatly, "I will die there."

It seemed to me as if the Sultan had heard this response many times, for he got up, went to the rampart, glanced over it, and then came back to the woman.

"I have to go back," he said, "and you have to come with me."

"Not to the town," the woman said in the same flat tone. "There will be roofs there."

The sun grew fiercer, and its heat mingled with the strong wind blowing through the tower. The Sultan glanced over the rampart once again, then came over to the other side of the tower and called out to someone.

"What is happening now?" he asked. "It's hard to see outside from here."

An imperial officer's voice could be heard echoing slightly in reply. I could not understand what he was saying, although the voice served to remind me that I was the chronicler of events for the Sultan's desert campaign.

"Let them make a circle," the Sultan said.

The officer said something else. The Sultan spoke: "No, she will go with us."

In response to another question from the officer, he said, "A memento." Turning to look at the woman, he added, "And proof as well."

After this, his attention shifted almost completely away from the woman and he spent his time in conversation with the officer. Sometimes I could hear the officer, but mostly not at all. At times I could understand him, and at times he was incomprehensible. But, from this exchange, I gleaned details of the desert campaign that made me feel I could chronicle them as if they were scenes I had witnessed with my own eyes.

I had already begun to arrange these scenes in my head when I heard the rustle of wings and saw shadows – that appeared to have long lines attached to them – passing over the roof. The shadows loomed over the ramparts, and then I saw that they were small flocks of desert birds, and that each bird in each flock was pierced by an arrow. The Sultan looked at them in astonishment. I was amazed too, because the birds were floating calmly through the air, their large wings spread out. The Sultan said, apparently to himself, "It seems as if they are flying with the force of the arrows."

But after flying over the ramparts the birds thrashed about in the air in torment, before plummeting to the ground. An occasional bird rolled about so fast that the arrow piercing its body described a circle in the sky. I had seen this happen in the Sultan's hunting lodges many times.

Many more flocks of birds flew over the roof. The Sultan, leaning against the rampart, was inspecting them attentively, as if he were counting them. Suddenly he pulled a dagger from his waist and moved forward.

"One of them is coming down very low," he told his officer from there, "and it has not been hit by an arrow."

Then I saw the woman spring at the Sultan. The Sultan pulled her roughly from behind him and arched himself backwards, his dagger poised in the air. The beating of wings was heard, and a desert bird swooped low over the Sultan and the woman. I was convinced that it would crash against the rampart and fall down there, but the bird flapped its wings and rose higher. When it had crossed the wall it spread out its wings completely and soared high into the air, rapidly vanishing from sight. All this happened at once, and at the same moment I heard the woman scream. The Sultan's dagger was trapped in her long hair, and she was in pain once more. The Sultan wrenched his dagger loose from her hair, jerking it about again and again. Tufts of hair were cut loose from her head and fell to the ground, and, perhaps because of the fierce heat in the stone, lay writhing there for a while.

The Sultan was scouring the air for the bird, his dagger poised in his hand, when from far beyond the ramparts a cloud of sand rose up and could be seen moving slowly toward the fort. This time I heard the officer's voice clearly.

"Something is about to happen," he said. "It's not safe to stay out in the open now."

"I shall stay here for now," replied the Sultan. "Let them make the circle."

"At least she should be sent inside."

"She too will stay here."

"They may want to kill her."

"They won't want to," the Sultan said with great confidence.

The officer began to respond, but his voice was lost in the noise of the wind. Hot gusts of wind were making it difficult for me to sit in my place. I had pressed down the bundle of imperial papers with both hands and was seated on the floor as if I myself were a weight made of stone. I was practised at doing this, but this was my first encounter with a sandstorm.

Gritty particles of sand were in my hair and slid down my neck, all the way to my back. The sunlight grew dimmer in places, and the cloud of sand which had risen up at a distance was now at the ramparts of the fort. The cloud was being blown about by the wind as well. It would fall, rise, dip about here and there, and then revolve in one place like an immense whirlwind. Then some arrows were shot from behind it and landed at the Sultan's feet.

With the same calm that appeared on his face when in the midst of fierce battle, the Sultan bent and, picking up one of the arrows, examined its point carefully for some time. He glanced casually at the other arrows lying there, threw the arrow in his hand in the direction of the officer's voice, and said, "What is the blood on this?"

In a little while the officer responded, "This is our arrow, and perhaps the blood ..."

But suddenly many other human voices joined his and at that very moment I saw what appeared to be a flock of desert birds on the fort's ramparts. The sound of arrows had come from the spot where the officer's voice had been. Tufts of feathers rose over the wall and then were overturned. I caught glimpses of human faces beneath them. Then the Sultan's voice rose higher:

"Of which feathers are their crests made?"

He received no response, and his voice rose again: "Whose feathers are these?"

But only the twang of bows and the whistling of arrows were heard. The crests of feathers beyond the ramparts began to rise and fall with greater rapidity.

"What's the situation now?" the Sultan called out loudly, but perhaps he was used to not getting an answer on such occasions. He advanced slowly toward the woman as she lay on the roof. Then, looking at her intently for a while, bent over and grabbed her. She seemed to dangle in his grasp.

"All this for your sake," he said in a growling whisper, "for your sake."

I heard his whisper despite the noise of the wind, and then for the first time my eyes fell on the woman's upturned, open face. Perhaps because her eyes were closed, she seemed dead to me. The Sultan dragged her to the spot from where the voice of the officer had come.

"Pull her under the roof," he said loudly.

The woman's body trembled slightly and she opened her eyes. For a while she stared disconnectedly at the Sultan's face. The suddenly rising blood-thirst in his eyes did not have any effect on her. Slowly but firmly she extricated herself from the Sultan's grip and walked with light steps in the direction of the officer's voice. But the Sultan moved deftly and catching her with the same firmness loudly said, "Ropes!"

He had barely spoken when two or three rope-ends fell at his feet. He tied the woman tightly by her shoulders and waist. I heard the soft sound of jewellery and saw the ropes grow taut, but then I looked at the ramparts.

A cloud of sand was poised on top of the rampart, the noise of arrows was louder than the noise of the wind, and the rising and falling bunches of feathers behind the cloud could not be seen clearly. I looked at the roof again. The Sultan was standing there alone. One hand cupping the opposite shoulder, he seemed to be waiting for some news.

For a moment I imagined I was in a dream, but at that instant a gust of wind hit my face and hot sand filled my open eyes. I bowed my head and let the water stream from my eyes until all the particles of sand flowed out with it and I could see again. Finally the wind abated, and the cloud of sand disappeared. There was nothing beyond the ramparts except the silent sky. The Sultan stood quietly, as he had before. At last the voice of the officer was heard, along with many other voices, congratulating the Sultan on the victorious end of the campaign. The Sultan raised a hand and acknowledged the congratulations, then turned and walked to the rampart, where he stood looking out for a while.

"Only the desert!" he finally said.

Once again I suspected he was addressing me. Since I could see no one else on the roof my suspicion turned to belief. But he was not looking at me.

"Everyone awaits your orders," said the voice of the officer.

"Return," the Sultan replied. Then he paused and said, "And tell her she is to come with us."

"She ..." said the officer's terrified voice " ... is dead."

The Sultan steadied himself against the wall of the fort. "How?" he asked.

"She was crushed."

"Did a roof fall?" the Sultan asked, coming forward.

"All the roofs are in place," came the voice, " but she has been crushed and killed. It seems that way from her face. Her face ..."

"Return," ordered the Sultan, interrupting him. "The fort must be completely emptied by nightfall."

"And her?"

The Sultan looked in the direction of the voice, and then up at the tower. Finally, turning his head toward the ramparts he said in a voice of great clarity, "Let her be thrown into the desert. In a few days she will be sand again."

I saw the rays of the rising sun run on the waves of sand. The tomb lay in front of me. My body was stiff from sitting on the stone platform in the cold of the night. I waited for the sun to get stronger, and when my body grew a little warmer, I went to the tomb once again to examine it. I entered its doorway, carefully noting the way to return through the labyrinth, and reached the last of the walls built in the shape of a semicircle. Looking at one of the walls I suspected that the stones used to build it were from the floor of the tower in which I had been made to sit to chronicle the desert campaign – and had written nothing. I had written the account of the desert campaign sitting in the garden in front of my house. At a time when there had been no tree casting its shade for me. And though most of my account was hearsay I had described it as though I had been an eyewitness. But there were also in it the things I had seen sitting in the tower. Because of which one imperial historian – my only enemy – had to die.

And now I had to chronicle the construction of a tomb I hadn't seen built. The custodian had briefed me on the details of the construction process, but I was seeing it completed with my own eyes. I remembered the new imperial historian and his youthfulness, and slowly walked back through the tomb leaving by the doorway. From the platform the tomb's serrated roof, which did not exist, looked beautiful. I stepped down on to the road on the other side of the platform. On my way back I met groups of people who were coming from great distances, to see the tomb. Above me flocks of desert birds flew toward the lakes of the town. I walked on through the bazaar without looking around and entered my house. The Sultan's official was waiting. He thrust a bundle of imperial paper bearing the Sultan's seal, into my hands. Together we counted the paper and then the official left.

I have written all this from beginning to end on numbered and counted paper stamped with the Sultan's seal, which will be tallied when it is taken back from me. The personal use of imperial paper by a chronicler is a new crime, for which a new punishment will have to be devised. The Sultan has a refined talent for inventing punishments, and I have chronicled these in the past. But now I have been commanded to write a chronicle of the construction of the Sultan's tomb. I think I have fulfilled his orders, even though in my days of staying at home I have forgotten many of the rules of chronicling events. I cannot even say how long I have spent at home, but the fruit of all that time is this umbrella-shaped tree under which I have often rested.

From its roots to its flower, from the skin of its fruit to the marrow of its kernel, it is poison. Perhaps that is why one grows sleepy in its shade.

This story was first published as "Sultan Muzaffar ka Vaqi'a-Navis" in the volume of short stories *Itr-e Kafur*, Lucknow, Nizami Press, 1990.

lamentation

I have spent my life in fruitless diversions. And these days I spend most of my time wondering what, if anything, I have gained from them. This is my latest, perhaps final and most fruitless, diversion.

For years I knocked about the country, perhaps out of a desire to learn more about our cities, large and small. The upshot was that all cities, save my own, began to look alike to me, and after my last trip I stayed holed up in my house for several months. Then restlessness got the better of me and I set out again. This time I headed for the rural settlements. But I soon realized that they weren't much different from the cities, not to me at any rate. I returned home and was for a long while haunted by the suspicion that I had lost my ability to distinguish between things. I let this doubt grow inside me, but I made every effort not to let it show in my actions or words. When, however, I noticed that the people with whom I was in almost daily contact had begun giving me strange looks, I set out on another journey.

On this journey I roamed the desolate areas of my ancient land. The weather there was harsh and the earth barren. There were no rivers anywhere near these areas, so they were practically uninhabitable for anyone used to more amenities. Still they weren't completely

translated by

muhammad umar memon

unpopulated. I also passed through areas which perhaps had never been home to anyone. These were merely immense stretches of uninhabited geography which, in a vague sort of way, resembled the seas and, though unpopulated, somehow didn't look so desolate. Rather, it was the areas where humans had dwelled from ancient times that looked truly desolate. Across these immense geographical tracts they surged abruptly into view, like islands, and looked desolate precisely because of their human habitation. Just as these humans affected their habitats, so too did habitats affect humans. So much so that even in bustling cities one could easily identify wastelanders. At least I could, for I had spent the greater part of my travels roaming among similar people.

These were small communities, each distinct from the other, or so they appeared to me. During this journey my main occupation was observing these communities and spending a few days with each of them. I was especially keen on this undertaking as these scattered colonies were slowly dying out. A sudden epidemic or a major shift in the weather pattern could easily wipe them out, and often did. It even so happened that, on a second trip to an area occupied by a community, I found it deserted and practically swallowed by the surrounding uninhabited geography. This was because the traces of habitation left by these communities tended to disappear rather quickly – or perhaps were never there in the first place.

I couldn't gather much information about these people, for though they could understand my language a little, I could not understand their variety of tongues. Our communication was mostly through gestures. But this didn't help me much either. Different communities expressed themselves through different gestures, and sometimes the same gesture meant quite the opposite in a different community. Where one community used a particular hand gesture to express happiness, the other used the same to express sorrow. Where a nod of the head indicated Yes for one, the other used it to indicate No. Thus, much time was required to understand their gestures accurately, and I never stayed long enough in any given community. So what little I was able to uncover about them simply could not be trusted, and by the time I returned I had already expelled from my mind whatever confused information I had gathered about them.

The only thing that clung to my memory was the congregational lament of these communities, which although different in each place, was nonetheless easily recognizable.

I am not sure whether it was merely a coincidence or whether these people were actually prone to a higher death rate, but the fact remains that within a few days of my arrival in a community, a death invariably occurred. This would be announced by the wailing and weeping of the deceased's nearest or next-nearest relatives. The other members of the community approached the bereaved softly, calmed them down, and left – just as softly. Still others occupied themselves with the funeral arrangements. These out of the way, the members gathered at a fixed time and place – in some communities after the disposing of the body and in others before – to perform a congregational lament. The lamentation of most communities began with an accusatory complaint against death and then moved on to a reminiscence of the departed, which gained steadily in intensity and tempo. At the lament's highest point, everyone would be overcome with emotion and their body movements, their voices, and, most of all, their eyes, all came to reflect anger rather than grief. At times it was as if they had all taken some potent intoxicants. In certain places I, too, was obliged to participate in the rites. At such times, I would clumsily mime their actions without feeling the least bit of emotion. Then the lament would end, with everyone trying to comfort and console each other. I, too, would be offered solace.

In some places the women outnumbered the men in the lament, in others the men outnumbered the women; but in one community their numbers were equal. This was the only community whose women I was able to observe, even touch, but only during this ritual. Short-statured and tawny, these women seemed to have been liberally endowed in those parts of the body that made them women. They looked like the originals of those ancient statues and mural paintings which, it is sometimes assumed, were fashioned by people who had never laid eyes on a real woman, or at least not from up close, and who certainly had never touched one. The lamentation in practice among this community went something like this: the men sat on their haunches in a row on the bare earth, with the women sitting likewise in a row facing them. Each man-woman pair would touch first elbows, then wrists, then slap each other's palms, then interlock their fingers, and then say whatever was needed to be said; they would then separate and once again link their elbows and repeat their words. Their lament would rise repeatedly in a crescendo, then begin to fall, then rise up again, like the ebb and flow of the sea, until everyone's eyes were rolling back in their heads. They all finished the lament in faint, quavering voices and, dripping with sweat, pulled away.

Three deaths occurred during my stay in this particular community. I had participated in the lament for the first two. The third time, death claimed my own host, a decrepit old man. I had tried to treat him with the medicines I had with me, but he couldn't be saved. It wasn't just his face, even some of his mannerisms reminded me of my father, and I had tried to communicate this to him, partly through speech and partly through gestures.

I have no idea what he had told the community about me, but a couple of the group who came to comfort and calm the bereaved made their way toward me as well, and even though I was silent, "calmed" me down. Their visit brought back the memory of the day my own father had died. The house had resounded with the crazed wails of the womenfolk, while I had been left to sit quietly by myself.

My host's death brought back the image of my father's face as he lay dying; I then began to recall the face of my elderly host. After the funeral arrangements, when the men and women of the community began to line up opposite each other, I got up quietly and left for the next uninhabited area. Once there I quickly decided to end my journey, and that very day I set out for home.

These days, as I mentioned, I spend most of my time wondering what I have gained from these diversions. Thus my life, the greater part of which has been spent lurching from one stimulus to the next, has for some time now been quite drab and monotonous. One day, though, a bit of stimulation did interrupt the monotony. The occurrence could be seen as something gained from one of my diversions, but turned out to be worse, I believe, than no gain at all.

That day, early in the morning, there was a knock on the door of my house that opens on to the bazaar. I got up lazily and opened it. The local crazy boy – a denizen of the neighbourhood – was standing in front of me with a crumpled scrap of paper in his hand. As soon as he saw me he stuffed it into my hand and took off, laughing. It was his custom to pick up any fallen item in the bazaar and then give it to the others as a gift. He called it "prize-giving." The market folk begged him to give them such "prizes."

Well, I've got a prize today without even asking! – I thought to myself as I closed the door, and got on with the day's routine. I also wondered, as I did from time to time, why people considered this boy crazy. There was nothing really unusual about him except that he always looked cheerful and laughed at everything; still everybody thought him crazy, so I did too.

Shortly afterwards there was another knock. I opened the door once again, and there stood the same boy. "They're calling you," he said, trying not to laugh.

"Who?" I asked.

"The ones who've come."

"Who have come?"

"The piece-of-paper-people," he said, then laughed loudly and sprinted off.

I closed the door and picked up the scrap I had earlier dropped on the bed. The paper itself was old; it bore my name and address in my own hand, and appeared to date back to the time I wrote very deliberately, forming each letter with flourish and elegance. Those days came to mind, and with them the time I had spent wandering among the wasteland communities. All the same, I couldn't recall exactly where or when I had written this scrap, though I did remember I had in those days liberally distributed similar slips among the various communities I had visited. This was the only thing I had done to repay their hospitality. I would emphasize, in our jumbled-up sign language, that if ever one of them needed something done in the city, he could come straight to me, bearing one of my handwritten scraps. I was sure I would never see any of those countless slips of paper again. Now, though, ages later, one had found its way back to me. I had been apprised that some people, aided by this scrap, had come calling on me, even though the news was brought by one who was considered crazy by everyone, myself included. In the span of a few seconds all the communities I had visited whirled through my mind like dream images and then vanished. I stepped out of the house into the bazaar.

It was time for the shops to open, but most of them were still closed. The shopkeepers, however, were present, standing in a group and whispering furtively. Seeing me, they strode over.

"Who brought this?" I showed them the piece of paper.

Wordlessly they pointed to the nameless dirt track which sloped down toward the north, its mouth nearly blocked off by the bazaar's overflowing garbage dump. I looked to where they pointed. At first glance it appeared as though the area beyond the dump was dotted all over with small heaps of garbage, but a second glance revealed them to be a group of people who sat crouching on the ground.

"Who are they?" a shopkeeper asked me.

"Looks like some community," I replied. I was about to walk over to them when another shopkeeper asked, "Did you invite them?"

"No," I said.

"But it's you they want to see."

"Even so, I haven't sent for them."

"All right, fine. At least get them to move their cart. It's blocking the way."

It was only then that I noticed the cart that stood in the paved street. It looked like a barrel cut lengthwise, to resemble a small round-bottomed boat, minus the tapering ends. Or maybe it was, in fact, a discarded boat on which they had stuck a couple of wheels – huge discs cut from the round trunk of some old tree – making it usable on dry land. On closer inspection, I discovered that what I'd imagined to be a barrel was actually a hollowed-out tree trunk. It had a big shapeless stone below it secured by a thick, coarse, tree-bark rope, dangling so low it practically scraped the ground. Most likely it had been attached to stabilize the cart; all the same, two men held the cart from both sides. Suppose they let go – I wondered absent-mindedly – which way would the cart tip, forward or back? Then I looked even closer.

The inside of the cart was completely filled with rags. A woman bent over it, continually rearranging them. Even though she was wrapped from head to toe in a chadar, she looked young. I had barely glanced at her and the two men holding the cart when I heard another shopkeeper ask, "Which community is it?"

I turned to look at the people squatting on the ground beyond the garbage dump. There were ten or twelve men in all, and so grimy that one couldn't tell the colour of their clothes. Seeing them brought no memories to my mind. Still I had no difficulty recognizing them as one of the wasteland communities. I stared at them for a long time. They were all looking at me indifferently, and with every passing instant I was more and more convinced that I had never stayed among them. I couldn't understand how they had chanced upon my name and address.

Once again I examined the scrap of paper. Just then they noticed the scrap in my hand, and a sudden surge of excitement swept through them. They exchanged a few words among themselves and quickly rose to their feet setting free a cloud of dust. Soon I was surrounded by them, as well as by the queries of the bazaar-wallahs, who had begun repeating their last question: "Which community is this?"

I told them that I didn't know these people, but they kept on questioning me as though they thought I was accountable for them. Their questions, however, were such that I could not possibly answer: Aren't they untouchables? There's been a rash of thefts in the city, do you think they are behind it? Where have they come from? Could they be beggars?

Now I asked: "Have they asked anyone for anything?"

"Well, not so far," I was informed. "When we arrived, they were showing everyone the slip of paper and asking about you."

"In what language?"

"Through gestures."

"So?" I asked, "Did any of the gestures look like they were begging?"

"But just *look* at them ..."

"I *am.*"

"And the cart ...," said the shopkeeper with the loudest voice.

"I'm looking at that, too."

"... And who is this they're hauling around in the cart? Suppose he dies this instant – wouldn't they beg us for help? They're all tricks to swindle something out of us."

At that point I peered at the figure in the cart. What, until then, had looked like a lump in the pile of rags, turned out to be a person's constantly drooping head, which the woman was trying every now and then to prop up but which always fell back. I strode over to them. While watching the woman trying to steady his head with both her hands, I heard the voices of the wastelanders, all at once, and turned around.

They were touching my knees over and over again, saying something. Their speech sounded like a corrupted form of my own language – or its primitive form before corruption had set in – which was unfathomable to me. They would touch my knees and then point at the cart, their tone sounding increasingly like a plea. This made me wonder too whether they might perhaps be a pack of beggars after all. A few words to them and I was convinced that they didn't understand my tongue either. Given my perfectly flat intonation, they couldn't even guess what I might be saying. Their own speech was varied in tone, but nonetheless I could easily sense that they were hugely afraid of something, that they had endured all manner of hardship to get here, that they were looking for some kind of assistance from me, and that all of this had something to do with the occupant of the cart.

All the while the woman kept arranging the rags around the occupant and supporting his drooping head. I edged closer to him. He was buried chest-deep in the pile of rags, his head too swathed in them. The woman moved to one side and, raising his head with both her hands, turned it toward me.

I saw the inflamed face of a child before me. His eyelids were incredibly swollen. One of them was open just a crack, and he was looking at me through the slit. The other was completely shut, but it had been smeared with lime, or some other white substance, and had a large iris painted in the centre with lampblack. This gave the illusion of an eye frozen in a stare of astonishment. I looked away from it and bent down to peer into the slit of the other eye. Hidden behind the matted lashes it radiated torment, entreaty, and disgust. I attempted to look more closely at his face, setting a series of tremors vibrating through the rags. The occupant jerked his face away. His lips drew back, exposing his teeth. To the shopkeepers standing at a distance he may have appeared to be grinning, but to me he looked like a sick dog whom the mean boys were coming to get. Rising behind me I heard the buzz of the bazaar-wallahs and the shrill voices of the community folk, which led me to suspect that the parties had perhaps begun sparring with each other. I whirled around to look. Both the parties were telling me something, but I couldn't understand a word. Just then the woman grabbed my hand and I turned toward her. She stuck her free hand into the pile of rags and rummaged through it, eventually pulling out one of the occupant's hands all the way up to the elbow. I had three hands before me: my own familiar hand, its fingers interlocked with the soft, white fingers of the woman, slowly turning moist, and between our two palms the hand of the occupant – small, withered, with motley strings of colour connecting the wrist and elbow; dead, wrinkled skin showing through.

Her fingers throbbed in mine like a heart, and my body quivered lightly. The occupant made a sound, much like the sick dog I had imagined.

One of the shopkeepers placed his hand on my shoulder and I turned toward him. "Tell them to move the cart," he was saying. "They're ruining our business. First thing in the morning these people ..."

I turned toward the wastelanders. They were staring at me mutely. I gestured to them to proceed westward on the straight road, and they understood right away. The men who held the cart on both sides turned it easily toward the west. The woman withdrew her hand from mine, put the occupant's hand back into the pile, and supported his head as the rickety cart lumbered noisily forward. The clan followed, holding their drab, dingy bundles and long clubs, while the shopkeepers and people from the neighbourhood – among them a few women and children – stood quietly arrayed on either side of the road. Hurrying ahead of the cart and leaving the line of shops behind, I came to the southern bend in the paved road and stopped. I turned around and motioned for them to halt at the bend. They followed slowly, dust hovering around them like smoke. And then I saw it all at once. Everyone and everything in its entirety seemed fragile and decayed and on the road to imminent disintegration. And yet, I thought, had it all not been so grimy, had the chipped stone suspended from the cart boasted the slightest finesse, the whole parade might have been taken for a royal procession.

They came up to me and halted. Behind them, some distance away, I saw the shopkeepers return to their stores and the line of onlookers start to break up. Now I turned my attention to the clansfolk. They too had perhaps surmised that I was now ready to listen to them in peace. They started to speak calmly. I could make out that they were trying to get across some details about the occupant of the cart, but I was able to comprehend only one thing: the person was the last one. During my forays into these small communities the meaning of the word "last" had been so frequently expressed to me in so many different tongues and through so many different gestures that I understood it immediately. Almost everyone of this community, after recounting the condition of the occupant to me, touched my feet and solicitously informed me that he was the last one.

Absurdly, I felt responsible for them, and even more so for the occupant of the cart. I motioned for them to rest easy. They grew silent and fixed their eyes on me; they gestured to one another to relax and in fact did so. I gestured to them to stay put and wait for me. Then, walking quickly, as if I'd be right back, I returned to my house.

The crazy boy was standing at the door. He looked scared.

"Who are they?" he asked in a choked voice.

"They're the paper-people," I replied. "You didn't give them a prize?"

"Prize?" he asked, puzzled.

I patted him on the shoulder and said, "Run along, find a prize for them quickly. Then we will go and visit them."

"No," he said, appearing more frightened than before.

"All right, go and play," I said. "I've got work to do."

"Who is that old man?"

"Old man?"

"The one hiding in the cart."

"He's not an old man," I said.

I was jolted once again. Why had I supposed the occupant of the cart was a child? He might just as well have been an old man. I recalled his appearance. His face was swollen and there were wrinkles on his hands. I strained to remember how his hands had looked, but what came to mind was the slowly moistening white hand of the woman, throbbing like a heart, its fingers locked in mine. I shook myself and tried to recall the words and gestures of the wastelanders. All I had been able to fathom was that he was the last one. The community's last child ... or last old man? The last emblem of some person or event? The last testimonial of some thing or some age? I felt increasingly confused. Perhaps I allowed myself to indulge in my confusion far too long, for when I did decide to go back and look again, the crazy boy was already gone and the afternoon was almost over.

Leaving the garbage dump and the series of shops behind me as I moved ahead, I finally saw them. They were walking toward me, with the cart ahead of them. The occupant's head was resting on the side of the cart, the rags wrapped around it having come undone in several places. The woman was repeatedly trying to climb aboard the cart, but each time one of the clansfolk grabbed her and pulled her back. I heard their voices above the clatter of the cart. They were singing something. Each person chanted something in turn, then the others took up the last few words and repeated them in unison. They had lined themselves in a row and their voices were gaining in momentum. One of the men stepped slightly out of the row and intoned something. The others chanted it back. Then he stepped back and another stepped forward. His voice and the following chorus were louder than before. And now their hands and their bodies had begun to sway, almost as if in a dance. Every now and then one of the men would step forward and intone some words; the others would join in and then shake their heads as if in applause. At least I took it to be a gesture of applause. Actually I'm not quite certain what the gesture meant in that community.

Perhaps they didn't see me, even though I was well within their field of vision. As they moved forward, I found myself moving slowly backward, my ears tuned to their voices, my eyes fixed on the movement of their bodies. They were recounting some ancient tale, whose hazy scenes formed and dissolved before me like images in a dream. I saw a newborn child held tenderly in someone's arms. The child is learning to walk, he wobbles along, tumbles down, cries. He's picked up and pacified. He's running about, climbing trees, and falls asleep, exhausted. He wakes up, rubs his eyes with his palms; his eyes have turned red.

I saw many pairs of red eyes advancing toward me. They were all screaming "Last, last!" in unison, in a single voice, with a single gesture, and their throats seemed ready to burst. A terrible agitation had seized them and they all seemed crazed with anger. Then a kind of drunkenness came over them. A gentle cloud of dust rose from their clothes and feet, slowly enveloping them. Behind the dust-screen the woman once again propped up the face of the cart's occupant. The slit in his eye had closed, but the other white-and-black painted eye was fixed on me in a stare of permanent astonishment, refusing to close though utterly covered with grime. The cart bumped over a rut in the road, jolting the person's head. A trace of reproach flashed in the eye, turned to anger, then to slight inebriation, and then, once again, fixed on me in a stare of astonishment.

Approaching the series of shops the wastelanders quietened down and halted. They appeared utterly exhausted and oblivious to my presence. After a brief consultation among themselves they pointed into the distance toward my house. I turned and quickly walked back home. Just before reaching the door I turned to look. They were pointing at me and telling each other something. They began to move ahead, straight toward me. I turned and walked away, stopping again only after I had left my door some forty paces behind. I turned slowly and looked at them. They seemed like a moving pile of refuse. Then they broke into a disarray and hung their heads low.

For a long time I felt I had seen a spectacle I was not likely to see ever again. I experienced a faint remorse that I was not included in it.

All the same I also felt considerably safer, for they were now descending the nameless dirt track to the north that sloped out of the city toward the wastelands.

This story was first published as "Nudba" in the journal *Quarterly Aaj*, Karachi.

the woman in black

My dreame thou brok'st not, but continued'st it
Thou art so true, that thoughts of thee suffice,
To make dreames truth; and fables histories.

–John Donne

Savar-e daulat-e javid bar guzar amad
'Inan-e u na giriftand, az guzar bi-raft
(The rider bearing the eternal treasure appeared on the path
No one bade him halt. He travelled on.)

–Anonymous (found in the papers of Fazl Allah Hurufi)

I do not remember the story of the bad woman now, but back in those days I took a keen interest in it. I remember I was overjoyed at learning that her case would be heard at our house, and that she herself would come to see it settled. Prior to this, the case of another notoriously bad woman had also been heard at our house, and my elders had brought it to a neat conclusion. But that had happened when I was still in my nonage. I had only heard others speak of her, and they continued

translated by
muhammad umar memon

discussing her case amongst themselves until the case of this second bad woman came along and absorbed their attention.

On the day she was due to arrive, the outer room of our house was given a thorough clean-up and then furnished with additional seats. Several curios, some of them centuries old, were added to enhance the room's decor. The elders also called on me to help tidy up the place, and I did what was required of me with considerable enthusiasm. As I was moving a chair, I gathered from the conversation of my elders that this was the chair the bad woman would sit on. My heart began to pound. I could almost see her sitting right there. In fact, what aroused my interest in the matter was the opportunity it offered of looking squarely at a bad woman.

The elders alone were not going to try her; a number of outsiders were also expected to take part in the proceedings. These were honourable men who had been our guests in the past as well. All the sumptuous reception arrangements were, as a matter of fact, intended for them. My instructions, trickling down from the elders now and then, focused chiefly on ensuring that the honourable guests were properly looked after. But that wasn't where my interest lay.

As the time for everybody to arrive drew near, a flurry of nervous activity swept over the elders. This obliged me to scurry back and forth several times from the side door of the house to the far outer room which formed a part of the house's facade. In the space between the side door and the outer room was a courtyard, the better part of which was overshadowed by a sprawling ancient tree that bore unusually tiny leaves. As the barrage of commands showed no sign of letting up, I too was infected by the same nervous tension and grew breathless from my repeated rushed trips to the outer room. And yet I never failed, each time I passed under the tree, to raise my hand and give its branches a shake. It was an urge I could never resist, even now when I was beside myself with excitement. I would then lift my eyes to look at the portico with the run-down roof which stood in a corner of the courtyard. The old surgeon lived in that portico. Every time I laid my hand on the branches he would call out:

"Why do you meddle with that tree for no reason at all?"

But today he did not utter those words even once. He just sat there amid God-knows-what kind of medicines and ointments. He was so preoccupied with the paraphernalia before him that he forgot to defend the tree against my assaults. That day I saw him, for the first time ever, with the full array of his armamentarium; the fact is he had given up practising surgery when I was still very young. He was an accomplished surgeon in his time, but I had only heard about his expertise. To me he was merely an old man who pestered us with question after annoying question about everything and anything that transpired in the house. Old age had enhanced his nosiness. But most of his inquiries brought him no satisfaction: the elders rebuffed him and I, for my part, gave him only incomplete and wrong answers which confused and befuddled him even more. As soon as the case of the bad woman surfaced, the old man was stung with curiosity. Every day he dragged himself out of the portico several times, only to walk back in, mumbling angrily. Today, however, when he should have been more excited than ever before, he was quietly engrossed in his work, as if nothing else mattered.

I would certainly have teased him a bit for this. But by now I was feeling worked up – mainly because it was well past the time the invitees should have arrived. The elders began to feel increasingly jittery; once more I found myself scrambling out the side door on my way to the outer room, giving the branches of the tree a tug as I made my way along. The tree, as always, showered me with tiny yellow leaves. Brushing them off my hair and shoulders I reached the outer room ... and saw there was nobody there.

I remained in the outer room for quite some time. Eventually the hushed stillness of the extravagantly decorated room began to bother me. Bored with the delay of the guests, I felt I no longer wanted to think about the bad woman, or the honourable guests either. It was then that I remembered Nusrat.

Hurrying by on my errands I had seen her, indeed every single time, sitting under the tree, leaning against it, staring straight ahead at the old surgeon or looking sideways at the ground, as her fingers traced lines in the dirt. And now I even seemed to recall that the first time I passed by the tree – or was it the second? – she had turned to look at me. Perhaps she had also greeted me. But at the time I was too flustered to have returned her greeting, or even to have realized that she had actually raised her hand to me.

She had a sweet voice and she moved about nimbly. She came to our house from time to time, to look after some sick relative of hers. Often I would notice how, when called by someone, she would pick her way from one part of the house to the other with extreme caution, as if afraid of stepping on something fragile and crushing it. When she was present in the house, her name was heard quite often. But I rarely spoke to her. For one thing she talked in an exceedingly low voice, and for another, she kept her eyes lowered when she spoke. Yet she never failed to greet me.

At any rate, I started from the outer room, came to the tree, stopped and stood near it. I tugged at the branches lightly. The tree was in the grip of autumn and most of the leaves had turned pale and fallen. Here and there the branches were covered with spider webs, which caught many of the leaves as they came spiralling down. I looked at Nusrat. She sat leaning forward now, her head resting on her knees, her fingers still busily tracing lines. But then I saw her hand slacken and become motionless. Tiny yellow leaves covered her hair and shoulders. She was dressed in white. It was bright and sunny under the tree, but too warm to sit outside.

"It isn't chilly outside," I said.

She raised her head to look at me, and I asked, "Are you feeling cold, Nusrat?"

She sat up, her eyes still glued to the old surgeon.

"Are you feeling cold, Nusrat?"

"Not really," she said with a faint smile.

"Then why are you sitting here, in the sun?"

She didn't answer.

"Why don't you go in?" I said, pointing to the side door. "It's very hot here in the sun."

"Baba asked me to be here," she said, looking at the old surgeon.

"Come on then. We'll go and sit with him," I said.

And although she seemed to be willing to follow my suggestion, she made no attempt to get up. I repeated my words and waited for a while for her to rise.

"I am not able to walk," she said softly and with a slight nod of her head pointed at her feet.

Only then did I notice that her feet were badly crushed. They were blackish green and so swollen that they barely looked human. The skin had cracked in several places, and a light red showed between the cracks. The right foot had been totally twisted out of shape, and the toes of the left foot were so bloated and curled around that they were half-buried in the right sole. Almost as though they were being sucked into the right foot with tremendous force and would break off completely and vanish into it. The sheer tension of the toes as they struggled to break free had caused a mesh of protruding blue veins to erupt ominously all across her calves.

"What happened, Nusrat?" I asked her again and again.

"Everybody says both feet will just have to be amputated," she said. "But Baba wants me to let him ..." Here her voice grew so faint I could not hear the words that followed. I looked at the old surgeon. He was busy picking up various iron instruments one by one, drawing them close to his eyes and peering at them. Something was coming to a boil in a clay pot nearby and the portico was filled with smoke.

"Baba said I'm not to let anyone know," I heard Nusrat say. "He said he would do it today, because everyone would be busy elsewhere."

"But, Nusrat, how did this happen?"

Thereupon she told me the whole story. I've forgotten some of the details by now, some others I couldn't catch as her voice dropped to a whisper every now and then. Perhaps she was in too much pain. She mentioned some men who had been in a vehicle and wanted to get to a certain destination in a hurry. Perhaps there had been an accident. But something was blocking the vehicle and had to be removed. Nusrat had promptly pushed whatever it was aside. But before she could get out of the way the vehicle had lurched forward and crushed both her feet. It rolled on without bothering to stop and Nusrat had lain there unattended for a long time.

"What kind of people were they?" I exclaimed after hearing her out. "Didn't they even notice they'd run over you?"

"As a matter of fact, they did," she said. "That's why only the front wheel passed over my feet. They quickly swerved the vehicle to one side, manoeuvring the rear wheel away from my feet."

"But they didn't stop?"

"They were in a hurry."

"You didn't stop them either?"

"They were in a hurry. Still I managed to say ...," her voice grew faint.

"What did you say, Nusrat?"

"But maybe they could not hear me."

"What did you say, Nusrat?"

"I said, You see how helpless I am."

I couldn't help laughing at this.

"What a pointless thing to say!" I said. "What good could it possibly do? It wouldn't have made a bit of difference even if they had heard it."

"But what else could I have said?"

I had no answer to that. All the same I said, "Men like them are not likely to be affected by such a remark. You see how helpless I am," I said, mimicking the way she'd said it. "Didn't you realize the sort of people they were?"

"That's what people are like," she said, and once again put her face back on her knees.

Sensing she was not going to cry, I continued. "So what happened then? How did you get out of there?"

Just as she started to tell me about it I heard a few sharp sounds. I turned around and looked at the surgeon. He was getting up, clutching his waist with his hands. Obviously, he wasn't making the noise. I looked back at Nusrat. Her lips were moving but the racket drowned out her soft voice. Finally I did manage to guess where the sounds were coming from. I moved a few steps back to get a better view. I saw vehicles pulling up in front of the outer room. The bad woman had arrived.

I sprinted off.

Most of the seats in the outer room had been taken. Nearly all the honourable guests had also arrived. Their faces looked unusually serious, almost grim. My elders, being the hosts as well, were in something of a fix as to whether to look hospitable or grim. A number of women were also present. The bad woman was there too, as part of the audience. Contrary to my expectations, she didn't look significantly different from the others. She had draped herself in several layers, one on top of the other, and the only thing her face betrayed was exhaustion. Although she was practically buried under her clothing, a part of her belly, with prominent blue veins, could be seen clearly. Her lips parted a little as she breathed. Her front teeth were fully exposed and remained visible as she continued breathing fast. I was disappointed. A girl sat right next to her, and every now and then the bad woman leaned toward her to say something. Following one of her remarks, the girl began to look around and her eyes fell on me. She got up and walked over to me. Then she said, "Would it be possible to get a drink of water?"

I hurried off at once. As I passed by the tree on my way to the side door I saw the old surgeon sitting in front of Nusrat and examining her feet very closely. Hearing my footsteps he raised his head and squinted at me in an effort to make out who I might be. Had I tugged at the branches, he would have recognized me at once. As I hastened back to the outer room after fetching the glass of water from the house, I saw the old man still studying Nusrat's feet.

The bad woman drained the glass in a single draught and handed it back to the girl, who then returned it to me. I had to bring her water three times over. There was time for all this only because some of the honourable guests still hadn't turned up. Every so often a sudden silence would descend on the room, prompting one or the other of the elders to dispel it by clearing his throat and uttering some stiff pleasantries to the guests seated near him.

The fourth time I brought the water it was the girl who took the glass from my hand and began to drink from it in small, unhurried sips. Two of her teeth, refracted and distorted by the glass and the water, appeared enormous. When she handed the glass back to me I casually put it down on the floor near the door, and the girl returned to the bad woman.

By now the atmosphere in the room had become so intolerably thick that I thought I might as well withdraw for a little while.

As I was passing by the tree I heard the voice of the old surgeon.

"Come here," he called to me. I turned to walk over to him.

"Come closer." I drew nearer. He put his hand on my shoulder, pulling me down toward him.

"Her feet are stuck together," he whispered. "The first thing is to separate them. That is usually extremely painful. She may writhe and thrash about. Perhaps I won't be able to hold her still myself. I may no longer have the strength."

I looked at Nusrat. There was panic in her eyes; still, she was trying to smile.

"Maybe if you talked to her and somehow kept her occupied ...," the old man whispered again. "Said things that would take her mind off me, completely off me. For if she suddenly jerked her feet, things would go badly for her. I mean her left toes would snap off. Don't let that happen. When I gesture to you, keep her mind off what I'm doing. Make sure she remains absolutely still, and I mean absolutely still."

Next he said something funny but couldn't make her laugh, so I began telling her some anecdotes from the old man's life. I spoke of his achievements in the field of surgery about which I'd heard; in the meantime the old man went on examining her feet from various angles and arranging them on the ground in different ways.

I talked for a long time. I told her interesting titbits about our family. Then I began to talk about her. But it could not have amounted to much, or been very coherent. What did I really know about her? All the same, I tried not to let her sense that thought. I now had the distinct impression that she was no longer thinking about the old surgeon. All this while I kept glancing at him intermittently. I saw him indicate that I should be ready.

"And do you know, Nusrat, what came to my mind the very first time I saw you?" I couldn't even remember when that had been. Nonetheless I continued: "Do you know what crossed my mind that day? It seemed to me that you were walking on flowers." I realized at once what an awful mistake this was and hastily proceeded to say, "Should I tell you something about your hands, Nusrat – something I believe nobody else could ever tell you?"

Right then I saw the old man make that unmistakable sign. I quickly took hold of both her hands and pressed them hard.

"Should I tell you?" I whispered. Almost at once I heard harsh voices rise from the direction of the outer room and then melt away. Precisely at that moment her hands trembled in my grasp. I saw her face turn blue, then red, and then ashen white. She bit her lip and her eyes expressed terrible agony.

"It's all right," I heard the old man say. "It's absolutely fine. Well done! I will be able to heal her now. Just wait and see."

I turned toward the old man. He had spread his hands over Nusrat's feet, hiding them completely. I wanted to see what, exactly, he had done, but he refused sharply.

"Don't look at her feet," he said, "and don't let her look at them either."

I turned my face away and looked up at the spider webs stuck to the branches of the tree. It was absolutely quiet all around, except for the occasional soft clinking of the surgical instruments. I waited in anxious anticipation for the old man to say something. And he did, finally.

"You may go now, if you like, and attend to your own business. I can handle the rest myself."

Only then did I realize I was still holding her hands. She had put her face back down on her knees and her hands were damp with sweat. I let go of them, got up and, even though aware that I was already too late, began to walk toward the outer room.

A deathly hush had now swept over the room. The chairs were in total disarray, and some hastily scribbled scraps of paper lay near some of them. I collected the scraps. The scrawled writing marked the consultations that had taken place among the elders and the honourable guests. I put the chairs back in order. I had a hard time deciphering the writing on the scraps, but once I had mastered it I tried to ascertain the events that had taken place during my absence. I arranged and rearranged the scraps in many different ways but failed completely to make any sense of them; as soon as I changed their order the events they were supposed to represent also underwent a complete change. I wasted a considerable amount of time rearranging the scraps and was none the wiser for my effort. My interest, tremendously aroused by the sight of them, began to dampen and then vanished altogether. The room, lined with antiques, began to suffocate me. I felt I couldn't stay there any longer. As I was leaving the room I noticed that the glass lay undisturbed near the door where I had set it. I didn't bother to pick it up; instead I headed straight for the tree.

But there was only the carpet of yellow leaves beneath it. I looked at the portico of the old surgeon furtively. It was empty, though still filled with smoke.

Soon after this, my house began to empty out. My people began to expire, in quick succession, one by one. The elders died even more swiftly, as though they were a heap of rice against a surface that was being cleared off by a damp hand that lifted them off the surface. I looked upon all this thinking I must be in a dream and hoping I'd wake up from it. Occasionally, I felt frightened. Anyway, in the end I found myself all alone in a rambling mansion, trying somehow to get used to my loneliness.

I would visit each part of the house, anxious, always anxious, not to let even the smallest space remain unoccupied by me for too long. Anyone watching me in those days would surely have thought I was looking for something I had lost.

But one day it occurred to me that I had somehow completely neglected the outer room. So I went there. The main door stood open as usual and the heavy curtain across it stirred slowly. The light inside the room was dim, which made the farthest chairs appear hazy. In spite of the poor light I could still see the heavy layer of dust which had settled on the precious curios. The walls too had become coated with dust, and the portraits of my elders looked faded and dull. I touched the curios one at a time, leaving my fingerprints on them. I wiped the dust off the portraits with my hand. They became so vivid that I felt like talking to them. And when I spoke I could hear my voice resonate in the room. I talked for a long time. At last, coming to one portrait, I stopped. The kind face in the portrait peered at me apprehensively. A sense of loss overwhelmed me and I gently touched the portrait with my forehead.

"I remember everything," I said. "Everything."

The anxious eyes just kept gazing at me.

"But nothing can be done now. I had no idea until now how the same house could look so completely deserted, and yet so full of people. This very room ...," my eyes swept the room, "this very room, once upon a time ...," my eyes caught the glass on the floor near the door, "why, even the bad woman ..." Just then I heard the rustle of a dress, forcing me to turn around and look.

Someone got up from a chair in the distant gloom and walked toward me. It was a woman. Is she the bad woman? – I wondered. But then I heard her voice.

"You wouldn't have recognized me," she said softly. She had drawn nearer now. I bent down and touched her feet to see if they were completely healed.

"This is wonderful!" I said. "I am so happy, Nusrat, that your feet are better now."

A long silence ensued during which neither of us said a word. Then I said, "I hope there are no scars."

One after the other she placed her feet in the light filtering through the bottom of the heavy curtain.

"Even the scars have disappeared," she said.

Another long silence followed which I felt compelled to break. "After a few days," I began, "you won't even remember the terrible pain you had to endure. The scars would have been a reminder."

"But I shall."

"That's what everyone imagines in the beginning. Without scars, though, one can't remember – neither the pain nor the old surgeon."

That seemed to disturb her and when she spoke again she did so hesitantly, as if trying to explain a mistake of hers.

"The scars would certainly have been there, but Baba himself ... He said there should be no scars." Then after a while she added, repeating her words two or three times, "I didn't say anything to him."

"You don't have to explain anything," I said, raising my hand. "I'm not blaming you at all. But the fact is that there are no scars now."

The stiffness in my speech was all too obvious to me. It was not right of me, I conceded to myself. But I couldn't help it. The loss of so many had left me saddened.

"You must be wondering, Nusrat, why I'm talking this way," I said. "You must be thinking it isn't the way I spoke to you that day under the tree."

"That was another day," Nusrat said, looking intently at her feet. Her voice grew softer as she added, "I was in a pitiable state that day."

She lifted her head to look at me. After a brief silence she said in a voice that was softer still, "That was a day of commiseration."

"And today?" I asked, my voice growing louder. "Is it not a day of commiseration also? Weren't you really looking forward to it?" I took a few quick steps forward and moved close to her. "But, Nusrat, let me tell you, my state is not pitiable."

"When did I ever say that?" There was torment in her eyes and her voice was tremulous. "I couldn't even imagine it would turn out like this."

Suddenly her voice choked. She seemed ready to collapse. I quickly caught her arm to support her. After I had steadied her, I released her and moved back. Her face lost all its colour and she stood there so perfectly still, so lost, for such a long time, that she began to look like one of the antiques. My dusty fingers had left marks on her arm.

I now began to feel contrite. "I am sorry, Nusrat," I said. "The room is full of dust and you are so fond of white clothes. And white does look lovely on you. I've heard many people admire you in white. As for me, I like black more. Do you know why?"

She raised her head to look at me. I repeated a line I had read somewhere – one I had never forgotten: "Because black is the colour of nothingness."

A sense of loss overwhelmed me once again. I have no idea how much longer Nusrat stood there, waiting for me to say something more. But finally I saw her turn around slowly and walk toward the door. I heard the muted sound of glass breaking and saw Nusrat hesitate for a moment near the door. Then she lifted the heavy curtain. The light outside invaded the room and, just as suddenly, vanished.

She was a soft-footed girl. I couldn't hear the sound of her receding footsteps.

I remembered that my prolonged stay in the room had caused me to neglect other parts of the house, and this prompted me to leave at once. Coming to the door my eyes caught the glass. It was broken now. I swept the pieces aside with my foot. The edges of some of the jagged pieces, I noticed, were stained with something I recognized at once, even in the faint light. Fresh blood.

Afterwards I had the opportunity to pass by the tree many times. It had filled out with dense foliage again. The branches, unable to cope with the burden of the leaves, drooped so low that I had to crawl under them to get across. And if, on occasion, I walked, totally absorbed in my thoughts, the soft leaves invariably struck me across the face. Which prompted me to think: Why not prune these branches which always get in my way?

One day I was going toward the side door. As I approached the tree I reflexively bent down a little. But the leaves struck me in the face all the same and I noticed that the branches had drooped lower still. I was irritated. I thrust out my hand and pushed them away right and left, only to have them bounce back and strike me more forcefully than before. I began to feel terribly itchy on my face and neck and snapped off several branches, yanking at them vigorously. I had to bend low to free myself and as I straightened up and brushed the twigs and leaves off my body, I noticed someone sitting huddled against the trunk. It was not possible to see the face of the figure because of the gloom cast by the thick foliage, but I recognized her all the same.

"Nusrat!" I called out, picking my way toward her. As I drew near I saw that she was dressed in black.

"Nusrat!" I called softly and my eyes fell on her. Her features were not visible. I couldn't understand why this was so. I leaned forward and took a closer look. Dry yellow leaves covered her face like a veil. I wanted to remove the leaves from her face but saw that they were held together by cobwebs and my hand stopped halfway.

"Nusrat!" I called again, my voice growing fainter. I saw that the black mantle covered her from her shoulders to her feet. One of her hands was free of the cape and seemed to be resting on the ground. Her fingers were coated with dust and there was a maze of lines drawn in the dirt.

"Nusrat!" I said, but like a man talking only to himself. I shook her in an effort to wake her up. I tried to move her feet slowly. It was then that I saw: her feet under the black mantle formed an odd protuberance. I didn't touch her. Somehow I knew that beneath the mantle her feet were misshapen again.

I looked around. My eyes came to rest on the portico of the old surgeon. The floor was covered with the debris of the caved-in roof. There was no voice to be heard anywhere. Not a thing seemed to move. The chill under the tree increased suddenly and a severe trembling seized my body.

I stood up and ran in through the side door. I had taken only a few steps inside when I turned back to close it. I grabbed both panels of the door and brought them together. As the door was about to close I peered through the crack that remained to see whether Nusrat was still sitting there as before. She was.

I shut the door and was never able to open it again.

This story was first published as "Nusrat" in the literary journal *Shab-Khun,* Allahabad, later anthologized in the volume of short stories *Seemiya,* Lucknow, Kitabnagar, Nusrat Publishers, 1984.

nosh daru

On the left, at the very end of the straight lane, was a courtyard. The takht lying in a corner of this yard seemed to be no longer in use. Sun and rain had long played on it, loosening its joints until all its legs bent in the same direction. Still, it could be used.

The only tree in the courtyard, festooned with chandelier-sprays of yellow blossoms and plump black seed pods, grew in the corner opposite the takht. The skirt of the tree was thickly carpeted, first with a coarse layer of dry yellow petals, and then with a sprinkling of fresh ones. On top of these lay scattered some frayed seed pods.

Near the tree trunk was the door to the devrhi, ajar. The doors of the room above the devrhi seemed shut. A few tired branches leaned on the slender parapet of the roof, as though pausing briefly for a rest. A hawk hovering in the sky veered down and in a flash landed on the parapet; it shuffled its outspread wings, then changed its mind, wafted up, and disappeared into the sky.

From the other side of the parapet, two hands could be seen, rising slowly. Crooked fingers groped the uneven bricks, clutched them frantically and held on. A weary old man raised his head between the hands and rested his chin on the parapet. For a long time he tried to peer

translated by

shantanu phukan

beyond the branches, then turned his face upward, extended a hand, and pulled a cluster of flowers slowly toward himself. Bending, he put his nose to them and sniffed the flowers, his eyes closed and his nostrils flared slightly. He let go of the cluster and shook the branches back and forth. A plump pod fell into his hand. With his eyes closed he sniffed the pod once, and then once again, now drawing in his breath more emphatically. In sniffing at it a third time he breathed in so deeply that his nostrils were almost pinched shut.

"Amaltas," he told himself, and let the pod go.

The hall door opened and a middle-aged man emerged from it carrying a canvas shopping bag. He had just stepped out through the door when a woman's voice was heard. Turning, he came back toward the inner door.

"What are you saying?" he asked loudly.

The woman inside said something. He listened silently for a while and then said, "Yes, yes, I'll ask everything, let me first meet him."

Then, turning once again, he moved toward the outer door. He had hardly taken a couple of steps when the shopping bag got caught in something. Muttering, he stopped.

A bike stood leaning against the left wall. Both its tyres had flattened and were cracked in several places. The inner tubes were protruding slightly and were covered with a film of dust. One pedal had been improvised from wood, and only a thin iron rod remained in place of the other. A dirty towel was wrapped around the seat. On both the handles hung faded burlap sacks filled with hay. A few spokes in the front wheel had come off the rim and were poking out; one of these had hooked the man's shopping bag. He tugged a few times at the bag and then, bending down, pinched the spoke and unhooked the bag from it.

Amaltas: The Indian Laburnum.

Turning toward the outer door he stopped yet again – a small air pump, tied to the bike frame with a string, had come loose with his tugs and was dangling free. When he bent to straighten it, it came away in his hand. He blocked the nozzle with the tip of one finger and with the other hand he pumped the handle a few times, then tossed it out of the door. The rusted pump landed on the ground yellowed by the petals and seemed but another of the Amaltas seed pods.

Stepping out of the door the man entered the courtyard, and then the long, straight lane. He walked some hundred steps, turned into the right lane, and then into the left. In just a little while he was standing on the eastern end of the main street. Glancing both ways he crossed the avenue and stepped on to the wide sidewalk at its western end. Ahead lay a stepped lane, through which he descended into yet another street. He now entered an open-air market on both sides of a plaza. Beyond the flower-sellers' stalls, he turned left into a lane where a few kids were playing marbles. He asked one of them, "Beta, is there a water-pump around here somewhere?"

"It doesn't work," the boy answered, pointing to the plaza, "but the tap over there must have water in it."

"And where's the pump that doesn't work?"

The boy gestured with his arms, pointing out the direction, and then added, "But it's not working."

Just then the boy spotted one of his friends cheating at the game and got busy dealing with him. The man entered the alley pointed out by the boy and, passing through several narrow lanes, finally reached the one with the defunct hand-pump. Here he saw that the door of the front room of the third house was slightly ajar. A man, roughly the same age as he, sat on a high wooden stool reading a newspaper by the devrhi. Hearing his footsteps, the man looked up.

"Excuse me, bhai sahib," the newcomer asked hesitantly, "Kishan Chand Attar's pharmacy, is it here?"

"This is it," the seated man answered him before he could complete his sentence. "The store's right here, but now ... of course, we also keep patented Western drugs."

The newcomer glanced about the room. Except for a few bottles and packages arranged carefully about the shelves of the built-in cupboards, the room seemed strangely empty.

"I just had to find out something about Kishan Chand Ji."

"Yes, yes, what is it?"

The newcomer was about to say something, but then ran his eyes over the room once again. This time he also saw, leaning against the door, a square signboard with the insignia of a red cross, and below it the words: KISHAN CHAND & SONS, ENGLISH PHARMACY.

"And you're his ...?" he was again at the point of asking something.

"I'm his grandson."

The newcomer seemed relieved, though still a little anxious about asking the next question. The shopkeeper looked at him expectantly. The newcomer said haltingly, "Well, I just wanted to find out if he's still ...," and then, changing his mind he said, "I've come from Yaqub Attar's house, I'm his son. You may have heard of him?"

The pharmacist seemed a little more interested.

"Yaqub Attar Sahib? Yes, of course, he was my Baba's guru. I mean, Baba had learnt the apothecary's trade from him. You're Yaqub Sahib's son? Well, then you're one of us."

Standing up he shook hands with the newcomer. He folded up his newspaper, stowed it away under the stool, and then, bringing another small stool from the room, said, "He used to come to Baba all the time – I can even remember him a little ... and *your* full name?"

"I'm Yusuf."

"I'm Lal Chand. Here, please sit. I'm really glad to meet you."

Attar: A druggist, an apothecary.

But Yusuf seemed uninterested in formalities; glancing at his watch he said, "Lal Chand Ji, I'm in a bit of a ... I just wanted to find out if ... well, it seems crude to just ask point-blank."

"No, no, certainly not."

"Lal Chand Ji, is Kishan Chand Ji still around?"

"Yes, by the grace of Bhagvan, he's still alive."

Yusuf sat down on the other stool.

"And does he meet people?"

"Meet? Well, that's a bit of a problem – he's very weak now; he's past eighty six."

"Does he move about on his own?"

"Ye-es, a bit here and there ... I mean he takes care of his own bodily needs."

"I need him for something really urgent, Lal Chand Ji," Yusuf said. "Actually, I had to ask him about something which goes back some thirty years."

"But you know, he doesn't remember much, he's also begun to lose his memory of late," Lal Chand said, and then repeated, "he's past eighty six."

"Still ..."

"And then there's another thing," Lal Chand began, then fell silent.

"Yes?"

"If anyone wants to meet him he refuses. He doesn't even meet relatives, keeps losing his patience with them all."

"I see, but if he is told that his Ustad wants to meet him, maybe then he won't refuse."

"Well, then he will rush over; even now he sometimes pesters us to take him to his Ustad."

"Lal Chand Ji, his Ustad ..."

Suddenly Lal Chand put his finger to his lips and, gesturing to Yusuf to be quiet, stood up. A short and extremely thin man wrapped only in a dirty dhoti was stepping out of the hall. He held incense sticks in both his outstretched hands and was advancing toward the room like a child walking gingerly with a burning candle in his hands. He entered the room without paying the slightest attention to the two men. A few wisps of fragrant smoke coiled in the air outside the room and then vanished. The old man had reached a corner of the room where he could no longer be seen by the two men outside.

"Baba," Lal Chand whispered to Yusuf a few seconds later.

Before Yusuf could respond, the old man emerged from the room. Stopping for a moment, he stroked his cheeks with his palms, threw a cursory glance at the two men standing there, then turned, and with slow steps retreated into the hall.

Both the men stood stone-still. Finally, Lal Chand sat down on the stool and signalled to Yusuf to do the same.

"He's grown really old," Yusuf remarked as he sat.

"He's past eighty six," Lal Chand reminded Yusuf, and then asked, "How old must Yaqub Dada be now?"

"He's still around," Yusuf said. "He's just turned ninety six."

Lal Chand was about to say something when he changed his mind and asked, "What did you have to find out from Baba?"

"Several things, actually, very old things. Let's see if he remembers them."

"Well, he does talk of the past sometimes, but it seems to blur together, he mixes things up."

"Still, Lal Chand Ji, I have to see him."

"All right, I'll try. I'll mention it to him the first chance I get, and he may agree when I mention Yaqub Dada."

"Then I'll come and check back with you in a couple of days," Yusuf said, glancing at his watch, and stood up.

"Oh, sit, have some tea."

"No, no, please, I'll come again, it's getting late for the office."

He was just about to raise his hand in a salaam and turn around when the old attar emerged from the hall yet again and came straight toward Lal Chand.

"Hey Lallua," he said, addressing Lal Chand without even glancing at Yusuf, "This wouldn't be our Ustad's son, would he?"

"Yes Baba, he is Yaqub Dada's son – Yusuf Sahib."

"That's just what I've been telling myself. When I saw his eyes I thought they were like Ustad's."

Then turning, he stared at Yusuf. Yusuf greeted him with a little bow, and said, "Kishan Chacha, my father speaks of you all the time."

"And why shouldn't he talk of me, his Kishna? If not me then whom should he remember? This oaf Lallua?"

Lal Chand squirmed like a child, and began to giggle. Yusuf said, "So, Chacha, come by our place sometime."

"I've asked so many times, but this scoundrel won't take me."

"I'll come and get you," Yusuf said. "When will you come?"

"Lallua, some paan and sharbat for our friend?"

"Not now Chacha, the next time," Yusuf interrupted. "No, no, I'm not just being formal; but tell me, when are you coming to our place?"

But the old man seemed not to hear him. He was talking to himself: "The first showers of the monsoons would begin and the Ustad ... O Kishna! Get the bike! Pack the bags! ... Then for days on end he would comb riverbeds, ponds, lakes, woods, even weed patches, leaving nothing out. He would fill entire bags with just rain bugs and ... and then upon returning would sort it all out ... Kishna, here, get to know this resin ... and tell me what type of pollen this is ... and, hey Kishna, if one can't tell one thing apart from the other blindfolded, then one really can't claim to be an attar ... Then, Ustad, I don't think I can ... Yes, you can, beta, you can; just keep at it, and you'll develop an eye – now that's it."

The old man stopped to catch his breath. Yusuf cleared his throat and wanted to say something, but Lal Chand silenced him with a gesture.

"And my! What an eye he had," the old man resumed speaking. "You could come and show him formulae a hundred years old ... Ustad, I don't get this ma'jun formula ... Ustad would look it over, sniff it, taste it and there it was ... Write this down ... and he would spell out the entire formula at one go – dozens of ingredients in their exact proportions. There were these hakeems from old families who hid their family recipes even from their own sons. How they would sweat at the mere mention of Ustad's name! Before they prescribed a drug they would make the patient swear: Now look, not even a whiff of this should reach Yaqub. And our Ustad, what can one say! He was something else – thought it a sin to steal others' formulae. If by chance a special formula belonging to some old family fell into his hands, he would turn away from it: No, that is wrong. But yes, if a family should begin to squander the tradition, or come to an end, then there was no holding back; but even then, he would prepare the formula only to shelve it away. At most, he would administer a dose or two of it to a patient, but he wouldn't dream of taking any money for it. When Hakeem Nabba Sahib's line came to an end, his formula Panja-e Ta'us died along with him. Our Ustad found a pinhead's worth of it lying about somewhere; and in the blink of an eye, my friend, that formula was ready. He also gave me a small jar of it. I said, Ustad, this is no mere ointment, it's a miracle, an absolute miracle; write it down. But no, he shrank from the mere suggestion: Kishna, it doesn't belong to us. And then there was this other formula, the Nosh Daru, developed by the family of the dark Kirmanis ..."

"Nosh Daru!" Yusuf broke in. He didn't notice that Lal Chand was making desperate signs for him to keep quiet.

"Kishan Chacha, will you be able to recognize Nosh Daru?"

Ma'jun: Something kneaded; here, drugs mixed with honey or syrup.

Panja-e Ta'us: *Panja* means a paw, claw; also clutch, grasp, and power; *ta'us* is peacock; here the two together stand for the name of a medicinal compound.

The old man stopped dead in his tracks.

Yusuf waited a few seconds for his answer, and then said limply, "You were just talking about Nosh Daru, Kishan Chacha."

"Nosh Daru?" the old man echoed glancing about himself.

"The one your Ustad had prepared."

"*My* Ustad? I *myself* am the Ustad," the old man muttered faintly, and looked toward Lal Chand. Then he said, "Lallua, I'd just come out to say that today I'll eat some makko berry bhujiya." He turned, and disappeared into the hall.

Both the men stared after him for a long while.

At last Lal Chand drew in a long breath and said, "Outrageous, to break him off while he's talking."

"I shouldn't have, what can I say, Lal Chand Ji? Actually, I couldn't hold myself back when I heard him say Nosh Daru."

"Nosh Daru," Lal Chand repeated, squinting for a while and then shaking his head. "I never heard that name from Baba. He often talks of Panja-e Ta'us; he even had it; stashed it away somewhere and then forgot about it. Even now he begins searching for it at times. But this is the first time he's mentioned the Nosh Daru formula, and it's also the first time he's talked on and on like this. Perhaps hearing his Ustad's name ..."

"Listen, Lal Chand Ji, the two of them have to meet. Who knows how much they will remember, once the master and student meet. And maybe in the meeting Nosh Daru also ...," breaking off he glanced at his watch. "Let me tell you the whole story, you're not busy, are you?"

"I sit here all day long," Lal Chand answered, "It's you who ..."

"Well, no, it's too late for the office anyway; I'll have to file an absence report."

"Well, then, go on."

Makko: *Physalis Peruviana*, Cape gooseberry, Brazil cherry, "winter cherry."

For a few long moments Yusuf was silent, lost in thought. Then he began to speak: "Father left his profession as an attar thirty two years ago. The truth is, he had begun to falter in recognizing drugs. One day a young hakeem came to our pharmacy and created a big scene, saying, What do you mean by showing off your know-how by embellishing my prescriptions? Abba said, It isn't a matter of showing off. It's just that one medicine inadvertently got added to the wrong prescription. The hakeem pounced back: If wrong drugs keep getting added like this, God protect my patients. What happens to me if a patient ups and dies? Abba said nothing. Even after the hakeem was done with his scene and had left, he said nothing. When at long last he did speak, it was to say that the hakeem sahib's father used to come to him to check up the exact proportions of the formulae in his prescriptions. The very next day he packed up the store. For a few days he held on to the drugs, extracts and other stuff, but one day he went out and sold everything off to other attars. Whatever was left he handed out with his own hands, going around on his bike. His takht used to be inside the house, he had it carried and laid out in the open. For a few days, he said nothing to anyone. Then he seemed to return to his old self. Mornings he would go out for a walk, and then for the rest of the day would turn the pages of the old hikmat books. So the years passed. Then one day he went out for a walk, but came back halfway through, saying – My legs aren't quite working. That night he didn't sleep a wink. The next day he called me very early, handed me a small jar, and said – Hold on to this very carefully, it has my Nosh Daru in it. I'm losing my senses, and even my limbs are beginning to give. Nosh Daru will cure it all; it's an old, old royal formula. I said, In that case, start it right away. No, no, he said, its work begins when all other cures have failed. Before that it actually harms

Hikmat: The practice of Arab-Greek medicine; also, wisdom, knowledge, science, philosophy.

one. You keep it hidden and in the meantime I will try other drugs. Only when you see me becoming totally useless must you begin the treatment, not a moment before. He then snatched the jar from my hands and, raising it to his mouth, whispered something to it which I couldn't hear."

"So, you also saw the concoction," asked Lal Chand. "What was it like?"

"Something like honey," Yusuf answered. "Pungent, with a touch of saffron to it. Anyhow, I took the jar from him and put it away in a trunk full of old clothes; this was many years ago. Now he's reached the point where he doesn't grasp anything. His vision's almost completely gone, he can hear very little, neither can he walk. But once a day he drags himself to the edge of the roof and somehow manages to stand up for a while, clutching the parapet. Then he slumps over right there. This bit of exertion drains him so much that he can't move for half a day."

"In other words, it's time for Nosh Daru," Lal Chand said.

"That's just what I'm getting at, Lal Chand Ji," Yusuf answered. "I'd long since forgotten about it and he'd been taking Western medicine. One day he poured out the medicine all over the floor and kept repeating all day long that no cure works, nothing works. It was then that I remembered Nosh Daru. But he hadn't mentioned the dosage to me – or maybe he had, and it was I who didn't remember. Anyway, I took out the jar, went up to him and said, This is Nosh Daru, you'd had me hide it away. But he didn't remember a thing. Take it, I suggested, it will help. He took the jar from me, opened it, drew it up to his eyes, and looked it over. Then he sniffed at it deeply and, losing his temper, shrieked, This is poison, sheer poison! I was startled out of my skin. I took the jar back from him and stashed it away again, but from that day he's got it into his head that I want to do him in. He keeps calling my wife and whispering to her, Go, go ask Yusuf what have I ever done to him? And from that day he won't even take a glass of water from me – just eats what she serves him. Now these last couple of days he's begun refusing even that. And so, it suddenly occurred to me that if Kishan Chacha ... Perhaps Kishan Chacha can help out in all this."

"Father's condition is also like that," Lal Chand said. "But you've got the right idea, Yusuf Bhai, the two have to meet."

"So when shall I come?"

"No, no. You don't have to run around. I'll talk Father into coming out to your place, in just a day or two. Are evenings a good time?"

"Yes, any evening, or any holiday. But, Lal Chand Bhai, don't take long."

"Don't worry, I myself am worried about it."

"Now, the address."

"I know the address. I sometimes go over there; I've a friend out that way."

Yusuf got up. Lal Chand shook hands with him and then watched him walk away down the alley. Then he drew a long breath, picked up the small stool, put it back in the room, picked up the newspaper lying on the floor, and sat down to read.

Greyish water flowed out of the door of the devrhi and spread slowly in the courtyard. Lal Chand tapped lightly on the door. It opened, and Yusuf leaned out holding a dripping broom and wearing only a tahmad around his waist.

"Lal Chand Ji! Come in, come in."

"I just found out when I came out here. I'm really sorry. When ...?"

"The day I came by your place, the very next day, sometime at night," Yusuf answered, opening the door fully. "Come in, come right in, I'll bring out the chairs."

"No, no, don't trouble yourself, I won't sit now," Lal Chand said.

Tahmad: A cloth worn round the waist and passing between the legs.

"The thing is, Baba's also with me."

"Kishan Chacha? He's come? Where is he?"

"He's out there, resting on the takht."

Yusuf began to come out of the door, but Lal Chand stopped him.

"No, Yusuf Sahib, better if you don't show yourself, because while coming here he forgot that I was bringing him here to meet his Ustad. Once he sees you ... He's sitting there peacefully."

"You're right," Yusuf admitted softly.

"But that matter of – I mean the Nosh Daru ...?"

"Lal Chand Ji," Yusuf said, "Finally he did remember Nosh Daru. That evening he called me and had me sit down next to him; he kept on talking to me – and very lovingly. I was convinced that he had come around to trusting me again. Then he suddenly said, Yusuf, so much time has passed and you've never given me my Nosh Daru. I ran to get the jar and handed it to him. He opened and sniffed it, and then softly he repeated that same thing: It's poison, sheer poison. Now he wasn't at all angry. He returned the jar to me and said, Yusuf, now what will you give me?

He fell silent. His condition was pretty bad, and that same night ... When I went and looked in on him that morning, it seemed as if he were asleep ..." The words caught in Yusuf's throat.

"I'm really sorry," Lal Chand said.

For a while both remained silent, and then Yusuf said, "And Kishan Chacha ...?"

"I'm taking him back," Lal Chand said. "Today he began fussing over his clothes quite early in the morning. He'd lain them out last night. He was ecstatic that he was going to his Ustad's. Now we can only wait to see what he does when he finds out. All right then. I know I should've stayed a bit, but ..."

"No, no, it's fine, you take him back," Yusuf said, wiping his hands on his tahmad before shaking Lal Chand's hand.

"If I can ever be of any help," Lal Chand said. "Either I or Baba ..."

"Certainly," Yusuf said.

He watched from the hall as Lal Chand crossed over to the other end of the courtyard.

The old attar, seated on the takht, was hidden from Yusuf's view by Lal Chand as he walked. Even so, Yusuf could glimpse the sleeve of his carefully creased, dazzling white kurta, and a corner of his starched, double-peaked cap. Lal Chand said something to him and then bent down to help him up.

The devrhi door slowly swung shut. And then, from behind it, was heard the swish of a broom on a wet floor.

This story was first published as "Noshdaru" in the journal *Quarterly Aaj*, Karachi.

the myna from peacock garden

It would happen every day. I'd get home and knock on the door. Jumerati's mother's coughing and hacking would be heard inching closer and closer from the other side. But even before that, I'd hear small feet run up and then stop right behind the door, and I'd call out from my side, "Open the door! Kale, Kale, Khan is here!" I'd hear gay laughter from behind the door, and then I'd hear the little feet run away again. Some moments would pass before Jumerati's mother would reach the door and open it. I'd go inside the house acting as if I were looking for something I'd lost. I'd peer into every corner and call out, "Hei! Where's the fair, fair daughter of the Black, Black Khan?" Sometimes I would call out, "Does a Princess Falak Ara live here?" And sometimes I'd shake the branches of the night-blooming kamni tree and ask, "Has anyone seen my pet, my little hill myna?"

Glancing out of the corner of my eye I'd see little Falak Ara, breaking into giggles, run from her hiding place in one corner of the house to another. But I would pretend to be blind and deaf and keep looking in all the wrong places. When at last I heard her laughter right behind me, I'd turn and pounce on her with a cry and sweep her up into my arms. Her chirps of delight sounded like a hill myna's then.

translated by

sagaree sengupta

Such had been the daily pattern of my life from the day the Darogha of the royal animals, Nabi Bakhsh, found me a job in the Peacock Garden of Qaisar Bagh – the grand royal complex of palaces and gardens. Before I found employment there, I had been in the habit of wandering aimlessly around the animal parks on the banks of the Gomti, watching the tigers and leopards pace behind the high wooden fences. I often wished that one of the tigers would leap over the fence, tear me to pieces and eat me up. And that was the other daily routine which began on the day my wife died, leaving behind the eleven month old Falak Ara.

Before that particular event, I had been an employee of the Holy Endowment of Husainabad. It was my duty to look after the lights in the Imambara building. The salary was low, but we got by. My wife was quite efficient. She managed to run the household and indulge in her hobby of keeping birds out of the money I earned – she raised several parrot-chicks in our house and trained them deftly. We also had mynas of the ordinary kind, but she had set her heart on a hill myna because she had heard that birds of that particular breed could talk exactly like human beings. To make her happy, I had promised I would bring home a hill myna the next time I got paid.

But four days before I received my salary a pain started in her chest, and the very next day she died. Life stopped mattering to me after that. I stopped going to work. I stopped looking after myself, so I could hardly take proper care of Falak Ara. If it wasn't for Jumerati's mother, our baby daughter wouldn't have survived. Jumerati's mother lived in an outer room of my house. Six months earlier her bread-winning son, Jumerati, had got caught in an eddy of the Gomti and drowned. My wife had looked in on the older woman regularly after that event. And now, Jumerati's mother considered herself responsible for Falak Ara's care. She'd stay in my house during the hours I was out and do some cooking as well; I gave her a bit of money, enough for two square meals a day, and a little paan and tobacco too.

Ahmad Ali Khan, the Darogha of Husainabad, had sent a man enquiring after me a few times, but I refused to have anything to do with him. The poor Darogha had no choice but to suspend my pay. Then, I began to take loans on interest from the bazaar moneylenders to make ends meet. I would go home only at night, and by then Falak Ara would be fast asleep. First thing in the morning, the parrots would rattle off the things my wife had taught them, thus making it too painful for me to remain in the house. Finally one day I got up, went to the bird market and sold all the birds.

One day during that particular period of my life Darogha Nabi Bakhsh summoned me for a talk. He had been watching me loitering by the animal parks for a number of days. He took such a warm interest in my welfare that I ended up telling him all my troubles. The Darogha was very comforting, but he was also furious about my taking loans from the moneylenders. I was mortified by the picture he drew of the future – with me unable to pay back loans – and I envisioned myself either banging my head on prison bars, or begging in the lanes and alleys of Lucknow with my little daughter's hand held in mine.

"Look, Kale Khan, it's still early in the game," said the Darogha. "Get a job or something somewhere, and start thinking about paying off your debts. Or else!"

"But Darogha Sahib, where can I get a job?"

"Why? For starters, the doors of the Holy Endowment of Husainabad are open to you."

"Yes, there might be a job there. But how can I ever face Darogha Ahmad Ali Khan? Do you know how many times he sent a man to fetch me, and I wouldn't even have anything to do with him? How can I possibly face the Darogha now and ask for a job?"

"All right. Can you work in the gardens?"

"I don't see why not," I said. "Even if it's ripping grass out of the ground, I'll do it."

"Then come with me right now," he said. "There's a job open."

The Darogha took me immediately to the Palace Secretariat, the Badshah Manzil. My name and description were entered in assorted documents. The Darogha had his own name entered in the space left for the guarantor's. Then we reached the gate, the Lakkhi Darvaza. There was a crowd of officials, sentries and such gathered there. The Darogha exchanged formal greetings with several people, and then said to me, "Wait right here. Your name will be called out soon." And gently lifting the maroon brocade curtain hanging in front of the door, he went inside. Meanwhile, I stood back and marvelled at the artistry of the Lakkhi Darvaza. Finally my papers were complete and were sent back from the offices. My name was called out. A khwaja-sara asked me several questions and matched my answers to the information entered in the documents. Then, he pointed toward the maroon curtains and said, "Go to the Peacock Garden."

I stood on the other side of the curtain a moment later. I was too flustered at the time to notice the splendours of the place, but I saw peacocks strutting on the grounds and figured that this indeed was The Peacock Garden. But Darogha Nabi Bakhsh was nowhere to be seen. I had no idea which way to go. The entire place seemed deserted except for the many birds in the trees and in the huge pavilion cages. From time to time the cooing of pigeons and the songs of nightingales could be heard, and every once in a while an elephant would trumpet from its distant enclosure, and these were the only signs of life. I was looking around nervously when I noticed several enormous green peacocks standing perfectly still. When I looked at them more closely, I realized that they were shrubs which had been trimmed into peacock shapes.

"The Peacock Garden!" I exclaimed to myself, and walked swiftly in to it.

Khwaja-sara: Eunuch palace officer.

Peacocks had been fashioned out of beaten silver even on the gateway to the garden. The Darogha was inside the entrance, standing next to a pile of marble slabs. "Come on in, Miyan Kale Khan," he called out when he saw me waiting outside the gate, and I walked over to him. In the middle of the garden, several masons were building a low platform. The Darogha gave them directions, then took me by my arm on a quick tour. I was astonished at the shapes the shrubs had been trimmed into. They were formed so exactly like peacocks that it seemed like the plants had been melted down and poured into some kind of mould! Even the triangular crests and pointed beaks could be made out clearly. The most wonderful peacock was the one that had its head twisted around to preen its feathers.

Each peacock had been crafted by bringing together the branches of two thin-trunked shrubs planted side by side. The woody trunks served as legs for the peacock, and some of the roots had been allowed to emerge from the surface of the ground in such a way that they looked exactly like peacock feet. The Darogha explained to me that every morning at the crack of dawn a troop of gardeners propped up ladders, set up bamboo scaffoldings, and trimmed every single shrub. He laughed when I gushed compliment after compliment for the work.

"You're impressed by just looking at the plain shrubs!" he said. "This month their vines have been taken down. When the new vines have grown over them again and have flowered, you should see the colours of the feathers then!"

After that he took me into another garden nearby in which all the trees were shaped like lions. "This is the Lion Garden," he explained. "The Badshah has given these trees names as well." Then he led me back to the Peacock Garden. "Your job is to keep the Peacock Garden as spotless as a mirror," he said, and pointed to the half-finished platform. "Once that's finished there will be a bit more work, but even then it won't be more than half a day's worth. Your shift will be from sunrise to noon for a week, and then the next week from noon to sunset."

Then he told me exactly what my job entailed, and finally said, "From today you are an employee of His Majesty the Badshah. May God bless you! That's all for now – you can go home. Start coming to work tomorrow, and stop loafing around!" I showered him with grateful blessings.

"The things you say!" he retorted, and set to directing the masons.

For the first time since my wife died, I took a good look at my Falak Ara that day. She had her mother's face and colouring. It was hard to believe that this girl who looked like a white china doll could be the daughter of a black devil like me whom people took to be a Black slave from Africa. I felt pity for Falak Ara, and anger at myself for not only had this tiny being been torn away from her mother, but she had been deprived for so long of her father's love as well. However, in two or three days' time she took to me so completely that it was hard to imagine that she could have ever been more attached to her mother. As for me, some days I too would come straight home from work instead of strolling through the bazaars, and would wait at the door for the sound of those little feet.

I never brought Falak Ara anything from the markets. Even though I got a higher salary than in Husainabad, so much was taken out every month to repay the moneylenders' loans that just enough was left to cover the cost of our daily meals. Anyway, Falak Ara had not learned to ask for things on her own yet. But one day while we were chatting, she suddenly said, "Abba, how I want you to bring me a myna!"

There was nothing I could say. After my wife had died I had taken a sort of oath that I wouldn't keep any pet birds; yet when I saw my daughter looking at me with eyes full of longing I heard myself say, "Of course I'll bring my little hill myna her little hill myna!"

Falak Ara would wait for her hill myna every day after that. I even took a turn through the bird market one day. Hill mynas cost more than the domestic variety, but not so much more that I couldn't imagine buying one. I just couldn't buy one with the fraction of my salary that came into my hands those days. I moved away from the birds and went over to the cage sellers. There was a big crowd of prospective buyers, and among them that day I heard the Royal Minister's Wondrous Cage mentioned for the first time. I found out from the things people were saying that the Minister had been occupied for a long time with a huge cage he was having built as a gift for the Badshah. I also learned the Cage was being talked about all over Lucknow. Several customers in the bird market claimed to have seen it under construction, and they also said that they didn't understand how such a big cage could be brought inside Qaisar Bagh. Hearing this, an old-timer said, "Look, Miyan, these are matters for ministers to worry about. When they want, they move entire sultanates from here to there. Why are you getting all worked up about a tiny little cage?"

Everyone laughed. One of the men who claimed to have seen the cage said, "Venerable sir, you are speaking without having seen it. A tiny little cage! If you had only seen how tall it was ...!"

"How tall could it be? Taller than the Rumi Darvaza?"

"Maybe not the Rumi Darvaza, but it's just as high as the gates of Husainabad!"

"Is that all?" the elderly gent asked. "Then he'll just hook it on the little finger of his left hand and lift it over the Rumi Darvaza."

Loud laughter broke out and I started toward home.

The very next day I heard about the Minister's wonderful Cage in the Peacock Garden as well. The platform was already finished. Its shining

---

Rumi Darvaza: "The Turkish Gate" – an ornate, 18th century, ceremonial gate near the great Imambara of Lucknow.

stony whiteness amidst the greenery of the garden was both pleasing and painful to the eyes. Darogha Nabi Bakhsh said that the cage would be placed on top of the platform.

"But Darogha Sahib," I asked, "how can such a large cage be brought inside the garden?"

"It is coming in separate pieces, understand?" The Darogha explained. "Then it will be put together here. The Minister's men should be here any moment. For the time being they will take over the Garden completely. They'll work all night, and tomorrow the birds will be released into the Cage ..."

"Released, or shut up?" I asked with a laugh.

"It's all the same. For Heaven's sake, stop playing word games and pay attention to the important things! The Minister himself is going to come, so it would not be of any surprise if Hazrat Sultan-e Alam, our Badshah, also graced us with his presence. Your real work will begin tomorrow. Understand? You've been appointed to look after the Wondrous Cage and the birds inside it. So make sure you show up tomorrow. Don't go taking the day off for any reason."

At that moment a chobdar entered the Peacock Garden and, going up to the Darogha, said a few words to him in hushed tones. By way of an answer, the Darogha said, "May he oblige us by coming! Our work is done."

He gestured toward the platform and said to me, "Let's go, my friend. Let's make way for the Cage."

The next day I started out from home well before the normal time. Like every other day, little Falak Ara reminded me as I was leaving, "Abba, my hill myna ..."

Chobdar: The macebearer of the king, whose job it was to carry messages and announcements.

"Yes, child, I'll surely bring it."

"But you always forget!" she said with childish obstinacy, as I went out through the door.

After walking a little way, I turned back to look at her. She was holding one of the door panels and gazing steadily after me, exactly the way her mother used to when I went off to work every day.

Walking by way of the animal parks, I went in through the northern gate of Qaisar Bagh; from there I went through the Lakkhi Darvaza and reached the Peacock Garden straightaway. A major commotion had started there. There were sentries standing outside the garden, and Darogha Nabi Bakhsh was talking to them. As soon as he caught sight of me, he said, "Come, my friend Kale Khan. I told you! His Highness the Sultan is indeed going to grace us with his presence! You did the right thing by arriving good and early today. I was about to send someone running to get you."

He took me with him as he entered the Peacock Garden. The Minister's Wondrous Cage was the first thing one saw. I had thought that it would be just some largish, fancy birdcage, and that's all, but once I laid my eyes on the real item I couldn't look away. Cage? This was an entire building! The frame was made of rails some four fingers wide. They were red when seen from one side and green from the other. I didn't know whether they were made of wood or of iron, but the high gloss on them could deceive one into thinking the material to be ruby or emerald. The wall, consisting of rails that were red outside and green inside, had a wall across from it made from rails which were green outside and red inside. Thus, if you looked at it from one side the whole cage appeared red. Looked at from the other side it would appear entirely green! In the spaces between the rails, flowers and birds had been shaped from thick silver wires, and between the wires there was a delicate netting of gold metal threads, with tiny doors and windows set in on all sides. The main door of the Cage was higher than a man's head, and on its lintel, mermaids held aloft the royal crown of Lucknow. A huge crescent moon was placed above the bulbous spire of the dome. The smaller spires over the smaller domes in the corners were set with stars.

Four rows of ten small round birdcages – each with one hill myna in it – had been set up a short distance from the main doorway of the Wondrous Cage. The Darogha said, "Take a good look at them, Kale Khan. They're authentic hill mynas. In fact, they're not mynas, they're birds made of solid gold! The Badshah had them ordered especially for the Wondrous Cage. You should think of them as royal princesses!"

In front of the Cage, there was a high and dainty-looking sandalwood table inlaid with ivory flowers, leaves and different kinds of birds.

"Now look over here," said the Darogha, pointing at the table. "Each cage will be placed on this. His Majesty will look over each bird. You will stand here next to the door. After His Majesty inspects it, each cage will be passed along hand to hand until it reaches you. Your job will be to take each little creature out of its small cage and put it into the big one. This is a job requiring you to be very alert – go slack for a moment, and the bird flies off!"

"Fear not, my Master," I said. "Even if I transferred a thousand birds from one cage to another, there's no chance of a single one slipping out of my hands."

"You're right, my friend," said the Darogha. "But still, you'll be face to face with His Highness – try to keep your wits about you."

He then went outside, and I began examining the Cage again. It looked like a miniature Qaisar Bagh inside. Red volcanic gravel was spread on the floor. In the middle there was a pond filled with water in which tiny golden boats floated, each with a little bit of water inside it. On the floor shallow china basins of red and green held low shrubs with long thin branches. Clinging to the walls were flowering creepers of basant malti, basant kanta, jasmine and some European varieties as well. The vines had more flowers than leaves, and were trimmed so that they brought out, rather than hid, the artistry of the Cage. Small star-shaped mirrors had been scattered through the Cage and, because of them, wherever one looked one just saw flowers and more flowers. Basins of water, bowls of birdseed, clay pots, little swings, revolving perches, tiny scaffolding platforms and nests were set all about: these were the only indications that this was a place designed for birds.

A breeze was blowing and the whole cage rattled faintly. I felt a sudden silence sweep through the Peacock Garden and I started out of my reverie. I saw that His Majesty the Badshah and the Minister were entering the garden with the favourites of the court. Darogha Nabi Bakhsh brought up the rear, walking with his hand placed on his breast and his head bowed low. The Badshah stopped when he arrived at the sandalwood table, and gazed at the Cage for a long time.

"Excellent job!" he said, and looked at the Chief Minister. "O Noble Minister of the Realm, was all this work done within Our own borders?"

"O Refuge of the World," responded the Minister, bowing low with a hand over his heart, "each and every wire was twisted by a Lucknow craftsman."

"So, did you reward them with something extra?"

"Seven generations of each craftsman's family will be blessed with plenty, due to His Majesty's graciousness."

"Good, you did the proper thing," said the Badshah. "Increase that a little and make it a gift on Our behalf as well."

The minister bowed even lower. I wasn't looking at the Sultan's face. No one was looking at his face. All the courtiers stood with their eyes lowered and a hand held over their hearts. A little later I heard the Badshah's voice:

"All right, Nabi Bakhsh – you can bring them on now."

I looked at the Darogha. With a very subtle movement of his head

---

Basant kanta, basant malti: Flowering vines.

and eyebrows he signalled me to ready myself. A servant brought forward the first cage. The Darogha took it in both hands and, advancing two steps, placed it on the table with the utmost care as if it were a delicate glass vessel, and then stepped back. The Badshah picked up the cage in his own hands. The myna inside the cage fluttered around. The Badshah laughed and said, "Why not relax a bit, Miss Feisty?" and put the cage down on the table again.

A courtier picked up the cage and handed it to another, the second handed it to a third and finally the cage reached me. I brought the small cage up to the chink of the door of the much bigger Wondrous Cage and with great alacrity, put Lady Feisty inside the Wondrous Cage. Yet another servant took the empty birdcage away from my hands. Meanwhile another birdcage had arrived on the table. The Badshah picked it up as well – the myna in this one was sitting on the perch with her head bent low. The Badshah made gentle kissing noises at her and she lowered her head even further. The Badshah said, "Dear madam, won't you let me see your face?" Then he put the birdcage down on the table and said, "This one will be called Bashful Bride." The birdcage came to me and I placed Bashful Bride inside the Cage with the other. Thus all the mynas came up to the Badshah one by one in their individual cages, and he gave a name to each one. One was named "Dainty Steps," one "Gazelle Eyes," one "Renunciant." A particular cage reached the Badshah and the myna inside it began to flap its wings and chirp; he named it "Fairy Venus."

The cages kept arriving for a long time, and the new names of the mynas kept ringing in my ears. I felt less flustered in the presence of the Badshah than in the beginning, and I would even take a quick look at each myna before putting it into the Cage. All the mynas looked the same to me but the Badshah saw something unique in each one and named it accordingly. After twenty two or twenty three cages, I suddenly heard the Badshah's voice say, Falak Ara – Ornament of the Sky! And a cage reached my hands. Deep in my heart I repeated, "Falak Ara," and looked intently at the myna. It seemed to be just like the other birds. I didn't understand why the Badshah had named this one Ornament of the Sky. I must have missed the things he had said when he first looked at the bird. She sat in her cage with her neck craning forward. She looked back at me too and I felt as if I were gazing at my own little daughter, Falak Ara. All this took a bit of time, and I was still holding her cage and the bird was still in it when I saw the next cage moving toward me. Flustered, I put Falak Ara into the Cage so clumsily that she almost slipped out of my hands. It was lucky that no one saw me, and that once inside the Wondrous Cage, Falak Ara settled down on a swing.

There were sixteen or seventeen more cages to go. Before putting each myna into the Cage, I would be sure to glance at Falak Ara. She was still perched on her swing the same way, and was still gazing back at me. I realized with some surprise that although I wouldn't be able to point out the precise differences between her and the other mynas, I could tell her apart from all the others. All forty mynas had been put into the Cage and were flitting around inside. After a while Falak Ara, too, took a little flight from her swing and landed on a branch in the eastern portion of the Cage. The Badshah was explaining something to the Darogha in a low voice when the sound of a tiger's roar came from one of the wild animal parks. He stopped in the middle of what he was saying and asked, "Nabi Bakhsh, with whom is Mohini displeased?"

Stealing a smile, lowering his head and casting a sidelong glance at the Badshah, the Darogha said, "If this slave felt certain that his life would be spared, he'd venture an answer to His Majesty's question."

"Speak! Speak!"

"She's upset with Your Majesty the Sultan."

"But what have We done, my man?" the Badshah inquired, and then

---

Mohini: A name meaning "enchantress."

his face flushed with pleasure. "I see! I see! I know what it is! We came here directly today without visiting her first. That's it, isn't it?"

The Darogha placed his hand on his heart and, bowing low, said, "Who knows her ways better than your Royal Majesty? It's true that her pride has been hurt on your account. And besides, she's just recovered from an illness and is feeling irritable. She doesn't even heed what this slave of yours says to her ..."

"You are right," said the Badshah. He looked at the courtiers, at the Minister, and finally at Nabi Bakhsh again, and said, "Well then, let Us go and coax her into a better mood."

The royal party left the Garden with the Darogha following behind. Meanwhile workers had placed sacks of seed and large jugs of water by the doorway of the Cage. I opened the door ever so slightly and, turning sideways, went inside. I reached through a smaller door and got the sacks and jugs and filled all the food and water containers. The mynas were flying from one branch to another. They all looked the same, but I had no difficulty recognizing Falak Ara. I stood near her for a while and made chirping noises.

"I'm going to call you Falak Myna," I told her in confidence.

I came out of the Cage and went over to the planted beds which formed the boundary of the Peacock Garden; they were fenced with latticework panels and roofed with lattice as well. Thousands of birds of every kind were cheeping and chirping inside. I filled the food and water dishes here too, swept away the debris on the ground, sprinkled the little bushes with water and then went back inside the Peacock Garden.

Meanwhile, the Darogha had returned from the animal parks, and was standing by the Wondrous Cage, perhaps waiting for me. "Thank goodness we're finally finished with this hazardous enterprise," he said, and began walking around the Cage to check it.

"What craftsmen there are hidden away in our own city, Darogha

Sahib!" I said. But the Darogha was preoccupied. He kept gazing at the Cage and strolling around it. "I'll say this much," he said finally, "the Minister really put his heart into getting this made."

My job in the Peacock Garden was not a difficult one. In a matter of a few days I got the hang of my chores. I would finish up quickly and spend the resulting spare time in further cleaning and scrubbing the Wondrous Cage. The mynas knew me quite well by now and as soon as they caught sight of me they would come and perch on the rims of the empty food vessels. Falak Myna may have guessed that she was a special object of my attention. She had become quite fond of me, and when she saw me at the door of the Cage she'd be the first one to come up close and chirp at me.

One day, who knows what was going on in the royal quarters, but no one came to stroll in the Peacock Garden or to see the Wondrous Cage. I had finished all my work and stood examining the Cage from a few steps away. Two of the little boats floating in the tank had run into each other and didn't look right. I went back inside the cage and separated the boats, then came back to the spot where I had been standing.

The chattering mynas flitted here, there and everywhere inside the Cage. They all had full crops so none of them paid any particular attention to me. But Falak Myna would come to me again and again, call loudly, and then fly off to sit on a distant perch or swing. Again, she'd take flight from that spot over to where I was, let out another call, and then fly far off again. Sometimes my little Falak Ara played with me in exactly the same way! I felt terrible for her, especially when I thought of how these days, when I got home from work, instead of running and hiding from me, she'd meet me at the door and ask, "Abba, did you bring me my myna?" Then she'd see my empty hands and her spirits would fall. Her disappointed face floated before my eyes. Suddenly, wickedness arose in my heart and I began to think differently. Forty mynas flitted around in the Wondrous Cage – it was not easy to take an exact count of them. Easy? – it was impossible! The star-shaped mirrors made each bird appear to be ten. And anyway, what was the difference between forty and thirty nine? If there was one myna less, no one would even know. Just at that moment Falak Myna came close and chirped, and with a swift yet gentle movement of the hand I caught her. I retreated into a corner of the Cage stroking her feathers all the while and tried to count the mynas still flying around me. Even after counting them several times, I couldn't tell if there were forty or thirty nine. I felt reassured. I placed Falak Myna on a swing, gave it a gentle push, and left the Cage.

That day, while leaving through the Lakkhi Darvaza, I firmly decided to bring Falak Myna home and, moreover, considered it a straightforward sort of thing which would cause me no shame or remorse later. Rather, if I was ashamed of anything, it was of facing my own Falak Ara after making her crave for a myna of her own for so long. If I had any regrets it was only that I hadn't taken Falak Myna out of the Cage today!

I stopped at the bird market and, after a bit of bargaining, bought an inexpensive cage. "What kind of bird is it for?" the cage-seller asked, counting his money.

"A hill myna," I said as my heart pounded softly.

The cage-seller answered, "If you've kept a hill myna as a pet, Mr Abyssinian, you should have bought a suitably fancy cage for it. But do as you please."

I took the cage and went on, but must have gone only a few paces when my arms and legs began to tingle and my throat to dry up. I seemed to hear someone say, "Kale Khan! Stealing one of the Badshah's birds!" in my ear. All the way home I kept hearing this voice. I decided to return the birdcage more than once, then I got the notion that somehow I would distract Falak Ara with just the empty cage. By the time I reached home I was amazed at myself and at the fact that I had even had the idea of doing such a dangerous thing. I was also relieved that I hadn't already extracted Falak Myna from the Wondrous Cage. I was still sure that the theft of a single myna could not be detected, but nevertheless it seemed as if I had just escaped the jaws of death. When I got home, Falak Ara saw the cage in my hand and screamed, "My myna is here!" But when she ran up close and saw that the cage was empty, her face fell. She looked into my face and her eyes welled up with tears. I took her into my arms and said, "Look, the cage arrived today. Tomorrow the myna will be here!"

"No! You're always lying!"

"It's not a lie, child. You'll see tomorrow," I said. "I've even bought your myna already."

"Are you really telling the truth?" she chirped and her face suddenly shone with delight. "So where is she?"

"She's in a really big cage," I said. "She insisted on coming to live with her sister Falak Ara immediately, but I said, Look, today I'm going to buy you a cage. Then Falak Ara is going to wash it, decorate it nicely, and put your food and water dishes in it – and after that I'll take you home with me."

Falak Ara's joy was something to see. She climbed down from my lap immediately and hugged and kissed the cage over and over; she immediately washed and wiped it carefully, laid a carpet of kamni leaves inside, and put in a clay water bowl and a small pot for seed. She wanted to know every little thing about the myna: the shape of her beak, the colour of her feathers, what phrases the bird could already say. Falak Ara didn't sleep well that night. She kept waking up and talking about her myna.

The next day, when I left for work, I could hear her voice for quite a distance – My myna is coming today! My myna is coming today!

All along the way I thought about what excuse I would give Falak Ara when I returned empty-handed that night. Even as I fed and watered the mynas in the Peacock Garden, I kept thinking up all kinds of excuses. I couldn't concentrate on my work that day, yet it was finished by the time of the sunset prayers, and I turned around once more to go inside the Wondrous Cage. It occurred to me that I hadn't even looked at Falak Myna that day. She was perched on one of the little filigreed platforms on the western side of the Wondrous Cage, and was quietly gazing at me. When I went up close, she turned her head and looked away. I made some squawking noises with my lips. She ruffled her feathers softly and gazed at me again. I glanced all around the Cage once more. All the mynas had settled down quietly in their own places. Yet counting them was still not easy because nearly half of them were hidden in the branches. The fear I had felt the previous day about stealing a royal myna suddenly vanished as did the excuses I had thought up to console Falak Ara with; stealing the myna seemed, once more, a reasonable thing to do. I looked this way and that. The Peacock Garden was empty and desolate; the gardeners had finished their work and left. No one was watching me. I made chirping noises at Falak Myna again. Once more, she gently ruffled her feathers and looked at me. In the blink of an eye, I reached out and grabbed her. She struggled to free herself, but when I made chirping noises and stroked her feathers, she shut her eyes and let her body go limp. For a while I held my breath and just stood there, then I put her in one of my long kurta pockets and came out of the Cage.

I encountered several sentries on guard at their respective posts up to the Lakkhi Darvaza, but they already knew that I was on the evening shift at the Peacock Garden. No one asked me anything and I left Qaisar Bagh and started for home with my hand stuck deep in my pocket the whole time. I felt an intense desire to run as fast as my feet could carry me, but somehow I managed to walk along with measured steps.

Falak Ara was already asleep. Jumerati's mother was waiting up for me. Giving her some food, I sent her off for the night. I shut the door from inside, took the myna out of my pocket and carried it to the cage. Falak Ara's decorations had become even fancier today. She had attached silver flowers between the bars, and had stuck a scrap of coloured cloth to a tiny stick from a broom and, following her own fancy, had made a little banner which now leaned crookedly against the wall of the cage. Inside the cage, the water dish was brimming, pieces of bread lay soaking in the clay feeding pot, and there were a couple of pieces of rolled up cotton to serve as bolsters for the royal myna to lean against. I gently put the myna inside and hung the cage from a peg. The myna fluttered around inside for a while, and then settled down in one place.

The next morning I opened my eyes to the sounds of Falak Ara's giggles and the myna's chirps. God knows when Falak Ara had dragged the wicker stool under the peg and taken the cage down. She had now set it on that same stool and, kneeling on the floor, kissed the cage over and over as the myna chirped again and again. As soon as she saw me, Falak Ara announced "Abba, my myna has arrived!"

She spent a long time explaining the things the myna said to her. I sat down by the cage and said a few words to the myna myself, but the bird looked at me as if she didn't recognize me at all. Meanwhile, Falak Ara asked, "Abba, what's her name?"

"Falak Ara" was about to escape from my lips, but I stopped and said, "Falak Ara, my child, her name is Myna."

"But, she *is* a myna!"

"That's why her *name* is Myna."

"But Myna is what they're *all* called."

"And that's why her name is Myna as well."

In this way, I confused my daughter's little mind. In reality, my own mind was confused. For several days in a row, I arrived at the Peacock Garden only to come back a frightened man. I would feel on edge the whole time. If anyone looked at me hard while I was anywhere inside Qaisar Bagh, I'd want to break into a run. At home, I'd see Falak Ara sitting with the cage in front of her, chatting about a whole world of things. As soon as she saw me she'd report everything the myna had said to her that day. Then slowly, my terror abated, and one day when Falak Ara was talking about the myna, I said, "But your myna won't speak to me."

"You don't speak to her, either. She was complaining about that."

"Really? What did she say?"

"She was saying, Your Abba is fond of you, but he's not fond of me."

"But the myna has a sister who is very fond of her ..."

"Which sister?"

"Princess Falak Ara!"

She laughed so gleefully at this that my fear completely evaporated and the next day I entered the Peacock Garden without anxiety. When evening came, I counted the mynas several times but I couldn't get an accurate count. On the pretext that the mirrors needed cleaning, I removed all of them from the Wondrous Cage and counted again, but once again I counted them wrong. After that, I would summon a couple of the gardeners over to the Peacock Garden every day on one pretext or another, and have *them* count the mynas. The numbers they came up with were so preposterous that I couldn't help but laugh.

I enjoyed making the gardeners count the mynas as much as Falak Ara enjoyed talking with her pet. It had become a daily ritual when one day the Badshah visited the Peacock Garden once more. Stopping near the Wondrous Cage, the King spoke with his courtiers and Darogha Nabi Bakhsh. There was no reason for me to fear anything, but my heart was pounding. The Badshah was saying something to Nabi Bakhsh about the elephants in the royal animal parks. From time to time, he'd glance at the Cage and look at the mynas flitting from one spot to another. One particular time he looked at the mynas a little longer, and then asked Nabi Bakhsh, "Have you begun their training?"

"O Refuge of the World, Mir Daud comes every day at the time of sunrise prayers to teach them."

Then the Badshah fell into conversation about the Cage with his courtiers. The skills the craftsmen had displayed in making it were mentioned. Some of the craftsmen's names were mentioned too, and several of them were famous Lucknow goldsmiths. My worry had abated now. I was thinking about how our Badshah spoke to even his servants so cordially, and how extremely gentle his voice was. Just at that moment I heard the Badshah's mild voice say, "Well, Nabi Bakhsh, I don't see Falak Ara today."

I felt as if someone had drained the blood out of my body. The Darogha said, "Refuge of the World, she must be hiding in a branch somewhere. She was flying all over just a little while ago."

The Badshah smiled gently and said, "She's not feeling too shy to come out before me, is she? And look at this one, Bashful Bride! How she's jesting and teasing! Bashful Bride, if this is going to be typical of your behaviour we'll have to change your name to Mischief Maker!"

All the courtiers present bowed their heads, put handkerchiefs over their mouths and laughed soundlessly. If it had been any other occasion, I too would have been pleased no end to see the Badshah in such an engaging mood, and I too would have repeated every single one of his words to all my acquaintances later. But this time only one phrase echoed in my ear – "Well, Nabi Bakhsh, I don't see Falak Ara today."

The Badshah was talking about the elephants again, and I was standing a few steps away from the Cage. When the Badshah's words first fell on my ears, I felt as if I had shrunk to less than a hand's breadth. But now it seemed as if my body had expanded and become so large that I couldn't hide myself from anyone. I kept clenching my fists to make myself shrink again. Struggling this way, I wasn't even aware of when the Badshah left. When I came to my senses, the Peacock Garden was deserted and there was just the sound of the mynas' wings as they flew around inside the Wondrous Cage.

I didn't have it in me to dash home instantly to get the royal myna to put her back into the Cage. Somehow I finished my work and went home by the time of the sunset prayers. All along the way I worried about returning the myna undetected to the Cage. But when I reached home and Falak Ara began her chitchat about how the myna's day had gone, I developed another worry. I could take the myna back, well and good, but what would I tell Falak Ara? That night I tossed and turned, and didn't get to sleep until very late.

When morning came and I awoke, it occurred to me that starting the next day my shift at the Peacock Garden would begin in the morning. Then for a whole week, returning the myna to the Cage would not be easy. Whatever had to be done had to be done today. Falak Ara was playing with the myna right there in front of me. It troubled me to have to separate them, but a solution instantly came into my head. I sat down next to the birdcage, looked intently at the myna, and said, "Child, don't your myna's eyes look a little funny?"

"They're all right," said Falak Ara, looking into the myna's eyes.

"They're not all right at all! They look dirty, and the corners are yellow. Aha, she's got jaundice too!"

"What's *chaundice*?" asked Falak Ara, worried.

"It's a very terrible disease. Who knows how many mynas from the Badshah's garden have died from it!"

Falak Ara looked even more worried, and said, "So go get some medicine from Hakeem Sahib."

"And you think the Hakeem Sahib would prescribe a cure for a bird? Certainly not!" I replied. "We're going to have to take her to Nasiruddin Haidar Badshah's English hospital. She might be saved if we can get her there. She's in very bad shape, but still ... let's see whether we can keep her alive until we get to the hospital."

In short, I frightened that innocent child to the point of making her cry, until she herself began to insist, "For God's sake, Abba, please take her there! And go quickly!"

"The hospital must be closed right now," I explained to her. "I'll take her along with me when I go to work."

When it was time to go, I took the myna out of the cage. Falak Ara said, "Abba, take her right in her cage!"

"Birds aren't kept in cages there. There's a whole house that's been made just for them. You clean this cage up. When she gets better and comes out of the hospital, she'll enjoy living in her own home again."

Falak Ara took the myna from my hand. She caressed the bird for a long time, then said, "Abba, say a good luck prayer over her."

"I'll do it on the way," I said. "Here, hand her to me. It's getting late, the hospital's going to close."

I took the myna from her and put it in my kurta pocket and quickly left the house. I knew that like on every other day, Falak Ara would cling to the door and watch me leave the house. But I didn't turn around to look back.

My luck held and I got my chance as soon as I entered the Peacock Garden. None of the gardeners paid any attention to me. When I entered the Cage, every gardener was busy with his own work. I coughed loudly once to clear my throat, but still no one looked at me. I entered the Wondrous Cage, went over to one side and, taking Falak Myna out of my pocket, tossed her gently into the air. She flapped her wings and steadied herself in flight, then alighted on a swing, and flew from there to a little scaffolding platform. From the platform, she plunged downward and ended by sitting at the edge of the pool. Wherever she alighted, several other mynas came and perched next to her and chirruped as if to ask, "Sister, where have you been all this while?"

This was the first day since the mynas had arrived in the Peacock Garden that my heart was completely free of burden. Even on the way to work, I had thought up all kinds of things to distract little Falak Ara with, and I was sure that at least for a while she would be satisfied with the idea that her myna was getting better in hospital, and after that would more or less forget about the bird. Today, I looked intently at the mynas in the Wondrous Cage and noticed some differences in them, and I knew I could have picked Falak Myna out from among thousands of others. She was sitting by herself on a gently swaying branch. I went closer, puckered my lips and made some chirping noises at her. She gazed at me silently.

"Do you miss Falak Ara?" I asked her.

She kept looking at me in the same way.

I said, "You're not angry with me, are you?"

Suddenly, I realized that I sounded exactly like the Badshah. I felt a secret rush of fear and, quickly finishing my work in the Wondrous Cage, I left.

Just as I had thought, I had no problems with the story I'd made up for Falak Ara. I told her with great relish how her myna had refused to take the bitter-tasting medicine in the hospital and how a special sweet medicine had to be mixed up for her.

"And, listen, when they gave her moong daal khichri to eat and she flatly refused, saying, No way I'm going to eat that! the doctor had to ask, Well, what *do* you eat?"

"She must have said, Jalebis and milk, that's all we eat!" Falak Ara interrupted.

"Yes," I said. "The doctor didn't understand. The poor fellow's an Englishman, you know. He began to ask me all kinds of things, like, Well, Mr Kale Khan, what is this jalebi?"

Falak Ara was rolling on the floor with laughter. She picked up the empty birdcage and hugged it, repeating the phrase "What is this jalebi?" and chuckled to herself for a long time. I told her tales about the hospital and her myna all night long. When she fell asleep, I took the birdcage together with all its decorations and hid it amidst the clutter of the store room. I wanted Falak Ara to forget the myna completely.

When she woke up the next morning Falak Ara seemed subdued.

After a long time she just asked, "Abba, is my myna going to get better?"

"Yes, she'll get better," I answered. "But, child, one shouldn't talk too much about someone who's sick, because that makes the illness worse."

After that she didn't even ask me what happened to her myna's cage. I was thinking of ways to distract and amuse her when there was a knock at the door. I came outside. One of Darogha Nabi Bakhsh's men was standing there.

"Is everything all right, Muharram Ali?" I asked.

"Darogha Sahib has summoned you to come in early this morning," he said. "His Highness the Badshah is going to grace the Garden with his presence."

"Today?" I asked, astonished. "Just the day before yesterday he ..."

"The birds have been taught to speak, you know," said Muharram Ali. "He's coming to hear them perform."

"All right. You go on ahead."

Hurriedly I changed my clothes. Leaving the house, I told Jumerati's mother to go stay with Falak Ara and hurried toward the Peacock Garden. Along the way I took the opportunity to congratulate myself several times for having taken Falak Myna back to the Wondrous Cage in time.

A small green satin canopy with a fringe of metallic-thread had been erected on ornate silver posts in front of the Wondrous Cage. The Darogha and many other employees had gathered in front of the Cage. In the centre of them all the elderly Mir Daud stood stiffly at command, as if he were the Badshah and we his slaves. Tales of Mir Daud's finicky temperament and pompousness were known all over Lucknow, but everyone also knew that he was next to none when it came to training birds to speak.

"There you are, Kale Khan," said the Darogha as soon as he saw me. "Take care of the Cage, quickly, please ..."

I had just cleaned the floor, sprinkled water on the plants, gathered up the fallen flowers and leaves, and come out of the Cage, when shehnais and kettledrums began to play in the jelo-khana.

I heard Mir Daud's voice, "I'm going to say it once more! No one should speak in the middle of the performance, or else the birds will become shy and clam up!"

The Darogha was a little irritated by this, and said, "Mir Sahib, I've already told you once, who on earth would have the nerve to make even a pip in front of His Highness? But there you go repeating the same thing over and over since God knows when!"

In response, Mir Sahib placed his finger on the Darogha's chest and calmly repeated himself: "No one should say anything in the middle of the performance or else the creatures will refuse to talk!"

"For Heaven's sake, Mir Sahib!" the Darogha made a face and exclaimed, "You're going on like a parrot!"

Mir Sahib was all set to make a testy reply when the royal procession appeared in the distance. We all lined up in two rows at the gates of the Peacock Garden and in a short while the procession arrived. There were some English officers from the Residency with the Badshah today, in addition to the Minister and the courtiers. The Minister promptly busied himself pointing out each and every feature of the Wondrous Cage to the visitors. Then the Badshah said something to him in low tones and signalled Mir Daud with a look. Mir Sahib bowed and came up to the Cage. He made a whistling noise with his lips. The mynas flying around in the Cage came toward him, settled on swings and perches, and began to chirp loudly. Mir Sahib puffed out his cheeks, then squeezed them in again until a strange noise came out. The mynas were silent for a moment, then all of their throats swelled and their voices were heard as one:

Long live King Akhtar, Beloved of the World!
Solomon of our times! King of the World!

Each word was pronounced with such crystal clarity that I was astonished. It sounded exactly as if a sizeable group of women were singing songs together at a family celebration. The mynas recited the verse again, paused for a moment and, this time using a heavy voice and masculine intonation, recited in English:

Welcome to the Peacock Garden.

The British officers enjoyed this so much that they raised their hands in the air and jumped up and down with joy. The mynas recited the first couplet again, and then another one, and then another. From time to time the Badshah would smile appreciatively and look at Mir Daud, who was putting on quite a show himself. He would spread and puff out his chest and then immediately lean forward and bow so low that he seemed about to somersault.

The mynas recited a new verse, and then recited the first rhyme all over again:

Long live King Akhtar, Beloved of the World.

But the verse wasn't finished yet when, from the eastern part of the Cage came a loud, childish voice, "Falak Ara's a princess sweet!"

Suddenly all the mynas fell silent and Mir Daud stood there with his mouth hanging open. Falak Myna was sitting alone on a branch and her throat was swollen; she intoned again:

Falak Ara's a princess sweet!
Milk and jalebis is what she eats!

It was exactly my little daughter Falak Ara's voice! Darkness seemed to spread before my eyes. I don't know how those words struck the

---

Akhtar: Literally, "star"; here, pen name of Wajid Ali Shah, the last king of Avadh.

Jelo-khana: The courtyard of a palace where processions assemble before starting out.

others, but I myself was horrified at the mere thought of the mares in the palace stables condescending to eat "milk and jalebis," and this heartless myna was ready to feed princesses the same thing! And in front of the Badshah at that! I heard a few people speaking softly, but I couldn't understand what they were saying because there was a whistling sound in my ears. And then I heard a separate whistle-like voice even sharper than the other whistling,

Falak Ara's a princess sweet!
Milk and jalebis is what she eats!
She's the fair, fair daughter of Black, Black Khan!

Then there were sounds of Falak Ara's giggling and clapping, and then the same:

She's the fair, fair daughter of Black, Black Khan!
She's the fair, fair daughter of Black, Black Khan!

Even before my vision had cleared completely, I could make out Darogha Nabi Bakhsh staring wide-eyed at me. I saw the Badshah look at the Darogha and then slowly turn his head and fix his eyes on me. My body trembled violently and my teeth chattered. At that moment the white stone platform under the Wondrous Cage leapt up and hit me on the head.

When consciousness returned to me the next day, I was lying in the English-style hospital of Nasiruddin Haidar, and Darogha Nabi Bakhsh was bending down to peer into my face. The instant I saw the Darogha everything came back to me and I tried to raise myself. But the Darogha placed his hand on my chest and stopped me.

"Lie down, lie down," he said. "How's the wound on your head today?"

"Wound?" I asked, and when I ran my hand over my head I realized that several bandages were wrapped around it, and that it hurt a bit too. But at the moment I didn't care about pain. I grabbed the Darogha's hand and said, "Darogha Sahib, please tell me the honest truth about what really happened there!"

"You'll find out all about it, my friend, you'll find out all about it. First, get well."

"I'm just fine, Darogha Sahib," I said, "I swear."

The Darogha put off giving me an answer for as long as he possibly could.

"What are you asking, Miyan Kale Khan?" he began. "You did well to pass out right there. You have no idea what befell us afterwards ... But first tell me this, when did you give her that training?"

"Who?"

"The myna, Falak Ara, who else?"

"I didn't teach her anything, Darogha Sahib, I swear."

"Then?" he asked. "Where else did she hear such coarse and idiotic words?"

I hesitated a while, and finally said, "In my home."

The Darogha's jaw dropped in amazement. "Are you serious?"

I told him the whole story from the beginning to the end. The Darogha was stunned. For a long time not a single sound came out of his mouth. Finally, he said, "You've really wreaked havoc, Kale Khan. Stealing a royal bird! Listen, was the bird still at your house when his Majesty said that Falak Ara wasn't to be seen the other day?"

I hung my head.

"You've slaughtered me!" the Darogha said. "I had no idea! I said to His Majesty that she had been flitting around right there just a moment ago! My friend, you were about to get me fired from my job as well! It all became clear to His Majesty when she started babbling all that nonsense in front of the Englishmen. My God! – what His Majesty said when he heard her showing off like that! All I can say is that I too was astonished that His Highness could be uttering such words."

"What?" I sat up. "What did His Majesty say?"

"He just said: Darogha Sahib, please don't send Our birds outside," said the Darogha, sighing sadly. "Darogha Sahib! Never has His Majesty called me Darogha in place of Nabi Bakhsh, let alone Darogha Sahib! After all this time in his service, I had to hear such a thing because of you! My ears are still cringing from those bitter words!"

"Darogha Sahib," I pleaded, "I'm guilty of the offence. Give me whatever punishment I deserve ..."

"All right, then." He raised his hand to silence me. "His Majesty left, along with the English officers from the Residency. Meanwhile, a veritable tumult broke out in the Peacock Garden. The Royal Minister was ready to devour each one of us alive, while Mir Daud leapt up and down like a maniac and claimed that his enemies had deliberately brought in an outside bird and stuck it inside the Wondrous Cage to startle the mynas. I kept telling him this was no outside bird, it was a myna His Majesty was familiar with! Mir Daud took no account of the fact that the Royal Minister was standing right there, and began to shout: I didn't train her! I didn't train her!

"On top of that, the Royal Minister sprinkled salt on the wound by saying: Mir Sahib, it's clear that you didn't train her, for the simple reason that she talks better than your mynas! Then Mir Sahib... what more can I tell you, Kale Khan? He hit his head on the Cage right then and was sent home with an escort of sentries, but he tried to leap into the Gomti on the way. And into any well that he passed. He pretty much did jump into Darshan Singh's stepwell."

What on earth had I to do with Mir Sahib's jumping and leaping? I said, "Darogha Sahib, just tell me this – what was decided about me then?"

"What else could have been decided?" he said. "His Majesty put the Royal Minister in charge of punishing the offence, and left. It was plain to everyone that this was some mischief of yours, since that erudite bird didn't leave anything to the imagination. The Royal Minister decided your fate then and there. But I begged – I took my cap off and laid it at his feet. Well, he cooled down somehow, and accepted my assurances. He rescinded the order for your arrest. Now he'll write up the charges and take depositions from the witnesses. Wait and see what decision he takes; you can assume that there'll be a fine, and beyond that ..."

"Darogha Sahib," I said nervously, "I don't have a single rusty coin to my name. Where will I find money to pay a fine?"

"Come now, my friend. Why get so anxious?" the Darogha said. "What am I here for? If only everything could be settled with a mere fine. The Royal Minister has been embarrassed in front of the English officers – who knows, he might lock you up, or have you exiled to the other side of the Ganga into British territory."

I was more terrified of exile than of prison. I had spent my entire life in Lucknow; if I had to live anywhere else I'd go mad. I said, "Darogha Sahib, it would be better if the Minister had me shot out of a cannon! For God's sake, think of a way out!" Then I had an idea. "Should I write a petition to the Badshah? He might forgive me ... What do you say?"

"My friend, as if petitions actually reach the Badshah!" said the Darogha with a sigh. "Every single piece of paper first comes under the Minister's scrutiny. The Minister does as he pleases – pronouncing the verdict on some himself, and submitting some to His Highness."

The Darogha stood up. As he was leaving, he paused and said, "But one thing is certain, Kale Khan. This petition idea of yours is a good one."

"Please, Darogha Sahib, for God's sake get me out of here," I said, "or the fumes from the drugs will kill me!"

"You have a point. I'll get you out right away. You go home and rest for a couple of days. Then, have a decent petition writer write up an appeal for you. Don't try to write it yourself!"

"I'm not an educated man, Darogha Sahib. Why should I write it myself and ruin any chance of success I might have?"

"That's exactly what I'm saying."

Darogha Sahib talked to the hospital people and then left straight away. I was discharged in a little while and went home. Once in my own house, I drew little Falak Ara into my lap and entertained her with stories and tales for a long time, but I have no idea what I said to her or what she said to me.

The very next day I went out looking for a decent petition writer. There were a number of famous "writers" in Lucknow those days. Munshi Kalka Prasad lived right in my neighbourhood and I knew of three other writers who had direct access to the Badshah's presence. One was Mirza Rajab Ali Sahib, another was Munshi Zahiruddin Sahib, and the third was Munshi Amir Ahmad Sahib. Mirza Sahib was something of a celebrity around town, and at one time his pen had commanded great renown. I couldn't muster the courage to talk to him. As for Munshi Zahiruddin, I asked around about his whereabouts and finally located his house, only to find that he had gone to Bilgram.

Now there was only Munshi Amir Ahmad left. I couldn't find anyone to show me the way to his house, but I did learn that every Friday evening he showed up at Shah Mina's shrine without fail. As luck would have it, it was a Friday, and a new-moon Friday at that! So at the time of the sunset prayers, I walked by the Machchi Bhavan Castle and arrived at the Shrine of Shah Mina. There was a huge crowd of people, but somehow I managed to get inside. A qavvali performance was underway and Munshi Sahib's own verses were being sung. He was there – I had seen him several times in Qaisar Bagh and had no trouble recognizing him. I stood in a corner and listened to the qavvali. When the gathering

---

Shah Mina: A Sufi saint

broke up late at night, people surrounded Munshi Sahib and a general conversation ensued. At long last, the Munshi Sahib managed to leave. I fell in behind him. Munshi Sahib turned from one alley into another, then into a third, twirling his prayer beads, and I followed right along like a shadow. He stopped in his tracks finally, and I approached him and uttered a greeting. He greeted me in return, then peered intently at my face.

"I crave your compassion," I said.

Munshi Sahib reached for his pocket. I joined my hands and said, "Your Honour, I am not a beggar."

"What is it, then?"

"I'm even more lowly than a beggar. But I can be saved from ruin by your will."

"My good man! Why talk in riddles? Use plain language!"

Standing right there I launched into my tale of woe, but Munshi Sahib stopped me. We were near his house by then and so he took me in. I said many times to him that it was very late at night, and that I would come back the next day, but he listened to the whole report right then, and expressed sympathy from time to time and, from time to time, amazement. Sometimes he'd break into laughter, and sometimes he'd chime in with praises for the Badshah. He fell into thought after I had told him the whole story and confided my plan to him. He said, "Listen, my friend Kale Khan, your story has touched my heart. I'll write the petition for you all right, and I'll put my heartfelt effort into it, but will it ever reach the Badshah ... that's the question. That's something you don't have power over. Do you have other means of getting it to him?"

"Means?" I asked. "Munshi Sahib, you're all the means I have. If you yourself could appear in His Majesty's presence ..."

"Yes, my friend, from time to time I do appear in His Majesty's presence. It is due to His Majesty's generosity to the humble that he calls for me."

Somewhat cheered yet still fearful I said, "Then, Munshi Sahib, if you yourself ..."

Munshi Sahib laughed.

"My friend Kale Khan! ... but then, what would you know of how the Badshah's court functions? It doesn't happen just like that, you know, showing up and saying: Your Gracious Highness, Greetings! Please look at this letter, and His Majesty reaches for it and ..."

My face flushed with embarrassment. I said, "Munshi Sahib, that's not what I meant. The truth is that there's no one I can ask except you to deliver the petition to the Badshah."

"Even if the petition reached the Badshah, it would do so only after passing through a thousand other hands. And besides, your case has been entrusted to the Minister. He wouldn't like it if – "

Munshi Sahib stopped and thought about something. He talked out loud to himself every once in a while, and mentioned names of several people – Miyan Sahiban, Maqbul-ud Daula, Rahat-us Sultan, Imaman and God knows who else. Finally he said to me, "Look, Miyan Kale Khan. If God wills, your petition will come before His Highness; after that, fate ..."

I thanked the Munshi many times, but when I dwelled on his virtues, he looked embarrassed and said, "My friend, my friend! Why are you making a sinner out of me? The One who sees the task through to the end is God. That's plenty for now. Why don't you go home?"

He stood up and came to the door to see me off. I bade him goodbye, saying, "Munshi Sahib, God will reward you for this. I am a poor man. Your payment ..."

"God forbid!" the Munshi bit his tongue in remorse. "Don't even allow that word to leave your lips!" He put his hand on my shoulder and repeated the sentence. "The truth of the matter is, Kale Khan, your story has touched my heart."

The last part of the night was being chimed in at the naubat-khana of

Asaf-ud Daula's Imambara. I thought of Jumerati's mother. The poor thing must have fallen asleep waiting for me to come home. It didn't seem right to wake her up, so I wandered around the city until daybreak.

Three or four days later whom should I see standing at my door but Darogha Nabi Bakhsh. I was startled, but he didn't give me a chance to speak. He began, "Listen, Kale Khan! You're the living end!"

Even more worried, I said, "Darogha Sahib, for Heaven's sake, I don't know anything! What has happened?"

"What has happened!" the Darogha asked. "What's happened is that your petition reached the presence of His Majesty the King, and as soon as it passed under his view a judgement was pronounced on it forthwith!"

"A judgement?" I asked impatiently. "What judgement was that, Darogha Sahib?"

"Is a royal decision going to be announced to lowly folks like us? What things you say, Kale Khan! But write this down ... Wait! First tell me this – did you have all that business written up in the petition? That your little girl is motherless, how she pestered you for a hill myna, and all the rest?"

"From the beginning to the end. I haven't seen the petition myself but Munshi Amir Ahmad Sahib said he would put his wholehearted effort into writing it."

"Munshi Amir Ahmad Sahib!" asked the Darogha with amazement. "You got hold of him? My goodness! I didn't know you had it in you! That explains it ... I was wondering how this petition reached His Highness at all!"

"Darogha Sahib, what was that you were talking about just now?"

Naubat-khana: A large gateway with a chamber above it for musicians, whose job it was to announce processions and times of day by playing their instruments.

"Good grief, I'm still talking about the same thing I was talking about then."

"No, what was it you were saying? Something like Write this down?"

"Oh, that," the Darogha remembered. "I was telling you to write down that you've received a pardon and your little daughter a myna."

"My little daughter a myna?" I asked with astonishment. "You can't possibly mean that, Darogha Sahib!"

"You still don't know the Badshah's true nature," said the Darogha. "I figured it out when his chobdar Bande Ali came this morning to ask the way to your house. My friend, it really brightened my day."

But I could well see that the Darogha was not very happy. He seemed hesitant, as though he wanted to say something more. I felt a little worried. I said, "Darogha Sahib, you've always looked out for me like a father. If you're not happy at a time like this then how could anyone else be? But ... Darogha Sahib, is there something else?"

The Darogha shifted uneasily, then said, "I can't say, Kale Khan. It could be nothing at all, or it could turn out to be something really big. Either way, it will all be to your benefit."

"Darogha Sahib, tell me for God's sake!"

Now the Darogha Sahib looked positively worried. "My friend," he said, "let me tell you about the latest event. Today three of Nawab Sahib's men came to the Peacock Garden."

"Nawab Sahib?"

"Oh, you know, The Royal Minister, the Holder of the Regime, the Support of the Kingdom, the Defender of the Realm, the Nawab Ali Naqi Khan Bahadur – understand?"

"Yes, I do."

"Or maybe it was four men who came ..." the Darogha tried to remember. "Well, anyway, they had me summoned to the Peacock Garden. When I got there I saw them standing at attention in front of the Wondrous Cage. As soon as they saw me they asked me in a most forward manner which among the mynas was Falak Ara. I got a little heated up myself and told him that she must be one of the mynas inside the Cage. I could hardly be expected to remember each of their names! These people seemed to think rather highly of themselves, and shot back things like: You've been the Darogha for so long but you don't know your own animals? I said: All right, I do recognize them – I just won't tell anyone which is which. What business is it of yours, anyway? It went on from there. One of them seemed to have landed his position in the Minister's official retinue only recently. His moustache hadn't even sprouted completely, and he was good-looking too. He started throwing his weight around a bit, so I said: Hold your horses, young man! I'm a descendant of the Pathans – you should watch your backside around me until your beard and moustache are fully grown!"

I laughed. "Darogha Sahib! God save us from your tongue!"

"What of it?" Darogha Sahib was really hitting his stride now. "That young fellow was braying at me by then. I said: My Prince, we feed the choicest pieces of meat to our tigers. That's enough out of you! Shut your trap or else I'll pick you up with my bare hands and throw you into Mohini's enclosure first and ask your name afterwards! On hearing the hullabaloo, many people came out of the royal palaces and calmed things down again."

For a while we were both sunk in our thoughts. Then I said, "That was quite an incident, Darogha Sahib!"

"Incident?" the Darogha asked. "My dear friend, you haven't even begun to hear about the real event. Now listen – there were also friends of the Nawab's men among the palace denizens who came out and they took them off to one side. It was then that the secret was revealed – one of the British officers from the Residency who had come to the Peacock Garden that first time had been charmed by the out-of-place babbling of your myna. He later spoke complimentary words about her to the Nawab, and the Nawab Sahib promised then and there that the myna would be sent over to the Residency! And not only that, he had already had a smaller cage made for her which is a miniature of the Wondrous Cage!"

In this short time, I had already begun to consider Falak Myna my personal property. "But His Majesty graciously granted the myna to my daughter," I protested.

"That he did, but the Nawab too has made a promise to the Great White Officer Sahib!"

"But is the Nawab going to disobey His Majesty's command and go by that ...?"

"All right, all right, that's enough, Kale Khan. Don't say any more. You have no idea what's going on in Avadh. While the Nawab can't override the Badshah's decision, what he can do is buy the myna from you, which he certainly will, and that at any price that you demand. Well, all right – royal gifts are given out just for such purposes, so that a fellow can sell them and make himself a little money. But remember this, Kale Khan: if the myna ends up in the Residency, the Badshah will feel bad."

"May his enemies feel bad!" I said. "If Nawab Sahib makes a move to buy the myna from me I'll tell him that my daughter doesn't agree to the sale, that the bird is like a sister to her!"

"And you think that alone will shut the Nawab Sahib's mouth?" the Darogha immediately retorted. "What kind of world do you live in, brother? Now listen carefully – do you remember Chote Miyan?"

"Which Chote Miyan?"

"For goodness' sake, the one who has an English box that makes pictures! Come on, what was his name? I just remember his nickname."

"Oh, that Chote Miyan! Darogha Ahmad Ali Khan," I said. "How could I ever forget him? I have worked at the Holy Endowment of Husainabad!"

"Fine. When the myna has arrived at your house, he'll come over. Do whatever he tells you to do and don't resist in the slightest. And look, stop worrying. Everything will turn out well for you in the end. All right, I'm off! Chote Miyan will explain the rest."

"Darogha Sahib, please tell me at least a little about what's going on!" I said. "I'm already terrified."

"Then listen, Kale Khan. We don't want one of the royal birds to end up in the Residency. You wouldn't want that to happen, would you?"

"Never in my life."

"That's all. Now sit back and relax."

The Darogha took his leave and I came back inside. I looked at Falak Ara carefully for the first time since the Peacock Garden mishap. She looked wan and pulled down. I knew that she was pining for her myna but was afraid to mention her by name. I had an urge to say "Your myna is going to come back to you," but I myself knew nothing – so what could I tell her? I just picked her up in my arms and walked around the house for a long time.

Darogha Nabi Bakhsh's hunch had been correct. The first thing the very next morning, the royal chobdar and two court officials showed up at my door. The Darogha himself had come along with them. After having the Darogha verify my identity, one of the officers began to read out the royal decree which went a little like this ...

Let Kale Khan, son of Yusuf Khan, be informed that his petition has been submitted to the Royal Presence. Whereas, on account of the following and by virtue of his own confession, it is proven that he committed the offence of stealing a myna by the name of Falak Ara from the Peacock Garden and then took it to his own home ...

Let it be further known that he is therefore being removed from the employ of the court but will continue to receive his salary ...

As a reward for training the myna named Falak Ara,' the selfsame bird has been granted to Lady Falak Ara, daughter of Kale Khan ...

In addition, for the feeding and care of the above-mentioned myna, a monthly allowance of one ashrafi from the royal treasury has been set ...

Furthermore, let it be known to Kale Khan, son of Yusuf Khan, that stealing is called for only in a house where requests go unheard.

The last phrase made me cringe with shame. I stood fixed to the spot and hung my head. Meanwhile, the other officer took the cage, slip-covered in red serge, from the chobdar and handed it to me. Then he took a small pouch out of his cummerbund and had me count out the twelve ashrafis that were in it. He said that this was for a year's expenses for the myna and, after writing out a receipt, he congratulated me. Darogha Nabi Bakhsh also congratulated me, and then said to the chobdar, "Well, Miyan Bande Ali, is my work done now?"

"Our work is done as well," he answered. "Why, Darogha Sahib, won't you come along?"

"No my friend, I think I'm going to go pay my respects at the Holy Endowment of Husainabad."

"Yes, yes. Please go ahead." Bande Ali added warmly, "Say a prayer for me too."

"Will you listen to that! Did you think you had to ask me?"

The Darogha looked at me and with a slight gesture of the head asked me "Remember?" I nodded gently back to say, "I remember."

They left and I went inside the house like a dreamer walking on air. Falak Ara was still asleep. I put the cage in the courtyard and took off the cloth cover.

My eyes were dazzled! "Gold!" I blurted out and the pure exquisiteness of the cage suddenly became obscure. I tried to guess what it might be worth. Just then I heard Falak Myna's faint voice. She looked

---

Ashrafi: A gold coin.

at me with squinting eyes. She bobbed her head up and down, flapped her wings and chirped. I ran into the storeroom and brought out her old cage. I had switched the myna from one cage to the other and was putting the new cage away in the storeroom when I heard Falak Ara's voice outside.

"My myna's all better! My myna's all better!"

When I came out of the storeroom she cheerfully told me the news as well. But I was worried about other things.

"Now go wash your hands and face first, and then you can chat with her as much as your heart desires," I said, and went and stood outside the front door.

The sounds of the myna's chattering and of Falak Ara's delighted laughter drifted out from inside the house. It really did seem like two sisters had reunited after a long separation. The voices stopped for a moment and then I heard:

Falak Ara's a princess sweet!
Milk and jalebis is all she eats!
She's the fair, fair daughter of Black, Black Khan!

Then there was laughter, and the sound of clapping. I couldn't tell if the voice was Falak Ara's or her myna's.

I spent that day sometimes coming inside and sometimes going to the door. Every other minute I would have a nervous premonition that Darogha Ahmad Ali Khan – Chote Miyan – was about to show up. But after waiting by the door for a long time, I would come in again. Finally, around evening, I saw him coming. There was another man with him who looked like a country bumpkin, dressed as he was in a lungi and a coarsely woven kurta, with a shawl wrapped around his waist and a bulky turban on his head. He had wrapped the end of the turban around his face so that only his eyes and the bridge of his nose were visible. The gleam in his eyes frightened me a bit. The two arrived at the door and greetings were exchanged. Ahmad Ali Khan quickly inquired after my health and welfare and then gestured toward the man with the turban and asked, "Do you recognize him, Kale Khan?"

"Perhaps I'd recognize him if I could see his face."

"No – do you recognize him like this?" he asked, and then asked, "If you ever saw him again somewhere, would you recognize him?"

"If I ever recognized his headwrap again, I would."

"You said the right thing," nodded the Darogha in approval. "Now, this is the buyer for the royal myna and the cage you were rewarded. What do you say?"

I was about to refuse flatly when I stopped myself. I said, "What can I say, Darogha Sahib? It is all in your hands."

"So you've made me your agent?"

"I have."

"Well then, I've sold your myna to him, and I've sold the cage as well. We'll think about it carefully before setting the price." And then Chote Miyan said to the other man, "Now come give him a deposit to hold the sale, and your oath."

The man put a rupee in my hand and said, "Kale Khan, son of Yusuf Khan, swear on the Holy Koran that you will never tell anyone how much you sold the myna for. You can mention the price of the cage however. If anyone asks about the price of the myna, say that you're under oath."

I took the oath. Chote Miyan said to me, "Go, distract your little daughter somehow and bring out the myna and the cage."

I went inside the house. Falak Ara was sitting next to the cage. I said to her, "Falak Ara, it's time for her to take her daily rest. If you don't let her sleep, she'll get sick again. I'll take her out for some fresh air. The doctor told me to."

Falak Ara got up quickly and went into the hall. I took the royal cage out of the storeroom, picked up Falak Myna's cage too, and came outside. Darogha Chote Miyan asked happily, "Did you switch cages? You did the right thing, Kale Khan."

He handed both things over to the man and asked, "Got the cage?"

"Yes," was the answer.

"Got the myna?"

"Yes."

"Now get going."

The man turned around with both the cages in his hands and set off. I was about to run after him but Chote Miyan grabbed my hand. I said, "Darogha Sahib, without the myna my daughter ..."

"Just hold on for a bit, Kale Khan, just hold on," he said and pointed ahead.

The man with the cloth wrapped around his face was coming back again. He carried the royal cage on his head, wrapped in the shawl previously around his waist; he looked exactly like a washerman. When he came near, he put the cage with the myna in it into Chote Miyan's hands and walked away rapidly.

The sun was setting and I couldn't see Chote Miyan's face clearly. He gave me the cage. I felt a little worried. He said, "Only good will come out of this for you, Kale Khan, as long as you speak with a level head. Don't get angry yourself and don't make anyone else angry. And, my friend, don't go to bed early tonight."

"Early?" I queried. "Could anyone sleep at a time like this, Darogha Sahib?"

"My friend! As I said, it will all turn out for your good. Just remember to remain calm."

He went away. I picked up the cage and went inside the house. While hanging it on the peg in the courtyard, I looked out of the corner of my eye. Falak Ara was peeking from behind one of the pillars of the hall. I went and laid her down on a takht. She went to sleep fast enough, talking about the myna. I had just stood up to find something to cover her with when Darogha Nabi Bakhsh knocked softly on the door.

"Everything's been arranged," he said. "Don't say anything, just come along with me! Bring your little daughter and her myna. There's no one else at home, is there?"

"No one else," I said and then I remembered, "except for Jumerati's mother."

"And who might that be? Well, bring her along as well, I've had a palanquin brought too. And please, Kale Khan, hurry!"

"And the household furnishings, Darogha Sahib?"

"But you're going to come right back again, Kale Khan. Just bring a few of the little girl's and Whats-his-name's-mother's things. If you want, bring a couple of items for yourself as well."

Behind the Seven Pillared Mansion – the Sat-Khandha of Husainabad – was a small house on a reed-covered, low patch of ground built during Muhammad Ali Shah's reign. We alighted there. It was a well-kept place. The floor had been swept out, the clay pots and pitchers had been filled with fresh water, and an oil lamp with a shade was lit over the sitting platform in the front hall. Falak Ara was fast asleep. I laid her down on a cot and hung the myna's cage at the head of the bed. It didn't take long to unload and put away the scant belongings we had brought with us.

Darogha Sahib had dropped us off and had gone somewhere. He came back after a while and called me to the door. He took a pouch out of his cummerbund and said, "The cage has been sold. The money has been entrusted to Chote Miyan. Here, count it – a hundred rupees of spending money. Or should I have the entire amount given to you now?"

"No, Darogha Sahib," I said worried. "My heart is about to stop just seeing this much silver!"

Darogha Sahib began to laugh, and then he said, "Have you forgotten about the gold allotted for the myna's food and water?"

Actually I had forgotten. Suddenly I couldn't even remember what I had done with the ashrafis. Darogha Sahib saw my confusion and asked, "What's the matter, my good man?"

Immediately it came back to me. I ran into the house, opened a bundle, picked up the ashrafis which were wrapped up in the cloth cover of the royal cage, then came outside and held the coins out toward the Darogha.

"Darogha Sahib, where can I put them?" I asked. "Please keep them with you. Or if you wish, give them to Chote Miyan to keep."

"Don't put so much trust in other people, Kale Khan," he said.

"Don't shame me, Darogha Sahib," I said. "Are you *other* people?"

"You really are a wonder," said the Darogha, and tucked the ashrafis into his cummerbund. Then he said, "Well, your dinner must be on its way. Go, eat and then go back to your own house. You should spend your nights there, but what you do in the daytime is up to you. And if the Minister's men come, talk to them with confidence and take care that Chote Miyan's name doesn't come into the discussion. He's a man of fearless temperament, and while he says that he doesn't care if his name comes up, what's the use of displaying unnecessary impetuousness? Anyway, you watch your words. Act like he never came to see you at home. Goodbye for now."

It wasn't long into the night when I arrived home. It didn't feel right without Falak Ara. I lay down and kept tossing and turning. My heart told me that something was about to happen. In the end I couldn't lie in bed any longer. I got up, went out of the house, and started pacing in front of the door.

When a little more of the night passed, I saw the lights of two torches approaching my house. I quickly went back inside, shut the door and lay down on the bed again. After a while there was a knock on the door.

There were four other men in addition to the torchbearers. They asked me my name, congratulated me curtly on receiving the royal reward, and then asked where the myna was.

"It's been sold," I said.

"Sold?" one of them asked with amazement. "In one day?"

"I'm a poor man. Where in my house could I keep an imperial myna?"

At this point, the men showered me with questions. The light from the torches fell straight on my face and my fear was growing but I kept my courage up and answered all the questions with promptness.

"Who bought it?"

"I don't know – his face was hidden."

"Would you recognize him if you saw him?"

"No, his face was hidden."

"How much did you sell it for?"

"I can't tell you, he made me swear."

"Why?"

"Only he would know."

"Did Chote Miyan come with him?"

"Which Chote Miyan?"

There was silence for a while, and then again the same question.

"Has the myna been sold?"

"Yes, it's been sold."

"What did you do with the money?" one of them asked. "We're Madar-ud Daula Bahadur the Minister's men. Be careful what you say! What did you do with the money, Kale Khan?"

"So far I've just taken an advance."

"How much?"

"One rupee," came out of my mouth.

Then I began to sweat. Would anyone ever believe that I had put a gold cage and an imperial bird in the hands of a total stranger in exchange for one rupee? At this moment one of them thundered out, "Kale Khan! Be careful what you say!"

The sound of that voice made people come out of several houses in the alley. I stood there silently. The torchbearer in front shifted his torch from one hand to the other, and the flame wavered and the light fell on the face of the man who was speaking. He was a young man. Not just young – one should say a boy. His moustache hadn't even completely sprouted yet. His face was handsome. Again, he roared, "Kale Khan, wouldn't you recognize that man?"

Suddenly my fear melted into the air.

"All right, I would recognize him," I said. "But I wouldn't tell anyone if I did. Who are you to ask?"

The men stood around silently for a while, staring at me. Then they all turned around at once and went away. The people from the neighbourhood came out and approached me. "What happened, what happened?" They wanted to know.

"Nothing," I said. "Bad times are upon us."

I didn't even bolt the door of my house from the inside. I lay down on my bed preoccupied with my thoughts.

"Things are all fouled up, Kale Khan," I finally said to myself.

And I had spoken the truth. Early in the morning the next day, I was arrested. A gold-and-silver bowl from the Wondrous Cage had been recovered from my house.

I forget how long I spent in prison. It felt as if my entire life was passing by in that cage. Most of the prisoners were members of Lucknow's low life or were petty thieves. I didn't get along with them at all. I stayed aloof from everyone. I missed Falak Ara very much. Sometimes I felt I heard the sound of her laughter and Falak Myna's chirping from somewhere very close by, and that would unsettle me. But I'd console myself thinking that at least she had her myna to amuse herself with, and that Nabi Bakhsh and Chote Miyan must be looking out for her welfare better than I could. Above everything, I felt at ease about the issue of money. Of course, I wouldn't have my salary any more but Falak Myna's monthly allowance with the price of the imperial cage thrown in seemed like so much wealth to me that I couldn't imagine how to ever spend it. Then again, I would wonder if I would ever get out to spend it, or whether I would die suffocating in prison? I really wished I could send another petition to the emperor. The case against me hadn't even been prepared yet. I had no idea when my trial would begin and, after that, if I got a prison sentence, how long it would be.

But one day, quite inexplicably, I was suddenly released. It occurred to me that perhaps Darogha Nabi Bakhsh had got hold of Munshi Amir Ahmad Sahib, but when I actually came outside, I saw that, like me, other prisoners – perhaps all the prisoners – had been freed. It was very noisy but I kept a low profile and, coming out, headed for the Sat-Khanda straight away.

I went along for some distance preoccupied with my own thoughts. Everything appeared somehow different. A strange, deathly desolation lay over the city. White military troops patrolled the high roads; the entrance of any alley I turned into would be guarded by two or three British soldiers standing sternly at attention. People had formed small clusters and were talking in hushed voices among themselves in the alleys. I was in a hurry to get home so I didn't stop anywhere. But all around the same thing was being talked about, and even without stopping to ask I realized that the Badshah's reign was finished in Avadh. Sultan e Alam Wajid Ali Shah had been removed from the throne. He had left Lucknow and gone away. Avadh had come into the hands of the British and in celebration they had released a large number of prisoners.

I was one of that multitude. It seemed as if I had come out of one cage only to be shut in another. I had an urge to turn around and go back to

---

Wajid Ali Shah (1821 – 1896): The last king of Avadh before its takeover by the British.

prison, but then Falak Ara came to mind and I began to run along down the straight road to the Sat-Khanda.

When I arrived at home everything seemed the same as before. At first Falak Ara shied away from me a bit, but then she climbed on to my lap and began to tell me the latest stories about her myna.

My not taking to life in the city of Lucknow again, my coming to live in Benaras within a month, the war of '57, the Badshah Sultan-e Alam's imprisonment in Calcutta, Chote Miyan's clashing with the British, the destruction of Lucknow, the British overrunning Qaisar Bagh, the hunting of the royal animals inside their enclosures, a certain tigress' wounding her British hunter and escaping, the British in their rage shooting Darogha Nabi Bakhsh – these are all other stories, and there are stories within those stories as well.

But the story of the Myna from Peacock Garden ends right here, with little Falak Ara sitting on my lap, telling me the latest tales of the bird's antics.

This story was first published as "Ta'us Chaman ki Maina" in the journal *Quarterly Aaj*, Karachi.

Notes on Contributors

ADITYA BEHL teaches Hindi in the Department of South and Southeast Asia Studies, University of California at Berkeley. He has co-edited, with David Nicholls, *The Penguin New Writing in India.* He received the Katha Award for Translation in 1993 for his translation of Naiyer Masud's "Remains of the Ray Family."

ELIZABETH BELL is a writer, editor and translator of French and Spanish, based in San Francisco. Her translations from the Spanish have appeared in *Light From a Nearby Window: Contemporary Mexican Poetry*, numerous Catalan Communications publications and *Kenyon Review.* She received the Katha Award for Translation in 1997 for her translation of Naiyer Masud's "Sheesha Ghat," which appears in this collection.

SHANTANU PHUKAN is a PhD student in the Department of South Asian Languages and Cultures at the University of Chicago. He is writing his dissertation on Jayasi's *Padmāvat.*

JAVAID QAZI was born in Pakistan in 1947, and is now based in San José, California. He writes fiction in English and his work has appeared in *Kansas Quarterly*, *Sequoia*, *Chelsea*, the *Toronto South Asian Review*, *Massachusetts Review*, and the *Anaïs Nin: International Journal.* A collection of his short stories, *Unlikely Stories*, will appear shortly from Oxford University Press.

SAGAREE SENGUPTA is a poet. Her work has appeared in the *Toronto South Asian Review.* She is a Visiting Assistant Professor in the Department of South Asian Studies, University of Wisconsin, Madison, where she teaches Hindi.

MOAZZAM SHEIKH was born in Lahore in 1962, and is now based in San Francisco. His stories have been published in the US and Canada.

His work appears in *The Dragonfly in the Sun: 50 Years of Pakistani Writing in English* (Oxford). He received the Katha Award for Translation in 1997 for his translation of Naiyer Masud's "Sheesha Ghat," which appears in this collection. He has just finished his first novel, *Sahab.*

The Editor

MUHAMMAD UMAR MEMON has a Masters in Near Eastern Languages and Literatures from Harvard University and a PhD in Islamic Studies from the University of California at Los Angeles. He is now Professor of Islamic Studies, Urdu and Persian, at the University of Wisconsin, Madison. Memon Sahab writes fiction and criticism in Urdu and English. A collection of his Urdu short stories, *Tareek Gali*, was published by Sang-e-Meel, Lahore, in 1989. His book on religious polemics, *Ibn Taimiyya's Struggle Against Popular Religion*, was published by Mouton (The Hague and Paris) in 1976. He has translated extensively from modern Urdu fiction. Some of his books are *Intizar Husain: The Seventh Door and Other Stories*; *An Epic Unwritten: The Penguin Book of Partition Stories*; *Abdullah Hussein: Stories of Exile & Alienation*; *Hasan Manzar: A Requiem for the Earth; Domains of Fear and Desire: Urdu Stories; The Tale of the Old Fisherman, Modern Urdu Short Stories; The Colour of Nothingness, Contemporary Urdu Short Stories; Abdullah Hussein: Night and Other Stories.* He has also edited Studies in the *Urdu Ghazal* and Prose Fiction.

He is the General Editor of the Pakistan Writers' Series, Oxford University Press; Editor, *The Annual of Urdu Studies*; Associate Editor, *The Journal of South Asian Literature.* Prof Memon also serves on the Editorial Board of several professional journals, among them *Edebiyat, Journal of Middle Eastern Literature* and *Toronto Review of Contemporary Writing Abroad.*

For Young Adults

Yuvakatha 1-4 ed Geeta Dharmarajan — Rs 30 each

Yuvakatha 5-8 ed Keerti Ramachandra — Rs 30 each

"Heady tales." – *Biblio*

A Unique Odyssey: The Story of the United Nations — Rs 120
by Geeta Dharmarajan, illustrated by Atanu Roy
"An exciting fusion of reality and fantasy." – *The Asian Age*

For Children

Tamasha! — Subscription Rs 60 (for 1 year)
India's only development quarterly with stories, games and activities for children. In Hindi and English.

Swapnasundari and the Magical Birds of Mithila — Rs 30
by Geeta Dharmarajan
A JALDI fantasy in Hindi and English.

The Secrets of Kalindi by Geeta Dharmarajan — Rs 50
A JALDI jigsaw puzzle adventure.

Dhammak Dhum! — Subscription Rs 80 (for 1 year)
A fun quarterly for 4-6 year olds

The Princesss with the Longest Hair — Rs 120
by Komilla Raote

For Neo-literates

Stree Katha — Rs 45
by Geeta Dharmarajan and Sheeba Chowdhary
An information-packed, interactive volume on women's issues.
"... imaginative and approachable." – *The Indian Express*

The Katha Vachak Series: Hindi adaptations of classic Indian stories.

Stree ka Patra by Rabindranath Tagore	Rs 15
Paro ki Kahani by Sughra Mehdi	Rs 15
Puraskar by Jaishankar Prasad	Rs 15
Thakavat by Gurbachan Singh Bhullar	Rs 15
Faisla by Maitreyi Pushpa	Rs 15
Bhola by Rajendra Singh Bedi	Rs 15
Samudra Tat Par by O V Vijayan	Rs 15
Sparsh by Jaywant Dalvi	Rs 15
Abhishaap by Pudhuvai Rã Rajani	Rs 15
Panch Parmeshwar by Premchand	Rs 15
Arjun by Mahasweta Devi	Rs 15
Do Haath by Ismat Chughtai	Rs 15

Special Offer

20% discount for Friends of Katha on all books!
For a postage-free delivery, send a DD/MO made out to KATHA at A-3, Sarvodaya Enclave, Sri Aurobindo Marg, New Delhi 110 017.

About Katha

Katha is a registered nonprofit organization working in the area of creative communication for development. Katha's main objective is to spread the love of books and the joy of reading amongst children and adults. Our activities span from publishing to education.

Kalpavriksham, Katha's Centre for Sustainable Learning, is active in the field of education. It develops and publishes quality material in the literacy to literature spectrum, and works with an eye to excellence in education – from nonformal education of working children to formal education, from primary through higher education. Katha also works with teachers to help them make their teaching more creative. It publishes learning packages for first-generation schoolgoers and adult neo-literates. Specially designed for use in nonformal education, every quarter Katha brings out *Tamasha!*, a fun and activity magazine on development issues for children, in Hindi and English. The *Katha Vachak* series is an attempt to take fiction to neo-literates, especially women. *Stree Katha* and *Stree Shakti* are illustrated, information-packed, interactive books on women's issues in a number of Indian languages.

Katha-Khazana, a part of Kalpavriksham, was started in Govindpuri, in one of Delhi's largest slum clusters, in 1990. Kathashala and the Katha School of Entrepreneurship have over 1000 students – mostly working children. To enhance their futures, an income-generation programme for the women of this community – Shakti-Khazana – and the Khazana Women's Cooperative were also started there, again in 1990.

Project Kanchi is Katha's effort to help forge linkages through academic interface programmes. It is working to develop syllabi and teaching material for courses in culture linking through translations. Launched in 1997, Kanchi has been conducting workshops in schools and colleges all over the country as part of this project. To further the objectives of this project, we have started an academic publishing programme – the Approaches to Literature in Translation series – as well as a Resource Centre for Teachers. Kanchi operates through six Academic Centres in various universities in the country – Guru Nanak Dev University, Amritsar, Bangalore University, Stella Maris College, Chennai, North East Hill University, Shillong, SNDT, Mumbai, in addition to its Delhi Centre.

Katha Vilasam, the Story Research and Resource Centre, seeks to foster and applaud quality fiction from the regional languages and take it to a wider readership through translations. The Katha Awards, instituted in 1990, are given annually to the best short fiction published in various languages that year, and for translations of these stories. Through projects like the Translation Contests, it attempts to build a bank of sensitive translators. Katha Vilasam also functions as a literary agency and works with academia to associate students in translation-related activities. KathaNet, an invaluable network of Friends of Katha, is the mainstay of all Katha Vilasam efforts. Katha Vilasam publications also include exciting books in the Yuvakatha and Balkatha series, for young adults and children respectively.

Be a Friend of Katha!

If you feel strongly about Indian literature, you belong with us! KathaNet, an invaluable network of our friends, is the mainstay of all our translation-related activities. We are happy to invite you to join this ever-widening circle of translation activists. Katha, with limited financial resources, is propped up by the unqualified enthusiasm and the indispensable support of nearly 5000 dedicated women and men.

We are constantly on the lookout for people who can spare the time to find stories for us, and to translate them. Katha has been able to access mainly the literature of the major Indian languages. Our efforts to locate resource people who could make the lesser-known literatures available to us have not yielded satisfactory results. We are specially eager to find Friends who could introduce us to Bhojpuri, Dogri, Kashmiri, Maithili, Manipuri, Nepali, Rajasthani and Sindhi fiction.

Do write to us with details about yourself, your language skills, the ways in which you can help us, and any material that you already have and feel might be publishable under a Katha programme. All this would be a labour of love, of course! But we do offer a discount of 20% on all our publications to Friends of Katha.

Write to us at –

Katha
A-3 Sarvodaya Enclave
Sri Aurobindo Marg
New Delhi 110 017

Or call us at:686- 8193, 652-1752